FINDER'S KEEPERS

"Who are you?" he growled.

"I could ask the same of you." She tried to head butt him. "Breaking and entering is a felony."

A felony? It was his trailer.

"How long have you lived here?"

Her muscles flexed, hinting at more fight to come. "Six weeks, if it's any of your business."

It concerned him greatly. She'd settled in right around the time he'd left for spring training. "My mobile home, my business," he told her. "You can't take over property without investigating ownership."

"Possession is nine-tenths of the law."

Triple bullshit to that logic.

She fought to sit up.

Strands of her wet hair slapped his cheek. Her peach-scented shampoo tickled his nose. He sneezed.

Her nipples poked his chest,

Kason sucked air.

Other *Love Spell* books by Kate Angell:

STRIKE ZONE
CURVEBALL
SQUEEZE PLAY
CRAZY FOR YOU
DRIVE ME CRAZY
CALDER'S ROSE

KATE
ANGELL

SLIDING
HOME

LOVE SPELL NEW YORK CITY

LOVE SPELL®

September 2009

Published by

Dorchester Publishing Co., Inc.
200 Madison Avenue
New York, NY 10016

ISBN 10: 0-505-52808-8
ISBN 13: 978-0-505-52808-7
E-ISBN: 978-1-4285-0737-1

The name "Love Spell" and its logo are trademarks of Dorchester Publishing Co., Inc.

Printed in the United States of America.

10 9 8 7 6 5 4 3 2

Visit us online at www.dorchesterpub.com.

ACKNOWLEDGMENTS

Anna Sugden—*Sliding Home* is for you! You're adorable, and I loved seeing you in San Francisco.

Alicia Condon, Vice President and Editorial Director—you are always appreciated.

Alissa Davis, Assistant Editor—I value your enthusiasm for my Rogues.

Jay T.—my favorite minor league ballplayer. Thanks for sharing your insight, humor, and intensity for the game.

Allie Mackay (and the clay pigeons)—there's always a little bit of you in each of my books.

Debbie and Ted Roome—exceptional friends. Sunny and Colby, wonder dogs.

All the Browns: Marion, Paul, Judy, Kristin, Grace, Mary, Paul, and Max.

Christopher—you put out the fires when I'm writing on deadline. Many, many thanks.

WELCOME TO JAMES RIVER STADIUM

HOME OF THE RICHMOND ROGUES

Starting Lineup

25	RF	Cody McMillan
18	C	Chase Tallan
11	3B	Jesse Bellisaro
21	CF	Risk Kincaid
7	SS	Zen Driscoll
15	1B	Rhaden Dunn
46	LF	Kason Rhodes
1	2B	James Lawless
53	P	Brek Stryker

One

Who'd been sleeping in Kason Rhodes's bed?

The left fielder for the Richmond Rogues had returned from six weeks of spring training in Florida to find someone had moved into his mobile home.

That person was presently in his shower. The bathroom door stood cracked open and steam curled into the hallway. The peach-scented shower gel suggested the intruder was female.

Kason took a moment and looked around his bedroom. Unmade bed, tossed brown comforter, rumpled beige cotton sheets, the imprint of her head on his pillow.

Lady was an uninvited sleepover.

A vintage Guns N' Roses T-shirt, a pair of stonewashed jeans, a pale blue bra, and panties lay across the foot of his bed. Black Converses were on the floor.

Kason's jaw locked. Damn, he hated intruders. He valued his privacy. No one came onto his land without his permission. He had No Trespassing signs posted throughout his thousand acres, yet this woman ignored his warning.

Whether con or prankster, reporter or baseball bunny, Kason wanted her gone. None of his team members knew where he lived. He used a post office box for his mail. Most people thought he lived in the woods with wolves.

He hated the fact she'd tracked him down.

But he was about to send her packing.

Within seconds he heard the shower shut off and the plastic curtain being drawn back. The medicine cabinet creaked as it was opened, then closed; silence followed as she stepped into the hallway.

Wanting to see her before she saw him, Kason backed toward the corner and faded into the late-afternoon shadows. The woman wouldn't immediately spot him when she entered his bedroom.

He'd positioned his eight-month-old Doberman by the front door. Cimarron was well trained and wouldn't allow an escape.

The lady had acute senses. Wrapped in a white towel, she stopped by the dresser, cocked her head, and listened. She knew she wasn't alone. Casual yet cautious, she looked into the mirror. She spotted him in two heartbeats.

Their eyes locked.

His narrowed, and hers went wide.

Amazingly, she didn't scream.

She turned around slowly, and in the blink of an eye, went apeshit on him.

Nothing surprised or shocked Kason. He'd lived life hard. Yet unease settled bone deep when she scooped her hairbrush, bottle of perfume, can of soda, paperback novel, box of Kleenex, porn-star vibrator, and gooseneck lamp off the top of his nightstand and fired them at him. He barely had time to duck.

She had the arm of a tomboy. The items came fast

and furious, forcing him back against the wall. She hit him five out of seven times. The perfume squirted on impact, and he instantly smelled fruity. The base of the lamp bruised his shoulder. The vibrator smacked his thigh and the switch turned on, and it emitted a low, slow buzz. Son of a bitch.

"You're trespassing," she shouted at him. "Get out or I'll call the police."

Call the cops on me? No way in hell.

"This is my trailer!" He grunted, barely managing to intercept an alarm clock aimed at his groin.

"No, it's mine," she shot back. "I found it abandoned."

Abandoned? The woman was crazy.

She showed no fear, only irritation, as she grabbed a tire iron off the floor. The tomboy was prepared for a burglary or home invasion. She was all threat and focus as she slapped the tool against her palm, her message clear: his head was about to roll.

Kason pushed off the wall and put on his game face. Mean and intimidating was second nature. He crossed to the bed, faced off across his mattress with the woman. He held up his hand. "Put the tire iron down before someone gets hurt. Let's talk this out."

The hard swing of the iron was her only response. She had power. The *whish* blew by his ear, standing his hair on end.

She gripped the tool low. Each swing loosened the knot on her towel above her right breast. The cotton fabric shimmied down her C cups.

A fourth flick, and the towel hung on her nipples. Pink nipples, puckered and pointed right at him.

Kason nearly got his brains knocked out for staring.

The woman pulled a face, then took her eyes off him for less than a second as she tugged up the towel.

The distraction was all he needed to make his move. He lunged low across the bed and tackled her. She twisted, and the tire iron went flying. A flip of her body and Kason had her pinned.

The lady was all slick skin, spread-eagled, and spitting mad. Wild brown hair and watercolor blue eyes registered as her shriek deafened his left ear. He blocked the jerk of her knee, but couldn't stop her bite to his shoulder.

He groaned, and swore she would draw blood through his gray pullover. She'd scored him with her teeth.

She was strong for a woman, yet he didn't want to hurt her. It took several attempts to secure both her hands with one of his own. *Tomorrow* was tattooed on her right wrist and a man's waterproof watch wrapped her left. The black leather band looked old and well worn.

She squirmed and bucked as he straddled her fully, then gnashed her teeth. Damned if she didn't prove slippery. Kason tightened his thighs against her hips, squeezed until she exhaled.

"Get off me." She fisted her hands above her head, probably wanting to blacken his eye.

He tightened his hold. He enjoyed fiery women, but the one beneath him would as soon unman him as draw her next breath. The tomboy was aggressive.

He might have considered her cute had she stopped screwing up her face. Her cheekbones were as sharp as her chin. A tiny crescent scar curved at one corner of her mouth. Her lips were flattened against her teeth. She was all snap and snarl, and flashed a lot of bare skin.

Her towel had parted, exposing her full breasts, a

gold-studded navel, and one pale hipbone. She dug in her heels and pushed up, struggling against his weight.

Kason was a big man. At six foot three, he tipped the scale at 220. He had three percent body fat, the remainder solid muscle. The lady would fight, but she'd soon tire. She wasn't going anywhere. Not until she explained her takeover of his trailer.

He leaned low, until their noses nearly touched. "Who are you?" he growled.

"I could ask the same of you." She tried to head butt him. "Breaking and entering is a felony."

A felony? It was his trailer.

He shifted his right leg, countered the slam of her heel to his calf. "How long have you lived here?"

Her muscles flexed, hinting at more fight to come. "Six weeks, if it's any of your business."

It concerned him greatly. She'd settled in right around the time he'd left for spring training. "My mobile home, my business," he told her. "You can't take over property without investigating ownership."

"Possession is nine-tenths of the law."

Triple bullshit to that logic.

She fought to sit up.

Strands of her wet hair slapped his cheek. Her peach-scented shampoo tickled his nose. He sneezed.

Her shoulder knocked his collarbone.

Her nipples poked his chest.

Kason sucked air.

He jerked on her wrists, and she flattened back on the bed. Sweet mother, she was soft beneath him.

"How could you live here?" she demanded. "No drapes, worn furniture, scratched linoleum, little water pressure. I broomed out a bat and two rats."

6 Kate Angell

He curled his lip. "The electricity was left on."

"And no doubt pirated," she countered. "There's been no meter reader."

Someone read the meter. An electric bill arrived every single month. "How'd you get inside?" he demanded.

"Unlatched the bathroom window—easy entrance." She rolled her shoulders, again tried to rise. "You're smothering me, jerk. Get the hell off."

He debated. He didn't want to go another round with this woman. "Truce?" he asked.

She muttered, "Until your back's turned."

He'd keep one eye on her at all times.

He released both wrists and swung off her. "Get dressed. Living room—five minutes," he ordered as he snatched up the tire iron, followed by the white plastic vibrator. Its size would shame most men. He lifted an eyebrow, tossed her the sex toy, the buzz now faint. "Needs new batteries."

Her whole body blushed.

Kason soon learned she couldn't tell time. Ten minutes stretched to twenty before she came to him, hair tamed, body clothed. She lived up to his tomboy assessment in her baggy shirt and jeans.

He preferred her in a towel.

He'd left the tire iron visible on the kitchen counter, near where he was standing. There was caution in her eyes, as well as a hint of daring. She wanted her weapon back. The tool would stay with him. The lady had tried to bust his balls and crush his skull. He wasn't taking any chances.

Cimarron gave a low bark, drawing her attention.

Kason watched her expression shift from stubborn to soft. "What's his name?" she asked.

He hesitated to tell her. "Cimarron."

She didn't ask Kason if the Dobie was friendly. She went straight to him and hit her knees, ready to win the big dog over.

"Hello, handsome." She let Cimarron sniff her hand before she scratched his ear. Within seconds, man's best friend had rolled onto his back to have his belly rubbed. Kason swore he heard Cim sigh.

Well trained and highly protective, Cimarron always took his cues from Kason. But Kason had yet to call the female intruder "friend," which was the dog's signal to back down.

The Doberman was already down, and so relaxed he looked asleep, with his eyes closed and tongue lolling from the corner of his mouth. Damned if he wasn't drooling.

Ticked that Cim was purring like a kitten under enemy hands, Kason gave a low whistle and the dog lurched to his feet, fully alert.

"Bed," Kason instructed, and Cim immediately headed down the hall.

"Great dog," the woman said as she stood up.

"Don't get attached," Kason returned.

"I never do," she replied softly with her chin down, the words said more to herself than to him.

His rumblings in the kitchen drew her notice as he raided the cupboards. Her disgust was obvious. "Trespassing, and now stealing my food. You are such an ass."

A hungry ass, actually. He was about to feast.

While she'd dressed, he'd remembered a leftover can

of tomato soup that was stuck high on the shelf. He was tired and hungry and not in the mood to be played.

He'd driven straight to Richmond from training camp. He'd stopped to feed Cimarron twice and to give the dog a run, then to hit a taco drive-through around noon the previous day. He hadn't eaten since.

What he found in his cupboards blew him away. The tomboy bought in bulk. She'd stored food for an army. Or a giant.

Sixty-four ounces of peanut butter and jelly spread a lot of sandwiches. Loaves of wheat, rye, and marble filled the bread box.

Family-size boxes of Hamburger Helper, macaroni and cheese, popcorn, and six types of cereal bowed the upper shelves. Cases of #10 cans of spaghetti sauce, tuna, mixed nuts, and peaches were stacked beneath the counter, along with an enormous tin of animal crackers that was as big as a small beer keg.

The refrigerator held eight tubs of butter, an enormous wheel of Swiss cheese, and a dozen cartons of eggs. Thirty pounds of hamburger wrapped in butcher paper jammed the freezer, along with fat bags of frozen vegetables. There was no sign of the ice-cube trays.

Kason hadn't seen this much food outside a grocery store or a restaurant. The items went on and on.

His intruder must have a tapeworm.

"Care to share?" he asked before he helped himself anyway. "Half my tomato soup for a grilled cheese sandwich?"

She glared at him. "Not an even trade."

"That's all I have to bargain with at the moment."

A second of sympathy passed with a blink. "Hard times?" she asked.

Not that hard. After a midseason trade the previous season, he'd signed a multimillion dollar contract with the Rogues. He was presently the highest paid outfielder in Major League Baseball.

His life was a work in progress. He'd chosen to live in the mobile home until he could build his house with his own bare hands. He considered the double-wide his construction trailer. It had all the basics.

He'd never pictured a woman living here.

Having the tomboy think he was poor had benefits. People treated him differently when they knew what he did. Strangely, he liked the fact she hadn't yet labeled him a Rogue.

"I'm in between jobs," he told her, which was partially true. Five days separated spring training from Opening Day at James River Stadium. There'd be meetings and workouts, yet a few hours belonged solely to him.

She straightened her shoulders. "I work part-time at Frank's Food Warehouse on Route Eleven. I get a discount on bulk items." She nodded toward the newspaper on the short breakfast bar, opened to the classifieds section. "I need more hours. I'm job hunting."

More than Kason needed to know. He didn't do personal on any level. He turned away from her and preheated the toaster oven.

"You have a name?" her question hit him between the shoulder blades.

"Kason." Last names weren't important. He planned to feed her, then release her. He'd never see her again.

"I'm Dayne."

Introductions over, he nodded without looking up.

Dayne Sheridan leaned a hip against the counter,

read Kason's expression. The man wanted her gone. A grilled cheese sandwich and he'd show her the door.

To hell with him; she wasn't leaving. The mobile home held her food. She wasn't about to walk away from her groceries. They'd cost her her last dime.

Kason claimed the trailer belonged to him, yet she'd seen no proof of purchase. She wanted to see the deed.

She studied him as he took a loaf of rye from the bread box and laid out eight slices. His hair was dark, his brown eyes sharp. Cheekbones slashed to an aggressive chin. He had a muscular build, wide shoulders, and thick thighs.

He wore a gray pullover and a pair of Wranglers that rode low on his hips. She could see the black waistband of his boxers when he bent to remove the wheel of Swiss cheese from the refrigerator.

Dark, dangerous, fallen, crossed her mind. And definitely a loner. She thought she'd seen his picture somewhere, but couldn't pinpoint the time or place. Maybe on *America's Most Wanted*.

The tire iron lay on the counter, midway between them. The tool was her primary means of protection should he show her the door. If she inched a little closer, she could swipe—

"Back it up," Kason said, cutting off her lunge. He moved the tool beyond her reach. "I like my head on my shoulders."

She held her spot at the end of the breakfast bar. If she couldn't get to the tire iron, there were always knives. The plastic ones available weren't a great defense, but she'd feel safer with one in her pocket. Or maybe a fork—prongs could jab.

Silence separated them as Kason made the sand-

wiches. He sliced thick wedges when she'd have con-
served with slivers. She hoped he wouldn't eat the entire
wheel of Swiss cheese in one sitting. She was on a very
tight budget.

Her mother had taught her to bargain shop. Buying in
bulk saved her from regular trips to the grocery store.
Large quantities were cheaper and stretched over weeks.
She could survive on what she had here for a month.

She watched as Kason slid the sandwiches into the
toaster oven and set the timer for three minutes. He then
popped the lid on the tomato soup and poured it into a
pan on the stove.

Dayne inhaled; there was something comforting
about soup and sandwiches. They said stable, homey,
family. She didn't let the feeling overtake her. A sense of
home had eluded her ever since her father had deserted
her mother when Dayne was twelve.

"How'd you land here?" Kason said, breaking into
her past. He'd collected paper plates and bowls, along
with plastic silverware. The man was ready to eat.

There was no reason to tell him about Mick Jakes,
radio personality, ex-fiancé, and weasel among men. He
had dumped her on the air. Dayne had heard the broad-
cast along with his million listeners.

Dayne had gone numb. She'd worked at WBT 91.2 as
Mick's assistant, promoting his talk show through speaking engagements and live on-site remotes. They'd talked
marriage in the fall, and she'd hired a wedding planner.

With their breakup, she'd lost her job. Mick had gone
as far as to change the locks on the condo they'd shared,
then closed their joint checking account.

Humiliation had sent Dayne packing. She'd had fifty
dollars to her name and a full tank of gas when she'd left

Baltimore. Heartbreak, self-pity, and her wedding file accompanied her south.

She'd changed the settings on her car radio. *Mick in the Morning* was dead to her. She'd sworn off men who lived in the public eye.

Dayne blinked away her past. Her good luck sucked. She'd drifted in and out of small towns for a week. Two flat tires, a lost wallet, and sleeping in her car had added insult to injury. She'd never been more miserable.

Without a lot of back story, she told Kason about the accident that had brought her to the trailer. "I was on the interstate, headed south, when a snowstorm hit. Zero visibility, no sense of direction—I got lost. The side roads proved slippery and I skidded straight into a snow bank. My Camry died. Once the blizzard let up, I walked until I came across this mobile home."

"*My* mobile home." He sent her a dark look. "You're not originally from Richmond, then?"

Baltimore, Maryland, no longer existed for her. "Richmond is my home now." Finding the trailer had given her hope. She'd felt comfortable in the woods. She had no plans to leave.

"Where's your car?"

She sighed. "I had it towed. The estimate on repairs would have cost more than the heap was worth. I sold it for scrap."

"How are you getting around?"

"On a bicycle with a basket. It beats walking."

She'd walked six miles each way her first week of employment at Frank's Food Warehouse. She'd formed blisters on her feet, and her arms had ached from carting home groceries.

She'd humbly requested an advance on her paycheck,

and with cash in hand, purchased a used Schwinn. As long as the bike didn't blow a tire, she was in good shape. She had pedal power.

The timer dinged and Kason slid the sandwiches from the toaster oven onto two plates. Three grilled cheeses for him, one for her. He then split the soup into bowls. Dayne swore she got the lesser portion.

"Kool-Aid or soda?" she asked.

A hint of a smile as he said, "I haven't had Kool-Aid since I was five."

Neither had she. She'd bought the Kool-Aid on impulse. Memories of her dad and her dipping their fingers into the packets and sampling the sugary granules remained as sweet as the drink. She could still see her father's purple tongue when he'd stuck it out after tasting the grape flavor. Her own tongue had been bright green from the lime food coloring. They'd both laughed so hard. . . .

"Raspberry or fruit punch?" Dayne offered.

"Fruit punch."

She found a pitcher, stirred up the Kool-Aid. No ice—they'd have to drink it warm. Two plastic glasses in hand, she moved to a small oval table situated before the west-facing living room window.

Kason made two trips to deliver their dinner. He dropped a spoon beside her bowl, then took the chair across from her. The man could eat. He'd inhaled two sandwiches before she'd finished her first half.

Outside the trailer window, twilight purpled the sky and shadows thickened. The darkening light gave Kason a dangerous edge. His skin was stretched tight across his cheekbones. His eyes glittered with an inborn toughness.

The man wasn't much for small talk. He ate his sandwiches, drank his Kool-Aid, then broke the silence on his last spoonful of soup. "Can I drive you to a hotel?" he asked.

She squared her shoulders. "No hotel." She felt safe in the secluded trailer. She had no plans to leave.

"You're not spending another night here." He pushed to his feet, pierced her with a look. "You've overstayed your welcome."

"I could say the same for you."

He collected the paper plates and bowls.

She dogged him to the kitchen.

He dumped their dishes in the trash.

She crossed her arms over her chest and tapped her foot, totally resistant.

Kason picked up the tire iron, slapped it against his palm. The air tensed and pulsed and her heart bumped hard. His eyes narrowed on her, and not in a good way.

Dayne suddenly wished she'd snagged a plastic fork when she'd had the opportunity. It was too late now. She had no protection against this man. He looked ready to strike.

Dayne flinched.

And Kason frowned.

Long seconds ticked by as he stared at her.

Her breath collected deep in her chest. She could barely exhale. Swallowing proved impossible. She'd gone cold.

The hands on the kitchen clock swept a full minute before he tossed her the tool. "I don't hit women. You keep the tire iron."

Relief swept her. She wouldn't have stood a chance against this man. He was ripped and rough and could've crushed her.

Yet he hadn't moved a muscle.

She'd misread him. "I can stay?" she dared to ask.

A shift of his jaw, followed by, "One more night, in the guest room."

"What about tomorrow?"

"We hitch a wagon to your bicycle and you pedal your food down the road."

Two

The butt crack of dawn rolled Kason Rhodes over on his bed. He stared up at the ceiling and listened. His bedroom was quiet—way too quiet. Where the hell was Cimarron? The Dobie had slept at the foot of Kason's bed ever since he was a pup. All night long, Cim chased rabbits in his sleep and snored like a water buffalo.

There was no sign of his dog.

Kason had slept alone.

He stretched his naked body and yawned deeply. Pushing off the bed, he slipped into a pair of navy sweatpants. He ran his hands down his face, then through his hair. It was April 2. Memories flooded him.

He'd shave his head today—after he located Cimarron and ran six miles.

Kason scoped the hallway and living room. No Cim.

He returned to the guest bedroom, knocked on the door. He was greeted by a bark. He turned the knob and walked in. Uninvited. What he saw pained him greatly.

Curled at the head of the bed, Cim wagged his tail, but didn't budge. His head owned a pillow.

"Still sleeping . . . scram." Dayne waved the tire iron at him in warning as she snuggled deeper beneath the covers. Kason caught a glimpse of her bed head and the pillow crease on her cheek before her body went soft once again.

Put out, he left the guest room. He shut the door with more force than was necessary. His dog and the tire iron had slept with Dayne. And were still in bed with her.

Cimarron's obedience suffered at the hands of the tomboy. The big dog had gone all protective over her. Kason wouldn't have a companion for his run.

He grabbed a cut-off gray sweatshirt and tied on his Nikes. He realized the longest relationship he'd had recently was with his running shoes.

Slipping out the front door, he took to the dirt road. Woods spread in all directions, dense with evergreen, white elm, and red maple. Wildflowers colored the ground in swaths of blue and purple.

The sun was barely up, the air crisp. He stretched his body until it was loose and fluid, then broke into a jog. He pushed himself hard, his mind blank, conscious of nothing but the race of his heart.

He returned to the trailer in forty minutes, breathing heavily, his chest fully expanded. He walked around his mobile home while his pulse slowed.

That's when he spotted Dayne's Schwinn, blue and rusty and locked to the trailer's hitch. Why she'd secured it was beyond him. No one in his right mind would steal a bicycle with a loose chain and bald tires. Even the white basket was lopsided.

The bike had a mile's worth of pedaling left in it, and that was if she rode slowly.

Kason stared at the Schwinn until he heard Dayne raise the kitchen window, and the scent of coffee crooked like a finger, drawing him inside.

He found her standing before the stove, fresh-faced and ponytailed. One step closer, and he was nearly licked by the tongue on her vintage Rolling Stones T-shirt when she bent to feed Cimarron.

She fed Cim a whole load of scrambled eggs.

Two cartons of Grade As lay open on the counter. One was completely empty. The Dobie wolfed down his breakfast, then wagged his stubby tail for seconds.

Dayne looked at home.

Kason didn't do *settled*. The tomboy had invaded his privacy. Spoiled his dog. All not to his liking. It was time to move her on.

She looked up and offered, "Omelet?"

He'd shared dinner with her, but wouldn't do breakfast. She'd be gone by lunch.

"Just a cup of black coffee." He tugged off his sweatshirt, swung it around his neck. He then blew on the Styrofoam cup she handed him; it was filled to the top and steaming-hot with a generic blend.

While he slowly sipped, her gaze cut to his shoulders, lingered on his pecs, looped to his abs. He was hot and sweaty, and she checked him out fully.

Most women went all flirty and suggestive in their appreciation of his body. Some went as far as to rub against him. Yet there was nothing sexual in the tomboy's look.

She took him in, and one corner of her mouth pinched before she looked away. Totally indifferent.

Apparently he wasn't her type. Not that he cared. "Shower time." Coffee in hand, he moved down the hall.

Twenty minutes later, towel-dried, Kason stood in a pair of navy boxers before the bathroom mirror and shaved his head. No one knew the reason behind his behavior. His private life was private. Most thought him mental.

The buzz of the shaver sent a strange calmness through his body. The tingle of his scalp brought back memories.

Memories of the events that had made him who he was.

Thick black hair fell into the sink and onto the towel spread at the sink's porcelain base. Both sides of his head were now smooth, the top spiked like a mohawk.

Five minutes more, and he was totally bald.

He brushed hair from his face and neck and stared into the mirror. He had a hard face, almost criminal.

This was his life. Bald was how he'd always started baseball season, even as a T-baller. The wounds had scabbed, but never fully healed.

He thought back on his birth mother and his prick of a stepfather. His family history was dark and unforgiving.

Raymond Rhodes had married Lana Anders when she was seventeen, and four months pregnant. She'd told Ray that he was the father, only to have DNA prove otherwise.

Ray had gone ballistic when the blood tests revealed he was raising his brother Joe's child. Ray had always envied Joe's popularity, intelligence, and athletic ability. Envy turned to hate when he learned his brother had been screwing Ray's high-school girlfriend.

Joe had joined the Marines before Kason was born. A week after Kason entered the world, Joe had been killed in a deployment overseas. Joe had never known he'd fathered a son.

With each birthday, Kason had grown more like Joe.

Ray had refused to let Kason call him Dad. Kason had grown up in Springfield, Missouri, under Ray's sneer and backhand slap. Kason became his stepfather's punching bag at age six.

A boot to the ribs was Kason's alarm clock. Knuckles to his chin reminded him to brush his teeth. The worst came when Ray caught Kason in camouflage pants playing combat.

Ray had grabbed Kason by the back of the neck and hauled him into the house. He'd told Kason if he wanted to imitate his dead military dad, Ray would shave him for boot camp.

Ray had held the boy down and buzzed him bald, then batted him on the back of the head. Kason now looked even more like the birth father he'd never known.

T-ball that year had been a killer. Ray made the shaving a yearly ritual.

Little league was a nightmare.

A baseball cap hadn't hidden his baldness. The Springfield Sox had looked embarrassed for him. The other boys kept their distance, as if his shaved head were contagious.

Kason had played hard, but never got close to his teammates. Over the years, he'd adjusted to being alone.

Throughout middle and high schools, Ray had attended Kason's baseball games. His shouts from the stands had been loud and abusive. When his team lost, his old man called him *Kassie*.

The girl's name triggered every bad memory from Kason's youth. In the end, humiliation had given Kason fight. He now expelled his demons from the batter's box and out in left field. Adrenaline pumped with every home run and fly ball caught at the wall.

Exhaling his past, he cast one last look in the bathroom mirror, then stepped out through the hall and into his bedroom. He pulled on an olive T-shirt and jeans. He had two hours before he had to report to James River Stadium.

Time enough to stop for breakfast on his way to the park. After practice, he'd help Dayne pack up her food and move her down the road.

Returning to the kitchen, he found her gone. The kitchen counter was wiped clean, the coffeemaker was turned off, and the eggs were put away. There was no sign of the tire iron.

Cimarron lay by the door, looking lost and left behind. Where had Dayne disappeared to? He'd wanted to talk to her before he left.

Kason let the Dobie out to do his business. While he waited, he shaded his eyes and squinted down the road. He concluded the dot in the distance was Dayne on her bike, running an errand or going to work.

He had six miles to catch her.

Once Cim was back in the trailer, Kason climbed into his battered black Hummer and took off after her. They needed to set a time for her to leave.

The gravel road made riding a bike difficult. He came up on her slowly, watching as she wobbled, caught her balance, then hit a rock and skidded. She nearly fell off her Schwinn.

He pulled up beside her, rolled to a stop, then lowered his window. "We need to talk."

"Can't, I'm late for work." She breezed past him in her yellow Frank's Food Warehouse shirt and khakis.

"I'll give you a lift." He pressed the accelerator, caught up to her. "You can toss your bike in the back."

"I'd rather ride." She threw more muscle into her pedaling. The wheels on the bike spun up dust.

What the hell was her problem? He didn't have time to chase her down the road. She'd pulled away from him now by three car lengths. Her shoulders curved low over the handlebars and her khakis pulled tight across her bottom. No sign of a panty line. Tomboy had a nice ass.

Kason drove by her, then cut the wheel sharply, forcing Dayne to stop. She jammed on the brakes so jarringly fast, the chain fell off.

"You jerk!" she shouted at him as he exited the Hummer. "Now I have to push my bike to town."

"I offered you a ride," he reminded her.

"Which I refused, *Prison Break*."

Her reference to his baldness spiked his temper. When she tried to push past him, he curved one big hand over the bike's basket and stopped her in her tracks.

He then took a step back when she balled a fist, ready to flatten his nose.

"God, you're obnoxious." He blew out a breath, did a mental ten count. "You moved into my mobile home without permission and are now riding your bike on my road. Let's wrap it up and call it a day."

"Not until I see the deed to the trailer," she huffed. "And unless your name's on the street sign, this is a public access road."

In actuality, the road was private. He'd scored a county permit and paid out of pocket to have the dirt road cut and graded to access the main highway when he'd bought the thousand acres. It was listed with the county as Rhodes Street, though an official sign had yet to be posted. His road formed a T with the highway, where a gas station, family diner, and the wholesale warehouse attracted local traffic.

Kason wasn't about to tell Dayne he owned acreage as far as her eye could see, and that he had legal documentation to prove it. Unfortunately, when it came to the trailer, she had him by the balls. There was no deed.

He'd picked up the double-wide for the towing fee. Dale Crenshaw, the original owner, had been older than God and on his way to a nursing home.

According to Crenshaw's caregiver, the man had advanced Alzheimer's and was alone in the world. He stared into space, eyes blank, shoulders slumped. Crenshaw couldn't remember his own name, much less where he'd stored the deed.

Kason's gut had twisted over the old man's memory loss. Kason understood *alone*. He'd been on his own since he was sixteen.

As much as he took to anyone, Kason took to the elderly. He'd grown close to his great-uncle Dave after his dad had kicked him out of the house. Dave had put a roof over Kason's head so he could finish high school.

Kason never took something for nothing.

Once Crenshaw's mobile home had been towed to his land, Kason had compensated the man in his own way. Throughout the last months of Crenshaw's life, Kason had visited him weekly at the Sunrise Center. He'd hired a private full-time nurse and seen to Crenshaw's comfort.

The week Crenshaw died, the man had locked eyes

with Kason for the first time in four months. In those fleeting seconds, Kason had seen Crenshaw's gratitude. He was glad the old man had finally found peace.

That didn't alter the fact that he didn't have papers on the trailer. Though he could show Dayne the deed for the land, he held back. There was no need to flash his bank account in her face. He lived low-key and planned to keep it that way.

There were no autograph seekers at the restaurants, grocery, and retail stores he frequented. People knew him, yet respected his space.

Space he wasn't about to share with the tomboy.

"If you're short on cash, I'll spot you a hotel room while you relocate." Kason thought his offer generous.

Her chin shot up, sharp, stubborn, and annoying. "You take the room. I'm happy at the trailer."

"I'm not happy that you're there."

"Too bad—so sad."

"Childish, Dayne."

"Adults don't leave their property unattended," she stated. "The mobile home was empty when I took it over."

"I left town for six weeks." He was rapidly getting tired of explaining himself to this woman. "I had business in Florida and have now officially returned. End of story."

She wasn't giving up. "There was no sign anyone inhabited the trailer. It smelled musty."

"I left furniture," he ground out. "A couch, dining room table and chairs, and a bed."

"You say it's yours, but why should I believe you?" she asked. "There were no clothes, no personal effects."

"I live light." All his clothes had fit in his duffel bag.

He carried no baggage. He'd never owned a knickknack. They only collected dust.

"I live to work so I can eat." She glanced at the man's watch on her wrist, then hit him with a look of disgust. "You've made me late. It's your fault if I get fired."

My fault? He wouldn't shoulder the blame.

"Take a hike, Kason." She pushed past him.

"Not so fast." He grabbed the bike seat, held fast. "I'll give you a ride."

"I'd rather walk." Lady was stubborn to a fault.

Her shoulders stiff, she inched the Schwinn forward. He'd wasted enough time arguing with her.

He jerked the bike back. He was giving her a lift whether she wanted one or not.

Kason's tug threw Dayne off balance. Her right arm flailed and her world tilted. She was an eyeblink from landing facedown on the ground.

Kason had lightning-fast reflexes. He twisted, grabbed her by the shoulders, and kept her on her feet.

The Schwinn tipped over, and chips of rust and paint went flying as the bike bit the dust. The pedals and wheels spun wildly. The white basket fell off and rolled into the ditch.

Kason turned her to face him. His expression was fierce, his chest brick hard. With his shaved head, he had "convict" written all over him. His intensity was both tangible and frightening. Dayne was certain there'd been a probation officer in his past.

She fought off her fear. She could take care of herself—always had, always would. She muscled an inch of breathing room, balled her fists, and thumped his chest. Her aggravation and frustration were at an all-time high.

No one told her what to do. She hated being bullied, even if taking his ride was to her advantage.

Like the men in her past, Kason was a control freak. His grip held firm; she had no wiggle room. The slight yet significant widening of his stance drew her snugly between his thighs.

She felt the full impact of his body.

Every nuance of muscle.

With a gentleness that betrayed his size, he tucked a loose strand of hair behind her ear. "Calm down."

Breath hissed through her teeth and her chest expanded. She regained her balance.

Time swelled, stretched, and her annoyance lost importance. She shifted toward his clean, raw masculinity.

Without the softening frame of hair, his features had a graphic harshness. He packed wide shoulders, a thick chest, and long legs into six-plus feet. He was pure strength and testosterone. And totally primed.

An unwanted heat streaked her spine.

Awareness punched like a heartbeat.

Attraction accelerated her pulse.

Her body did the unthinkable: it flirted with him.

Her breasts pressed his chest and her hips lightly bumped his zipper. His warmth licked her belly and skimmed like fingertips across her abdomen. Her V-zone tingled.

One heartbeat, and his big hands made their move. They skimmed her spine, curved and cupped her bottom. His fingers locked over the crease of her ass. He clutched her close.

For an insane instant, her mind blanked and she allowed his touch. Full watts of electricity charged her nerve endings. It would be so easy to lean into his palms, let him lift her so she could wrap her legs about his hips.

She wondered how they'd fit.

A sudden twitch between his thighs and his hiss blew by her ear. Anger and annoyance clearly marked his features. Aroused, he'd had a lapse in judgment. He was visibly mad at himself.

Dayne was equally furious for going so deep in the moment. After Mick Jakes, she'd sworn off men. She shoved against his chest and he released her.

"Go about your business and let me go about mine," she forced out.

He narrowed his eyes. "I can't move on with you standing knee deep in my life."

"I'm knee deep and staying," she stated. "I like living in the woods. It's quiet and peaceful." The land soothed her broken heart. The solitude pieced her soul back together.

Kason Rhodes also lived for peace and privacy. Dayne's similar preferences weren't a strong enough bond to make them roommates, though. Not now, not ever.

She scuffed the toe of her tennis shoe in the dirt, confessed on a sigh, "I need time to heal."

Heal? Was the tomboy sick? He hadn't seen any medication in the medicine cabinet. She looked healthy.

A dozen questions came to mind, but Dayne ended their conversation by jumping into the ditch and retrieving her crumpled white basket. Once reattached to her bike, the wicker rode low, rubbing the front tire.

She assessed the damage, concluded, "You owe me a new chain."

"Sweet mother." He snatched the bike, threw open

the back door of his Hummer, and fitted it inside. "I'll have it fixed and drop it off at the warehouse."

"Can you afford it?"

Her concern surprised him. She believed him unemployed and poor. He shrugged. "Shouldn't cost too much."

"Maybe we should go halves." She didn't want to stick him with the entire bill.

"I'll take care of it," he insisted. "When do you get off work?"

"Around four."

He nodded toward his vehicle. "Get in."

Breath in; breath out; move on. She repeated the mantra six times as she climbed into the Hummer.

The remaining miles were completed in silence.

Total pain in the ass, Kason thought as he dropped Dayne off at Frank's Food Warehouse. The tomboy was more trouble than she was worth.

A call to the sheriff's office would evict her from his trailer. Yet a small part of him hated to go to the law. He knew what it was like to survive on little money. Outside of her bulk food items, Dayne didn't have much going for her.

Well, maybe one *thing,* he quickly recanted. He backtracked twenty minutes. Her body had left an imprint on his own, a very memorable one.

They'd stood on the dirt road, tempers high, and his only choice to avoid a power struggle had been to pull her close.

Her body had fit his, tight, compact, and sun-warmed sweet.

Her temper could've set fires.

Tomboy was mercurial.

Kason shook his head. He didn't have the time or inclination to figure her out. She was too damn complicated.

He located a bike repair shop on his way to James River Stadium. He debated buying Dayne a brand-new ten-speed, but the expense would blow his cover. Besides, he doubted she'd accept it. She had too much pride.

He requested a new chain, two fresh tires, and a shot of spray paint. The rust had eaten away much of the blue. The remaining letters of Schwinn now spelled *Sin*.

A short time later, he took the turnoff onto Rogues Parkway. He parked in the stadium lot, then entered through the players' entrance.

The walls of the spacious locker room had heard men joke, rejoice, cry, and swear in living color. The lockers were large and constructed to give the players breathing room.

Dead silence greeted Kason as the professional ballplayers in various stages of undress stared at his shaved head. Total surprise crossed the men's faces.

Bald wasn't new to the game of baseball.

Bald was, however, new on Kason.

Until today, he'd worn his hair longer than most.

"Hare Krishna." A smile tipped one corner of third baseman Romeo Bellisaro's mouth.

Romeo belonged to the Bat Pack, made up of the three hottest batters in Major League Baseball. Psycho McMillan and Chase Tallan rounded out the group of friends. The men bonded like brothers.

Center fielder and team captain Risk Kincaid cut a

glance over his shoulder and raised an eyebrow. "Criminal, dude." Risk was a decent man. He played hard, gave time and money back to the community.

Psycho McMillan, radical right fielder and known nudist, had major testies. "Shaved head—are you manscaping? Waxed chest? Trimmed hedge around your lawn ornament?"

Psycho baited and waited.

Kason never gave Psycho the satisfaction of a response.

The two men had butted heads from the moment they'd met. From grand slams to snagging fly balls out of thin air, they had daily pissing contests.

They were rivals on the same team.

Kason had yet to fit into the organization. Within the fraternity of sportsmen, he was considered antisocial. He kept to himself, preferred it that way.

The more Psycho razzed him, the stronger Kason's game. His palms itched to slam the first home run of the season into the upper deck. Let Psycho match his batting stats.

Crossing to his locker, he caught Rhaden Dunn's double take. The first baseman's locker flanked Kason's. Dunn was one of few players Kason tolerated.

"Damn, bro, you lose a bet?" Dunn asked as he stepped into his sliding shorts.

"More a win-win." Kason methodically prepared for the morning workout.

In twelve minutes flat, he'd changed clothes, grabbed his glove, and hit the field. He was the first man out. The stillness settled his nerves. No breeze. No fans in the stands. No grounds or maintenance crew. No general manager or coaches.

He leaned against the dugout, looked out toward left field, where he made his living. The grass had been mowed, a checkerboard of light and dark squares. The warning track was smooth. The outfield walls were heavily padded.

He scanned the advertising billboards on the outer walls and inwardly grinned. The left field sign promoted a major insurance company. An international tennis shoe line stretched across center. A hemorrhoid cream backed right.

The sign couldn't have been more appropriate. Psycho McMillan was an asshole.

Rolling his shoulders, Kason inhaled the new season.

The playing field was level on Opening Day.

All teams had the same goal: to win the World Series.

He would contribute all he had to the Rogues.

Born under an athletic star, he'd known at an early age, winning was everything. Losers weren't celebrated.

By age eight, Kason had played with heart.

At ten, he'd grown thick skinned and kicked ass.

Turning twelve, he'd known baseball was his future.

He didn't, however, always play well with others.

He did solitary best.

Solitary. The word drew his thoughts to Dayne.

His time with the tomboy had come to an end.

After practice, he'd see her off.

Kason stretched, then worked the outfield for ninety minutes. He caught every ball batted into left, as well as stole a couple pop-ups meant for Risk Kincaid.

"Damn, Rhodes, play down," Kincaid shouted at him. "It's not October."

Kason preferred to play flat out from day one.

He spent another hour in the batting cages, until his shoulder felt fluid and a little tired. Next the players divided up, each choosing a dugout for their three-inning scrimmage.

Kason looked down the home team's bench. Rhaden Dunn and starting pitcher Brek Stryker stood with him in the dugout.

He and Stryke had a history. Prior to signing with Richmond, Kason had played for the Louisville Colonels. During a game in Louisville the previous season, Kason had turned Brek's no-hitter into a one-hitter. Back in Richmond, Stryke had bare-handed one of Kason's hits for an out.

Brek had broken nearly every bone in his hand on that catch. Surgery and a six-week rehabilitation had followed. Afterward, respect connected the men, and now they played on the same team.

Presently, they were six players short for the scrimmage. The coaches grunted, sent several second stringers their way.

The Bat Pack leaned against the railing in the visitors' dugout, all cocked eyebrows and shit-eating grins. They believed the scrimmage an easy win.

"They're out for blood," Rhaden predicted.

"Psycho's got that kick-ass look in his eye," Stryke agreed. "Someone needs to remind him that we're all on the same team."

Kason understood Psycho. At that moment, they were two very separate teams competing for the scrimmage title.

A growl rose from deep in his gut.

He grabbed his glove and jogged to left field.

Game on.

With the first pitch, the men became boys. They got down and back-lot dirty. The coaches allowed a few broken rules as adrenaline rushed and competitiveness charged the field.

An hour later, both dugouts emptied into the locker room. Psycho's practice uniform was grass stained and bloody.

Romeo's pants were ripped at both knees.

Catcher Chase Tallan had cleat tracks up his shin.

Kason's team had won, 2–1.

"Your bald head gave you superpowers." Psycho's sarcasm hit Kason as both men snagged towels on their way to the showers. "You totally unleashed."

Kason's need to win had proven strong. He'd fired a ball from left-center to put Psycho out at home plate. A showcase throw worthy of any pennant race.

Psycho had slid home headfirst. He'd scraped his forearm and jammed his little finger. Called out, Psycho had gone apeshit on the coach/umpire. His protests had fallen on deaf ears.

The wild man had leaped high to catch a ball meant for the lower deck. Psycho had slammed the wall with such force, he could've dislocated his shoulder.

"You robbed me of a home run," Kason had said as a backhanded compliment. "You fired your jet packs."

"Butt bruise." Chase Tallan checked out his backside in a mirror over the sink. "Stryke nailed me with an eighty-mile-an-hour changeup."

"You're lucky it wasn't his fastball," said Psycho. "He'd have reamed you a second."

Kason caught his own reflection in the mirror. He'd have a shiner by morning. As Kason was rounding third,

Romeo had stuck out his elbow. The poke to Kason's eye had blurred his vision before he'd headed home.

He rolled his shoulder now, felt the soreness that came from compressing nine innings into three. Rivalry brought out his warrior, even in scrimmage. He'd ice his shoulder once he got home. He refused to show weakness in the locker room.

"Rematch," Psycho called to Kason as the men left the showers.

Kason cut Psycho a look. "You must like losing."

By two thirty, Kason realized he'd lost Dayne. He'd picked up her bike, which looked as close to new as it was going to get. Then he'd pulled into Frank's Food Warehouse and had her paged.

Instead of Dayne, he'd gotten the store manager. The man said business had been slow and she'd volunteered to punch out. After some quick shopping, she'd split.

The manager went on to add she'd faced a long and tiring walk with two big bags of groceries. Yet she'd insisted on leaving.

Kason shook his head. The last thing Dayne needed was more food.

He hopped back into his Hummer and drove home. He didn't see any dropped cans or a trail of bread crumbs along the road, so whatever she'd purchased had made it back to the trailer.

Cimarron's bark greeted his arrival. He caught a glimpse of the Dobie in the front window, right before the drapes were drawn.

Drapes? What the hell? He'd never had curtains.

Kason tore out of his vehicle and jogged to the front door.

Something felt off. Very off.

A cardboard box sat by the steps. Inside it, he found his duffel bag, the zipper open, his clothes thrown in. A replacement can of tomato soup topped a pair of brown boxers.

Tomboy was trying to bounce him.

A twist of the door knob, and he realized she'd changed the locks. A marbled gray knob had replaced the worn brass.

Kason would bet his paycheck she'd set a dead bolt as well.

If the tomboy thought a change of hardware would discourage him, she was greatly mistaken.

This was his mobile home.

He was about to toss her ass.

Three

Dayne Sheridan pinched back the curtain and peered around the frame of the front window. She'd heard Kason approach, had pressed her ear to the door as he'd tried the knob. Then there'd been silence.

Silence was not good. Silence suggested sneaky.

Where had he gone?

She nearly jumped out of her skin when her cell phone rang. Without checking the number, she flipped it open and whispered, "Hello."

"Dayne, baby." Mick Jakes's radio-tempered voice stopped her heart. "I've given you a shout every morning on my show for a week. Why haven't you called in?"

She hadn't listened to the radio since he'd dumped her. She hated the fact that his call made her chest squeeze. And that she couldn't catch her breath.

"We have nothing more to say."

"Give me five," he pleaded. "I've boxed the books and clothes you left behind—"

"Which I would have packed, had you not changed the locks on the condo," she reminded him.

"Where are you living?" he asked. "I need your address for shipping."

A mail service kiss-off. UPS was impersonal. Slap on

a packing label, and a brown truck would deliver her past.

"Donate the items to charity." There was no reason to tell Mick she'd moved to Richmond.

His softly spoken, "I've missed you, Dayne," surprised her.

"You're dead to me." She wanted to kick him in the nuts.

"We had good times," he returned. "I've never worked with a better Baby Gherkin."

The dancing pickle? The memory remained vivid. The radio station had sent Mick and Dayne to an on-site remote at Pinelli's Deli. While Mick interviewed the owner and wrapped his jaws around a mile-high sandwich, a costumed Dayne hip-hopped and handed out sweet gherkins.

She'd felt silly, and her hands had smelled like pickle juice for a week. Yet she'd have done anything to promote Mick's career.

"Life happens and situations change," he said.

"*You* changed, and it affected me most."

"It was a business decision with benefits." His remorse was minimal. "I guess you've figured it out by now. I had an affair while we were engaged."

"Who'd you do?" *You son of a bitch.*

"You don't want to know."

Oh, yes, I do. "You owe me a name."

His confession stabbed her in the back. "Willow Clarke."

Sex for career advancement. Mick Jakes had screwed the big-breasted, bottle-blonde station manager to reach syndication. Dayne had trusted Willow. She'd shared her wedding plans with her boss. And Willow had betrayed her.

Sick to her stomach, Dayne turned off her cell phone. She should never have spoken to Mick. He made her feel like a loser.

Several seconds passed, and her cell again buzzed. She saw Mick's number was the incoming call. She dropped her phone and stomped it to death. Fragments and wires soon scattered the floor.

A faint beep indicated he'd left a message.

She kicked the cell against the wall.

No more beeping.

She inhaled a ragged breath.

Exhaled Mick Jakes out of her life.

She never wanted to hear from him again.

The trailer would help heal her. No way was Kason putting her out on the street.

"Temper, temper."

Speak of the devil. His voice hit her from behind, low and menacing. Her heart kicked so hard, she swore she broke a rib. How had Kason gotten inside? She turned so slowly, and time seemed to stand still.

There he stood, big, broad, and black-eyed.

"Bathroom window," he said, answering her unspoken question.

The same way she'd snuck inside when she'd taken over the mobile home.

Cimarron moved halfway between them, not taking either's side. Dog was diplomatic.

She stared at Kason. His eye was red, the rim darkly bruised. Concern took hold. "Were you in a fight?"

"Minor confrontation, nothing serious," he stated.

She shook her head. "Fists first thing in the morning—

very manly." She took a step toward him. "You need frozen peas on that eye."

One brow rose and his good eye narrowed. He seemed surprised she would help him. Without a cold press, the lid would soon swell shut.

She kept plenty of space between them as she edged near the kitchen counter to reach the refrigerator. Then, swinging open the frozen food door, she removed a big bag of peas and tossed it to him.

"Thanks." Kason pressed the bag to his eye. He shifted his gaze to the floor and the destroyed cell phone. "Some stomp. Care to explain?"

She scooped up the phone, dumped it in the trash. Then she shook her head. "No more than you want to detail your fight. It's personal."

"You're in my trailer," he reminded her. "If something bad is about to go down, I'd like advance warning. Pissed-off boyfriend? Angry husband?"

"No involvements." Which was the truth.

"You wanted by the cops?"

"I could ask you the same." She could picture him behind bars in an orange jumpsuit. He was already bald.

"I'm law abiding," he told her.

"You're out to steal my trailer."

He ran one hand down his face. "You're one dense woman. I'm tired of explaining myself. It's time to toss your ass."

"My ass isn't ready to be tossed."

"Your ass has no say in the matter."

She stood her ground. "You're mad about the change in locks."

"I damn sure am. That, and the fact you kidnapped my dog."

"I'd have eventually returned Cimarron."

He flipped the bag of peas, placed the colder side over his eye. "You have to go."

"I can't. . . ." She desperately needed to stay. "A coin toss for the trailer. Your call—heads or tails?"

His neck and shoulder muscles tightened.

"Rock, paper, scissors?" she asked hopefully.

He snarled, "Get real."

"Thumb war?"

He held up his thumb, which was twice the size of her own. She wouldn't stand a chance.

"Monopoly? Scrabble? Winner takes all."

His lips flattened against his teeth. "I don't do board games."

She jammed her fingers in her hair, clutched her skull in frustration. He made her want to pull her hair out. "What do you do?" she hissed.

He took his sweet time replying. His one-eyed stare was direct, serious, sharp as he debated their dilemma. She crossed her arms over her chest in a protective gesture. The man gave her goose bumps.

His mind made up, he tossed the bag of peas onto the counter. The vegetables were fully defrosted from his body heat. Male arrogance set his shoulders, the shift in his stance supported by thick thighs. His words hit her belly low.

"Sex settles my arguments with most women." One corner of his mouth lifted, stopping short of a smile. "Whoever ends up on top wins."

Sex. The air thickened with his suggestion.

His brown eyes ran over her body, holding on her breasts until her nipples puckered; then his stare slid even lower. His gaze tangled with the ties on her sweat-pants. Her V-zone warmed.

Sexual intimidation. Was he out to scare her? Or was he trying to turn her on? Whatever his intention, she wasn't riding his thighs. "Sex is to your advantage. You're stronger than me. One flip, and I'm flat on my back."

He shook his head. "Not necessarily so. Strength means little in sex. A woman could kill a man with a slow ride. The trailer could be yours in thirty minutes."

A naked half hour with this man would strip her of common sense. She knew without a doubt he'd be in total control.

She wouldn't stand a chance against him.

She'd start on top and end up missionary.

His weight would hold her to the mattress.

He'd dominate her orgasm.

The visual image was all too real. A blush threatened. She'd never dealt with a man as physical as Kason.

He was all testosterone.

He also disliked her. His *true* desire was to kick her to the curb. "No sex."

"No trailer."

Stalemate. Dayne's mind went blank. She had no alternative plan. The man was a ticking time bomb.

Cimarron's sudden whining drew her to the couch. The big dog lay on his belly, pawing the worn shag carpet. Cim swiped his front paw near the short wooden leg in an attempt to retrieve something.

"What's under there, boy?" Curious, Dayne moved to the sofa and dropped to her knees. She lifted the leg, and the world according to Cimarron came clear.

Six toys resided beneath the couch. Cim sniffed out

his favorite: a ten-inch wooden butcher's bone, heavily teeth-marked. Once it was retrieved, the dog turned toward Kason, his stubby tail wagging as he showed off his prize.

"So that's where you hid it." Kason patted Cimarron's head. "Good score, buddy."

Dayne's hand shook as she looked beyond the dust and slowly took in the remaining dog toys, all well chewed. The roped legs of a plaid octopus were nearly shredded. Two tennis balls had been bitten in half.

Cobwebbed in one corner, a dirty pair of men's socks, a gnawed leather belt, and a jock strap had also gone missing. A torn scrap of paper from an electric bill showed Kason's first name, amount to be paid, and the date issued.

January 16.

The snowstorm had driven her down the road in February.

Realization stalled her breath and she grew lightheaded. The items beneath the couch were *old,* used, and proved Kason had lived in the double-wide long before her arrival. She'd trespassed in her takeover.

"You need to vacuum," was all she could manage as she lowered the sofa and died a slow death.

"Cim likes to chase dust bunnies." Kason's voice was barely audible over the onslaught of her headache.

The pounding at her temples forced her to press her palms against her eyes and push back the pain. Loose strands of hair swept her cheeks, hiding her face from him.

"How long have you lived here?" She kept her head low.

"Nine months, off and on."

"I showed up when you were off."

"I spent six weeks out of town."

"And I took over your trailer."

"I tried to tell you." His tone was even, direct.

She tucked her hair behind her ears, cut him a glance. "But I wouldn't listen."

"You're stubborn to a fault."

In this case she had been. She'd needed to escape her past for a short time and regroup. The forsaken trailer had provided a safety net.

Kason's ownership pedaled her down the road.

She eased to her feet, in need of an aspirin. "I'm hungry," she stated. She thought better on a full stomach.

His lip curled. "You've worked up quite an appetite hanging curtains, changing locks, kidnapping my dog, and smashing your cell phone."

"All in a day's work."

"Add packing and moving to your work list."

She brushed passed him, her chin in the air. "It's at the bottom of my to-dos."

Kason Rhodes studied Dayne closely. She should have looked dejected, even frightened, yet determination squared her shoulders as she went about fixing dinner.

"Breathe in; breathe out; move on." The softly spoken mantra seemed to center her.

"You sharing food?" he asked as she opened a family-size bottle of Tylenol and tapped out two tablets.

"Is the guest room open for another night?" She downed the medicine with a glass of water.

"Depends on what you're cooking."

"Macaroni and cheese."

A boyhood favorite. He scruffed his knuckles over his jaw. "I'll give it some thought."

"Decide before you eat."

His gaze hit on her belly as she stretched to retrieve an enormous box of mac and cheese from the top shelf in the cupboard. Her stomach was flat and tight, her navel now pierced with a tiny pink butterfly. He was disappointed when the white Alice Cooper tank top again settled over her sweats. Tomboy had a thing for rockers.

Resting one hip against the counter, he crossed his arms over his chest and contemplated how best to get his share without committing to another sleepover.

While the noodles boiled, Dayne heated the defrosted peas. She then went on to make dessert, a batch of butterscotch pudding.

Kason wasn't much of a sweet eater, but pudding took him back to the one good memory of his childhood. To the time he lived with his great-uncle Dave.

Dave had been a man of habit. He'd made the same dessert every Sunday for the two years Kason had lived with him. When Dave had worked overtime, they'd splurged and topped the pudding with whipped cream.

Kason remained standing until Dayne finished cooking. He felt a heartbeat of relief when she withdrew two paper plates from a packet of five hundred and piled each with dinner.

His relief was short-lived.

"Cimarron," she called to the Dobie.

Cim left his butcher bone and went to her.

Kason stood, immobile and disbelieving, as Dayne set *his* dinner before his dog. Cimarron wolfed the macaroni and cheese in two big gulps.

Son of a bitch.

"Seconds?" she asked Cimarron.

"He's full," Kason stated.

"Maybe Cim would like some peas."

"Not his favorite," said Kason. "He spits them like a peashooter."

"More for me." She poured the peas into a large plastic bowl.

Kason wasn't a big fan of peas, but when a man was hungry, food was food. He'd yet to pick up his own groceries. He had no desire to drive to the restaurant at Tri-Corners. "What about me?"

"You eat, I sleep." Tomboy played hardball.

Another night in his trailer? What the hell? Macaroni and cheese and butterscotch pudding mellowed his mood. "Agreed."

Visible relief softened her features. She looked almost pretty. Until she scrunched up her nose, jabbed the bowl of peas into his chest, and commanded, "Make yourself useful."

Kason carried the bowl to the table.

At the counter, Dayne divided the remainder of the mac and cheese between them, then went as far as to give him the bigger portion of butterscotch pudding. Bribery was good. He might let Cimarron sleep on her bed again tonight.

She drew two glasses of tap water and gathered plastic silverware. They soon sat across from each other at the small dining room table. Her gaze fixed on him from his first bite.

"Something on your mind?" he asked.

She scooped her peas, blue-eyed and inquisitive. "Do you really settle arguments with your women in bed?"

He swallowed his smile. "Fight with me and find out."

"I don't like confrontation."

"Sex eases the tension."

Dayne didn't look convinced.

She had every right not to believe him. He'd mentioned sex earlier to see how far he could push her. Girl on top would have lasted as long as it took her to climb on; then he'd have flipped her.

His first time with a woman, he wanted her to forget her name and remember his. He liked to control her orgasm.

"Do you bring your dates here?" Her curiosity made her chatty.

"Never have," he admitted. "The mobile home's rundown. I doubt I could talk a woman through the door."

"You'd have to talk fast." Her smile revealed straight white teeth and a tiny dimple in her cheek.

"The trailer's a temporary roof over my head," he stated. "I'll be here a year, no longer."

"You're transient?" She sounded sympathetic.

He'd signed a seven-year deal with the Rogues, and planned to put down roots in Richmond. Dayne, however, saw him as unemployed and penniless. That was fine by him. The less she knew about him, the better.

"Don't worry about me." He blew her off. "I survive."

"I'm not as concerned about you as I am about Cimarron."

"Does he look like he's missed a meal?" Kason grunted.

Dayne twisted on her chair to look at the Dobie. Cim was solid and still growing. He now gnawed his butcher's bone in utter contentment.

"Cimarron liked the mac and cheese," she noted.

"So did I." He swallowed his last bite.

Dusk soon shadowed the woods visible through the back window. The window without drapes. Deep burgundy and muted orange scored the sky as night crept up fast.

Kason caught Dayne's long looks through the glass followed by her heavy sigh. She set down her fork and absently rubbed the *Tomorrow* tattoo on her wrist.

"Tell me about your tat," he said, drawing her gaze from the window.

She pursed her lips, turned thoughtful. "My tattoo's connected to my watch." She raised the cracked face and worn band for his inspection. "The watch belonged to my dad, the aging rocker. He played bass for Wicked Riot. It took years before the band was recognized beyond a local neighborhood tavern. He taught me to appreciate rock and concert T-shirts. When fame hit, my dad split."

Her voice slowed. "I caught him sneaking out the back door of our apartment on Christmas Eve when I was thirteen. He winked, told me that he was going to the convenience store for a gallon of milk. Dad insisted Santa needed milk with his sugar cookies. Cookies my mom hadn't baked.

"I didn't believe him for a second. Who went for milk carrying a duffel bag and guitar case? I begged to go with him, but Dad refused. He took off his watch, handed it to me. He told me to time him, that he'd be back in thirty minutes. A half hour passed, then an hour. Soon it was midnight."

Her shoulders slumped. "My dad didn't return for Christmas or for New Year's. My mother sat in a rocking chair by the tree and cried for a week. I fixed her peanut butter sandwiches for lunch and microwave popcorn for dinner. I returned to school after the holidays.

"Times were tough and money was tight. My dad never paid a dime in child support. Somehow we kept it together. Mom got a job and bought food in bulk—it was cheaper and lasted longer. She always told me that in a bad situation, I should breathe in, breathe out, and move on, and that tomorrow would always be better. Thus the tattoo."

"Ever see your dad again?" Kason asked.

"Not a phone call, not a letter. He chose single and the spotlight over marriage and a kid. His band opened for lead artists, but never cut an album. Six years on the road, and drugs took his life."

"Your mom?"

Dayne sighed. "She died shortly after my dad. Her heart grew tired of waiting for him to return."

"Sorry." It might not be enough, but it was all he had.

Silence wrapped up their meal. Dayne soon rose and removed their paper plates so they had a clear shot at dessert.

Kason's first bite of butterscotch pudding made him feel sixteen. For instant pudding, it went down smooth and easy. He wished there had been seconds.

He watched as Dayne rocked back in her chair and stretched her arms over her head. She had a lean line to her body. He'd hoped to catch another glimpse of the butterfly at her navel, but her top didn't ride beyond her hips. The ribbed white cotton did, however, pull across her breasts, showcasing her as ample, firm, and braless.

He liked a woman who set her tits free.

Catching his stare, Dayne lowered her arms and protectively crossed them over her chest. "No television, no radio—what do you do in the evening?" She wanted to know.

"I keep my own company."

She gave him a small smile. "I like being alone too."

Kason's nights passed quickly. He often worked out, was prone to read the newspaper or buy a book. Once a week he met with his architect to go over the plans for his home. He was always available to the Dream Foundation when it came to charity work for the Rogues. He was a busy man, but chose not to share his activities with the woman who would pack her food at dawn.

He rolled his shoulder. Hours after the Rogues scrimmage, his right rotator cuff had tightened up. He'd spent enough time at the table. He needed to ice down.

Kason scooted back his chair and hit his feet. He jammed his hand into the pocket of his jeans, scrounged for a five spot, passed it to Dayne. "Can I buy a second bag of peas?"

"For your eye?" she asked.

He hesitated, hating to show weakness. "For my shoulder."

Dayne Sheridan stared at the man towering over her. His earlier fight had left more than one injury. She took the money. Five dollars was five dollars. "Ace bandage?" She had one to sell. For the right price.

He shook his head. "I have a shoulder wrap." Which he retrieved from his bedroom. Back in the kitchen, he shrugged off his T-shirt, packed peas over his shoulder, then fit on the elastic brace. His body heat melted the veggies faster than a microwave.

Gathering the remaining dishes, Dayne left the table.

She dumped the garbage, leaned back against the sink, and took a moment to appreciate the big man's chest. His body went beyond perfect, all thick, cut, and close enough to touch.

His shoulder soon became slickened with condensation. She watched as one fat droplet took a slow slide down his pectoral, tipping on his nipple, a tongue lick away.

In the dim light of the kitchen, the urge to pop the droplet was strong. She clasped her hands tightly. Breathed deeply. Fought temptation, and lost.

She tapped the glistening drop with the tip of her finger. The barest touch and the droplet split into two. Slow motion trickled the water over his six-pack before it pooled at the slit of his navel. Spilling over, the drops were absorbed in the waistband of his navy boxers.

The water spots made Dayne blink. Her finger was still pressed to his nipple, and given the depth of Kason's breathing, the man was turned on.

She pulled back, mumbled, "Sorry."

No words from him, just a heavy-lidded stare, hot enough to set her panties on fire.

"Touching is dangerous and complicates our living arrangements." His baritone made her belly shimmy.

She should never have been so impulsive. "It meant nothing, nothing at all," she was quick to assure him. "We're roommates for one more night. Nothing sexual. I can picture you as a girl."

"A definite stretch of your imagination."

"I can and I will . . . Kassie."

He went utterly still, and his face bled pale. The corners of his eyes pinched, as did his mouth. A haunting hurt scarred the silence. A flash of vulnerability and pain crossed his face. She'd struck a nerve, unsettled him.

His chest heaved, and his words were ground out. "What did you just call me?"

"Kassie," she slowly repeated.

He iced over. "Don't call me that again."

His command pushed her buttons. Mick had dumped on her earlier, and now Kason wanted to steal her freedom of speech. Pain and anger lifted her chin. "I'll call you whatever I like."

"I'm asking you nicely to stop."

Nicely? He looked ready to kill. Dayne would not be bullied. Fool that she was, she went for the fight. "Kassie."

"Damn, woman, very unwise." The words were said darkly, tightly, and threaded with violence.

"Kassie." She couldn't stop herself.

He was on her, so fast and furious she never saw him coming. As he forced her back against the refrigerator, both his hands slammed on either side of her head.

The air around them thickened, as charged with her taunt as his reaction. A reaction stemming from anger and deep hurt.

Breast to chest, his weight crushed her.

Air caught in her lungs and her heartbeat raced.

His exhale came slow and hot on her cheek. His eyes were now glazed. "I warned you—"

"Kassie," she dared, knowing she'd lost her mind.

He shoved her words back down her throat with his tongue. He was out of her league the moment he kissed her. His kiss burned, bruised, punished. The intensity of the moment shook her. She couldn't fight his full-body press. The refrigerator handle jabbed the small of her back while his erection jammed her belly.

He kissed with a violence that should have scared her. Somehow, it didn't. He was mad as hell, yet she sensed that his anger came from pain. She'd triggered a memory that sought revenge.

He was taking his past out on her.

She clutched his upper arms so tightly, her nails scored his flesh. His big body held her against the refrigerator door.

The appliance was cool against her back.

The man was hot against her front.

His gaze was hooded and distant when he released her mouth. He wasn't fully seeing her.

He was, however, moving on her body.

Curving one big hand about her neck, he set his thumb to the pulse at the base of her throat. The wild beat sent him stroking lower, a primal slide of his palm over her collarbone, his fingers soon touching her nipple.

His touch slowed, somewhat gentler, yet firm with purpose. Dayne closed her eyes, pressed her face to the hard bulge of his bicep, as he captured her breast.

Squeezing, kneading, Kason was good with his hands. Raw, racing need rose off him, as thick and straining as the ridge of his sex. His anger now sought physical release.

His hips rocked against hers, solid, grinding, rhythmic. In no time he would be inside her.

She had to stop him. Sex against the refrigerator with a near stranger stretched beyond crazy. But the thought was vague as his long fingers dipped beneath the waistband of her sweats, then slid within the silk of her panties. He stroked her with a skill that shut off her mind and forced her to do nothing but feel.

She went wet for him.

Wet, but not willing. A part of Kason Rhodes sensed her hesitancy. He mentally distanced himself from the woman he now fondled with the intimacy of a lover.

He fought to catch his breath.

Tried to reclaim his sanity.

She'd provoked.

He'd punished.

Yet he'd only hurt himself.

He should never have allowed the tomboy to return him to his childhood. He was a man in control of his emotions, his feelings wrapped tight. Yet the taunt "Kassie" opened a wound and he'd bled out. He regretted it now.

He looked down between their bodies. The neckline of her top still hung off her nipples and the drawstring on her sweatpants was tugged low off her hips.

The exposed skin was flushed as pink as the wings on her butterfly navel stud.

The slickness between her thighs had invited him to enter her. Yet her dazed expression hadn't held the same naked lust that fired his belly. Her hands clutched his arms; her legs were stiffly locked.

He'd gone off on her, all wild and wounded.

She'd let him rage on her body.

She hadn't tried to fight him.

His hand was still down her panties.

He swore, pulled free, and dropped back a step. He was acutely aware how small she appeared. The perception reset reality.

Tension born of his adrenaline and her vulnerability

filled the air. He watched as Dayne adjusted her top and sweatpants. Her hands shook and her cheeks burned.

Once fully covered, she cleared her throat, and cautiously met his gaze. "I know what not to call you."

"We can't repeat what just happened." He owed her an explanation, which he reluctantly gave. "You jarred a bad memory that brought out the worst in me."

She touched her fingers to her lips—lips now swollen from the grind of his mouth against hers. "We all have our demons," she said softly. "Some that won't die. I didn't mean to be cruel."

"I didn't mean to jump you."

Cimarron took that moment to nudge himself between them. The dog dropped to his haunches beside Dayne, then leaned into her thigh. She immediately scratched his ears.

Kason noted the naturalness between Cim and the tomboy. The Doberman sensed something about her that Kason had yet to put his finger on. The earlier cell phone call had brought out the fight in her. She'd then gone on to challenge him for the trailer, win or lose.

In the end, he might have lost more than she. Her scent, taste, and feel soon followed him to bed. A bed where he slept naked and alone.

Cimarron had settled on the foot of the mattress, only to desert Kason within minutes for the guest room.

He'd heard the springs on Dayne's bed squeak as she'd edged over and welcomed his Dobie.

Cim was one lucky dog.

Four

Kason Rhodes kept company with the dawn. He'd always been a fan of mornings and rose with the first fingers of light.

He stretched out on his back, jammed a pillow beneath his head, and fought the full press of his erection. Damn, he was stiff.

Dayne had infiltrated his dreams. She'd aroused him in a fantasy of foreplay and sweet panting. Yet there'd been no satisfaction. Boners sucked.

His flying solo fell flat.

He hadn't taken himself in hand since he was sixteen.

There wasn't enough soap on the planet to satisfy him this morning.

Today, Dayne will pack and depart.

The thought jacked him from bed. He had every reason to want her gone, yet his gut tightened at the thought of her eviction. He hated to be the bad guy, even with good reason.

Kassie. He'd never imagined the childhood name would cause such a knee-jerk reaction. The previous evening he'd gone all animal on her. He'd shut her mouth with a punishing kiss, then proceeded to stroke her wet.

Lady had gone slick for him.

He'd had no business touching her.

He felt like an absolute ass.

He didn't seek forgiveness often.

Yet a second apology might set things right.

He'd shower and shave, and afterward they'd talk.

Female laughter captured the dawn, just outside his window. He glanced out.

He located Dayne just beyond his Hummer. A red Woodstock '69 T-shirt hung loosely off her shoulders and black sweatpants with Key West across her bottom draped her hips. She stood barefoot in the dewy grass, one arm raised, ready to throw a tennis ball for Cimarron to chase. Cim was so excited, he quivered.

Tomboy had a good arm. She powered the ball a fair distance, giving the Dobie a solid run. The dog retrieved, returned, and dropped the ball in her palm, ready to go again. Twenty tosses, and they changed games.

Hide-and-seek came next. Dayne made Cim sit and stay while she hid behind the Hummer. She whistled, and Cim charged to find her. Once spotted, Dayne took off. The Dobie loped at her heels. Cimarron lived to give chase.

In his exuberance, Cim sideswiped her hip, knocked her down. Dayne landed flat on her back in the grass. Cim dropped down beside her.

She was so out of breath, her laughter came choked and thin. The Dobie licked her face, and she wheezed even harder.

Hand over her heart, she slowly calmed. She shaded her eyes against the sun and looked at the crystal blue sky. She inhaled deeply—fresh air and the scent of the woods—and sighed with contentment.

"Eat." She knew the way to Cimarron's heart. Both woman and dog rose and returned to the trailer.

The scent and sizzle of hamburger made Kason's stomach growl. Lady was cooking breakfast.

He drew on a pair of gray athletic shorts, rounded the bed, and stepped into the hallway. The sight of Dayne feeding Cimarron two enormous hamburger patties on a paper plate brought him up short. The Dobie looked at her adoringly before devouring his breakfast.

She was spoiling his dog.

Dayne sensed Kason before he could move. Her gaze flicked up, then down, taking him in. Familiarity darkened her watercolor blue eyes. She'd known his kiss, his touch, the press of his erection.

There was no moving beyond her stare.

Her look dared him to face her after the previous evening. He met her challenge. His shoulders squared and his abs flexed.

His hands fisted.

He widened his stance.

Heat circled his groin. His dick strained to impress. He was nearly the size of her porno vibrator.

She blushed, and was the first to look away.

His neck burned.

There was no reason to stand in the hall and point at her. He sidestepped into the bathroom, cracked the door, called out. "You're up early."

"I wanted to shower before you got up." Her words came around the wooden frame.

Damn. "Any hot water left?"

"It's a very small tank."

The tank heated water for one shower, not two.

The icy cold tamped him down. After skrinking and shivering, he shot from the shower. He toweled off and dressed.

Back in the kitchen, Kason found Dayne bent low before the cupboards, itemizing her groceries. Her T-shirt climbed her spine, revealing a symmetrical display of soft, smooth skin and a nicely curved ass.

Cimarron had become Dayne's shadow. She nearly tripped over him as she collected several #10 cans, then staggered toward the front door. She stacked the items beneath the living room window.

Twisting toward him, she said, "I'm clearing the shelves so you can bring in your own food."

He hadn't planned to shop today. "What you don't want to haul, I'll buy," he offered.

She circled back to the kitchen. "I'm getting boxes from Frank's Warehouse today. I'll load up, see what's leftover, and cut you a good deal."

He moved to the coffeemaker, poured himself a cup. "How do you plan to get the boxes back to the trailer?" he asked with his first sip.

"I'll make several trips on my bike."

"That could take days."

"I could get a couple of people from work to help me."

"I don't want strangers in my mobile home."

"I was a stranger once."

She was familiar to him now. He had kissed her deeply, stroked her intimately. He'd almost taken her against the refrigerator. In the aftermath, they'd connected. She'd recognized and understood his pain.

"Where will you go?" His need to know proved stronger than he liked.

"I just might camp on your doorstep."

"Bad idea."

She sighed, concentration furrowing her brow. "I plan to buy a newspaper, scan the classifieds, and see if there's a one-bedroom available close by."

"Or maybe a place across town? North is nice."

"I'm healing," she reminded him. "I need alone time. This area is less traveled than most."

There was little traffic because he owned a thousand acres and no one trespassed. No one until the tomboy.

He again wondered about her illness, and if he was being a total jerk in tossing her ass. In his thirty-two years, he'd never rehashed, contemplated, or questioned his decisions. He lived by his gut. Yet Dayne had him second-guessing himself.

He glanced at his watch. "I have places to go and people to see."

"Job interviews?" She looked hopeful for him.

"I have a strong lead." He hated lying to her.

"Good luck." Her words sounded sincere.

"I'll be back around two."

"I'll have everything packed and ready to go."

Kason locked his jaw against offering her another night in his double-wide. He was glad Cimarron couldn't talk. The Dobie would be in Kason's face, campaigning for Dayne to stay.

Her mantra followed him out the door.

"Breathe in; breathe out; move on."

The Rogues practice strained both his muscles and his restraint. Psycho was more of a dick today than he'd been yesterday. His digs and jabs crossed to left field, then centered on the batter's box. The man liked to needle.

Kason tuned out Psycho until it came time for the team's daily scrimmage. Closing in on noon, the manager instructed the ballplayers to form into two different teams from the previous day. Center fielder Risk Kincaid and shortstop Zen Driscoll crossed to the home team's dugout.

The Bat Pack hung as one.

"Deserters," Psycho shouted from the visitors' side.

"You've got us." First baseman Rhaden Dunn, along with the back-up catcher, begrudgingly crossed the field.

Psycho grunted. "Two batters hitting .280 can't replace grand slammers."

Kason took his first at-bat against pitcher Sloan Mc-Caffrey. The man had never liked Kason. His wife, Eve, was an artist. The previous July, Dog Days of Summer, a charity silent auction, had brought out advocates for animal rescue. Sloan and Eve had been on the outs. Kason had pushed Sloan back into Eve's life by bidding on her oil painting of James River Stadium. Kason had driven up the price, forcing Sloan to compete for his woman.

Wildly jealous, Sloan had bid extravagantly. At the end of the night, he'd won both Eve and her painting.

Delighted by the outcome, Eve had gifted Kason with Cimarron, one of the rescued pups. A nice gesture on her part, yet one that suggested Kason might still be a rival for Eve's affection. Sloan continued to keep a sharp eye on Kason, even after the couple wed. Eve still dog-sat Cim whenever the Rogues played out of town.

On the mound now, McCaffrey wound up, hoping to draw Kason outside his strike zone.

Kason was selective.

He was known to often go to full count before he took his swing. Three balls and two strikes, and he nailed a fastball between first and second. The hit drew Psycho in from right to scoop and throw.

Kason slid cleats high into second for a double.

Risk Kincaid's single got Kason to third.

Zen Driscoll's solid hit to center dropped behind the fielder. Kason sprinted home. His team led by one.

The three-inning scrimmage ended when Kason laid down a bunt, and Zen scored from third. The home team took their 2-0 win to the locker room.

"Game was rigged," Psycho bellyached. "Damn, I hate to lose."

"The best team won," Kason tossed over his shoulder as he shucked off his pants and sliding shorts, down to his jock.

Psycho flipped him off. "I can spit farther than you can bunt."

"Try spitting a home run." Kason then stripped to his skin and headed for the shower.

"Dickhead," Psycho grumbled.

When Kason returned, he found a note taped to his locker, a summons from Revelle Sullivan from player promotions. Her reputation preceded her. Her newly established department had created major locker room buzz. Game's On connected players with high-profile promotions. The woman played hardball in the game of corporate endorsements and served the Rogues well.

Due to her efforts, Oat Berry Clusters featured Risk Kincaid on its organic cereal box.

Romeo Bellisaro had become the new hood ornament for Autobahn Elite, a German-based automaker. The low-slung sports car hit high speeds and hugged corners. The campaign had gone worldwide. Romeo was an international spokesman.

Psycho McMillan scored big with Dinkies Dog Biscuits. He howled as loudly as his Newfoundlands and miniature dachshund in the nationwide commercials. Dogs across the country barked for the treats. Even Cimarron found them tasty.

The Rogues had lined up to be showcased.

Everyone but Kason. He didn't seek the spotlight. He had no desire to be a household name. His statistics in the batter's box and skills in left field were syndicated in the sports section of every newspaper. Yet he'd never done an interview. He felt questions pertaining to his favorite music and movie, best color, and astrological sign were intrusive.

Some called him dark and mysterious. Others a dick for not sharing his innermost thoughts. His life outside the park was his own. He had no plans to be linked to a multimedia blitz. No matter how lucrative.

Revelle Sullivan, however, had leverage. She was Guy Powers's niece. What went down in her office traveled to her uncle. The team's owner liked his Rogues front and center in the community and recognizable to all. National promotions pleased him greatly.

Kason had ignored Revelle's phone calls and avoided her at the stadium. Today she'd twist his left nut.

"I need to see Revelle too." Rhaden Dunn produced a similar note. "I'll go with you, if you don't mind."

The two men rode the elevator to the sixth floor, then crossed the skywalk to the corporate offices located in the penthouse suites of Powers Tower. The team owner had invested heavily in real estate. Fanning out from

James River Stadium, he now owned every building and parking lot in a five-block radius.

The teammates sauntered down the hallway to player promotions. Revelle's office was situated between public relations and business affairs.

Kason heard a door creak and sensed stares. He glanced over his shoulder and found two women standing in the hallway, checking him and Rhaden out. A third peered around the jamb.

Rhaden smiled, and Kason shook his head. Both men kept right on walking. They were used to the once-overs.

As they stopped outside her office, Kason's thoughts were on Revelle. They were about to face off.

He wanted to walk out of her office the same way he would walk in: without a campaign.

"You can go first," Rhaden told Kason as he crossed to a cluster of chairs centered between hallways. "Take it easy on Revelle." His comment turned Kason around. Dunn looked worried. "She gives eighty hours a week to the organization. She's pro-Rogue."

"Lady needs a hobby or a boyfriend."

Rhaden shuffled the magazines on a side table. "She has neither."

"Maybe you could qualify as her hobby."

Rhaden ducked his head. Heat reddened the back of his neck. The magazine he picked up and pretended to read was upside down. The man was distracted.

Kason knocked on Revelle's office door, then entered before she could officially welcome him. Dark green leather and mahogany made the space elegant yet businesslike. An enormous black-and-white photograph of James River Stadium circa 1935 covered half a wall.

The picture captured a time before the luxury suites, concession stands, and press boxes. Fans had taken stairs to the upper decks, prior to the elevators and escalators. The stadium had been renovated three times since its construction. Yet it still hadn't lost the Roman Colosseum architecture favored by so many sports facilities.

All sportsmen were warriors in their own right.

Noting his arrival, Revelle half rose from behind her desk. A redhead with violet eyes and classic features, she wore rimless glasses and a tailored black power suit that left her sexless.

Her lips parted, then closed. She frowned when he threw his body into a green leather club chair and met her gaze squarely. Game on.

She nodded at him. "Kason Rhodes."

"Revelle Sullivan." He nodded back.

Greetings over, they stared at each other until Revelle blinked. "You're bald."

He cracked his knuckles. "You're observant."

"You look mean."

"You look stressed."

"I've a lot to do and little time to do it." She swept her hand across her desk. Three stacks of file folders fought for space amid a computer, desk lamp, and a bouquet of lavender roses. "Sorry about the mess. My assistant quit without notice. I'm trying to regroup."

She slipped off her glasses, forced a smile. "Know anyone looking for a job? Someone who could start tomorrow?"

Dayne immediately came to mind. She'd mentioned needing more than the part-time hours offered at Frank's Food Warehouse. He didn't, however, know her qualifications. He had no idea whether she had office or computer skills.

He also wasn't ready to tell her that he was a Rogue. So he shrugged, said, "No one at the moment."

"If you think of someone, send her my way. Hours and pay are good and we have great company benefits. I'm also willing to train."

She pulled a file from the middle of the pile closest to her and withdrew a blank piece of paper. "I need your Five Fun Facts for Rogues Highlights. You promised to send them in, but apparently they got lost in the mail."

Highlights was the free fan brochure available at the stadium's main gate. It featured the ballplayers' pictures, statistics, and personal info.

"Mail can be slow." Kason blew her off. "I'm sure the Fun Facts will arrive in a day or two."

"Highlights goes to press tomorrow," she said evenly. "To be on the safe side, let's do the facts now."

"Now isn't good for me."

He pushed forward in his chair, and she hit him with, "Go for the door, and I swear I'll tackle you."

Lady had guts.

"Five questions, Kason, quick and painless. Fans like to identify with their favorite players. These are the people who fill the stands and pay your salary." She poised her pen over the paper. "Favorite candy bar?"

"Butterfinger." He spoke between clenched teeth.

"Movies?"

"*Blade Runner* and *Raiders of the Lost Arc.*"

"Music?"

"Bruce Springsteen and early Bob Seger."

"If you didn't play baseball you'd . . . ?"

"Be an architect."

"Quote or philosophy?"

"Play hard, as if Opening Day were October."

Revelle peered at him over the rim of her glasses. "Single or seeing someone?"

"That's more than five questions."

"The women on the sixth floor want to know."

The women who'd come out of their offices to check him out. "I'm presently living with someone."

"That will break a lot of hearts."

He didn't think of himself as a heartbreaker. Dayne, however, did provide a good excuse. She hadn't officially moved out. If women thought him involved, a few might respect his relationship.

Revelle set the paper aside, moved on. "Promotion time, Kason Rhodes. Ever hear of Platinum?"

He shook his head.

Revelle filled him in. "It's an upscale jewelry shop. Gayle de Milo is known for her designer pieces, commissioned for an elite clientele. She's recently branched out to a cosmopolitan, more moderately priced line as well. She's planning a television commercial, and she wants to feature you."

Pimp jewelry? Not in this lifetime.

The thought was so ludicrous, Kason hit his feet. He wore a ten-year-old watch that lost five minutes over the course of a year even with a new battery. He couldn't tell the difference between fourteen-karat gold and gold plated.

He stood tall, arms crossed over his chest. "I'm not your guy."

"Gayle believes you'd be perfect."

"Gayle doesn't know me."

"She's seen you play ball. You're hard faced and your

intensity is staggering. Her idea for the commercial centers on romance: the bigger the man, the harder he falls when he meets the right woman."

"Get real."

"Gayle hopes to shoot five thirty-second commericals," Revelle continued. "In the first—"

"No 'first,'" he said, cutting her off. "I'm not interested."

She narrowed her eyes, fight in her features. "It's my job to offer you the promotion. So hear me out."

Kason admired the corporate woman. She was all business and no bullshit. Because she was Guy Powers's niece, she got one more minute. "Wrap it up."

"The first television segment will air in May. You'll enter Platinum, looking for a Mother's Day gift."

"My mother passed away ten years ago."

"It's television, Kason, not true life."

"You're asking me to play someone I'm not?"

"It's acting, for all of thirty seconds."

"I'm not an actor."

"Be yourself, then." She dismissed his concern. "Once inside the jewelry store, you'll check out the other shoppers. You'll notice a pretty woman looking at earrings. You stare long and hard until she looks up. Your eyes lock, sparks fly, and the shot ends."

His lip curled. "Is this your idea of a joke?"

"Not, it's not a laughing matter." She straightened her shoulders. "With each segment, the scenes get more and more intimate. By the fifth, the two of you will be engaged."

"I don't do romance, rings, or weddings."

"Not even for a hundred grand?"

"I don't need the money."

"Give it to charity.

"Get someone else."

"Gayle de Milo's a good friend," Revelle confessed. "If she wants you, I'll nag you to death."

"Nag away, Miss Sullivan."

Her lips pinched. "Are you always so uncooperative?"

"I gave you Fun Facts."

"Give Platinum some thought," she urged. "I don't need your answer today."

"My answer will be the same tomorrow. Player promotions are optional. I opt out."

"We'll meet again, Kason Rhodes."

Not unless it is court ordered.

He nodded to Rhaden Dunn on his way out, then headed for the elevator.

The afternoon had worn on. It was time to move Dayne down the road.

Kason didn't look forward to her departure.

Yet he knew, deep down, he did alone best.

Five

Rhaden Dunn's eyes fixed on Revelle Sullivan the moment he entered her office. He was a big, strong jock, yet in this woman's presence, his chest tightened and his palms grew sweaty. The lady was so beautiful, she made him ache.

He'd unbuttoned women's blouses and hiked enough miniskirts to know the difference between a one-night stand and someone special. His days of instant gratification were long behind him. At thirty-four, he wanted to take a woman to bed and draw out the intimacy.

The second Revelle had been introduced as head of player promotions, he'd known she belonged to him. For life. She just didn't know it yet.

He admired her strength and sense of purpose. She brought intelligent conversation, occasional humor, and simple elegance to the organization. Her presentation to the Rogues had been straightforward and held his teammates' attention. No man had laughed or made a snide remark. They'd all listened and lined up for promotions.

Now she sat behind her desk with shoulders slumped and features pale. The diamond studs in her ears twinkled with a brilliance that usually characterized her as well. Yet she'd momentarily lost her sparkle.

He needed to fix whatever was wrong. "Did Rhodes upset you?" he forced out from the doorway. "You look beat."

She cut him a glance as she cleaned her glasses on a soft cloth. "Ever gone a round with Kason?"

Rhaden nodded. "The man's intense."

"A brick wall with eyes."

"I gather he turned you down."

She sighed. "A slam-bam, no thank you, ma'am."

"The man's all baseball."

"I'm all about promotion." She took her job seriously. "I'll track down Kason after the home opener."

"Maybe Guy should be present."

She shook her head. "Game's On is my baby. There's no need to involve my uncle. I want Kason to take the Platinum Jewelry account willingly, not by ultimatum."

"You'll wear Rhodes down," he assured her.

"Maybe, maybe not. I'll give it my best shot. Promotions aren't mandatory. They're meant to give players visibility and pad their paychecks, though many donate the money to charity."

She set aside her glasses, invited him in. "No need to stand with three chairs available. Have a seat, Rhaden."

He preferred the door—a little distance kept him sane. Control of his body went south quickly with this woman. He had a hard-on barely hidden by the untucked tails on his white button-down. The slightest shift and she'd catch him stiff.

He jammed his hands deep in the pockets of his khakis, let his fingertips hold everything in place. His steps toward her desk were stiff and awkward. Not smooth for an athlete who could sprint around the bases and stretch like Gumby to catch a wild throw to first.

"Why'd you want to see me?" He managed to lower his body into a leather chair without embarrassing himself.

"Two reasons," she stated. "First, to thank you for the beautiful bouquet." Pleasure brought pink to her pale cheeks, which softened the sharp symmetry of her hair-cut and the black stiffness of her business suit. The blooms remained velvety and tight, and were the exact color of her violet eyes. "Each week is a celebration of color."

"The team appreciates all you've done."

"The flowers came from you."

He shrugged, forced a casualness he didn't feel. "I'm grateful you connected me to Cora Dora Pies."

"That's second on my list," she said, moving on. "You've been a great spokesman for the family-owned company. Cora and Dora want to extend your promotional contract."

"A unanimous decision?" he asked.

The seventy-year-old twins never agreed. The women were apple-cheeked, plump, and highly opinionated. They argued for the sake of argument.

Once, in their test kitchen, the ladies had fought over a secret ingredient. Cora had thrown salt, and Dora let loose with the flour. Rhaden had been the one powdered white.

The sisters were as crotchety as they were sweet. They kept their fingers on the pulse of their business. Every decision was monumental and demanded mutual consent.

"Cora and Dora both called, claiming you as their spokesman." Her grin curved. "They plan to fatten you up."

Rhaden massaged his abdomen. Over the last three months, he'd eaten a whole lot of pie.

Revelle caught his stomach pat.

And he froze. He didn't want her attention anywhere near his groin. He still packed a boner. He cleared his throat, drew her gaze up. "The national campaign before Valentine's went well," he said. "We shot television commercials prior to spring training. Then Cora's great-grandson traveled with the promo team to ten major cities, playing Cupid. The kid handed out carnation-tipped arrows and candy hearts while we served slices of chocolate-cherry cream. Everyone fell in love with the pie."

From coffee shops and bakeries to delis, major grocery chains, and the occasional street corner, Rhaden had socialized and shared dessert with total strangers. He'd hand sold three thousand pies.

"Even with gym access at the hotels, I gained ten pounds in one month," he concluded.

"You don't look like you have a weight problem," she complimented.

Rhaden disagreed. "An entire homemade pie each day packs on weight. Cora said I was too lean and didn't do justice to her desserts."

The man *was* lean, all sinewy and tight-skinned. Revelle Sullivan took him in, from his light brown hair and dark green eyes to his broken nose. A nose that gave him character. She'd witnessed the play the year prior that had caused his injury.

The injury had changed the way she looked at him.

It had been the last home series of the previous season. The Rogues had been playing the Pittsburgh Pirates. She'd watched the game from the team owner's private box. In the seventh inning, the second Pirates batter slammed a line drive to the shortstop. It had been a tough catch for Zen Driscoll, who had backhanded the ball, then fired it to first.

It had been a wild throw, in the dirt.

A throw that sent Rhaden to his knees just as the runner slid into first.

Rhaden had taken a batting helmet to his face.

Revelle remembered the spray of blood and stadium boos. The fans had gone ballistic, seeing one of their own take a hit.

His teammates had clustered quickly. Rhaden had covered his face with his glove. He'd been escorted to the dugout with the infield coach and team physician, then headed into the tunnel. The crowd had cheered, and Revelle had choked up. She'd barely known the man, yet she'd hurt for him. Her pain had been physical.

She'd been a bundle of nerves as she waited for word on his condition. Her mind had been on Rhaden and not on the game. She'd missed Kason Rhodes's grand slam and Psycho McMillan's vertical leap that stole the tying run from Pittsburgh.

Rhaden's diagnosis came with the Rogues' win. He suffered blurred vision and a fractured nose. In all her years of watching baseball, she'd never tracked a player's recovery. Yet she'd downloaded the injury roster daily.

He'd missed three games, and returned for the play-offs. His face was bruised, his nose heavily taped.

Rhaden Dunn appealed to her. She'd never been attracted to jocks. She didn't like cocky, nor did she believe major league players were God's gift to women.

She dated the corporate elite. Men of prominence and power. Her life appeared to be perfect on paper. A strong financial background. Solid career. Phenomenal networking. The ability to choose her own path.

She believed in controlling her destiny to the last detail, which included her sexuality. She'd made herself the perfect businesswoman, only to recently realize that somewhere along the way, the real woman had gotten lost. A part of her felt unfulfilled and empty.

She couldn't remember the last time a man had kissed her and her knees had buckled. One look at Rhaden and her fingertips tingled. So much so, her hands shook.

They trembled now as she produced a set of contracts for his signature. "It's a deal, then. Cora Dora will soon feature a St. Patrick's Day pie, pistachio-peanut."

"The ladies are definitely inventive."

Revelle released a soft breath. With Rhaden re-signed, she had every right to attend his photo shoots or drop by any locale where he might be promoting a dessert. Time spent with him related to business.

Her uncle's unwritten rule banned corporate and player involvement, yet she would walk outside the line for him.

She passed Rhaden her Montblanc fountain pen, a gift from Uncle Guy. She watched the first baseman finger the jeweled and outrageously expensive pen. "Does it ever run out of ink?" he asked.

"Hasn't yet," she said. "It keeps on writing."

He drew the contracts to him, smiled. "Can't believe I get paid for eating pie."

Revelle's telephone rang. She caught the number of the incoming call and recognized it as Collage, a one-room schoolhouse in the historic district preserved as a children's art gallery. A patron of watercolors, clay statues, and papier mâché, she donated heavily to keep the gallery alive.

Each month the curator sponsored a new elementary

school exhibit. It was time for Revelle to judge the show.

She'd take the call while Rhaden reviewed and signed his contracts. "Excuse me," she said to him. "Revelle Sullivan," she announced into the phone.

As expected, the call was quick and ended with her agreement to review the drawings that very afternoon. More often than not, she took a guest judge with her for a second opinion.

If the opportunity arose, she snagged a Rogue. Risk Kincaid and Psycho McMillan had accompanied her in the past. The kids grew an inch taller when the athletes praised their artwork. This time she'd been too busy to plan ahead.

Team practice was over for the day. Players were scarce. She disconnected, and looked directly at Rhaden. He'd scrawled his name on the bottom line of the last page of the contracts and pushed to his feet, ready to leave.

"Do you like children?" she blurted out.

He blinked, bumped into his chair, looked uncomfortable. "I'd like to be a father someday," he returned. "Every guy wants his own baseball team."

Nine boys. Her uterus clutched. "I need a guest judge for an art show," she was quick to explain.

More unease. "What kind of art?"

"Elementary school."

Relief shone on his face. "I was afraid it was abstracts, which I've never understood. I can do crayons and stick figures."

"I'll owe you one," she said, hoping he'd make a move, ask her for a later date.

He nodded, noncommittal.

Rhaden Dunn would give his left testicle to take Revelle Sullivan to dinner. It was rumored several Rogues had asked her out, yet she'd declined, and discouraged any second passes.

He refused to be shut down. Success was all in the timing. He'd ask her out when the moment was right, and not before.

"Where is it?" he asked. "Should we take two cars?"

"I rode in with Guy this morning," she told him. "I'm supposed to call for a limo when I'm done for the day."

"Or you could ride with me."

"Does your car have a cappuccino machine and CNN?"

"No, but you can sing along to the radio if you like."

"Soft rock?" she asked as she closed down her computer and grabbed her patent leather shoulder bag, no doubt designer and costly.

"I'll let you pick the station." He was up and behind her in a heartbeat. He stood at the door as she locked up for the afternoon. He breathed her in. Her fragrance was sophisticated, light, classic. And all woman.

"Chanel." She caught him sniffing her.

"Nice," was all he could manage.

At the exact second she turned, he shifted his stance. They bumped. The back of her wrist brushed his zipper and his dick jumped to shake her hand.

Her eyes went wide, her blush hot.

He ducked his head, embarrassed by the flagpole in his pants.

He mumbled an apology.

She bit her lip, eyes downcast.

All conversation died as they descended in the elevator and stepped into the parking lot. Four vehicles remained: a silver BMW, a black Porsche Cayenne, a green Land Rover, and a dark blue Ford pickup, jacked-up with oversize tires.

Her gaze hit his, direct and assessing, and filled with humor as she picked out his vehicle. "Has to be the monster truck."

"Not monster, but an off-road racer."

"Do you compete?" she asked curiously.

"Not professionally, but I like the challenge of dirt tracks and mountain trails."

She strolled toward the truck. "Looks like you."

Beat up, rusty, muddy, with a broken headlight. Rhaden wasn't certain her assessment of him was all that complimentary. He did, however, like the way she ran her hands along the suspension. The way she admired the enormous tires.

He followed her to the passenger side. "Let me give you a hand," he offered as she stretched to open the passenger door.

She went up on tiptoe to climb into the cab.

He curved his hands about her hips.

Revelle was all tight calves and hiked skirt. He caught the lace on her thigh-high stockings as he lifted her up. The bounce of her bottom nearly undid him.

He slowly made his way around the hood, sucking air and talking his dick down, with little success. He was one hard, sorry bastard.

Inside the cab, she gave him directions to Collage. Fascinated by the height and vibration of the pickup, Revelle chose conversation over the radio and shot him a dozen questions. She'd never driven off-road and wanted details.

Traffic moved quickly. Green held at every street-light.

He parked two blocks south of Jacy's Java, a coffee shop owned by Risk Kincaid's wife and frequented by the Rogues. He assisted Revelle from the cab. He'd have loved to slide her down his body. Yet a simple touch and his south would rise again. He held her at arm's length, played the gentleman.

The one-room schoolhouse was situated on the old town square. The building took Rhaden back to the days of hand-sawed and hand-planed timbers. Square nails held the boards together.

Inside, pointers, maps, yardsticks, and ten antique desks were set up for class. Framed behind the teacher's desk, black-and-white photographs depicted early Richmond.

An antique potbelly stove stood in one corner. The stove had once provided both warmth and a hot meal for students. Rhaden could hear the long-ago echo of the school bell as the children walked a short distance from home or arrived by horse-drawn hacks.

Rules were posted on the chalkboard. Discipline had called for a ruler rapped across a student's knuckles or a face turned toward the wall. The dunce cap looked well worn.

Revelle introduced him to the curator, Anne Malone, a woman who looked as old as the schoolhouse. In period costume, her vintage calico dress hung loosely; the toes of her sensible brown shoes peaked from beneath the hemline.

"Mrs. Potter's second-grade class will arrive in thirty minutes," Anne informed them. "I'll set up a table for juice and cookies while you review the artwork."

"Let me help you," Rhaden volunteered. Anne looked brittle. He didn't want the curator lifting anything heavier than a teacup.

He dragged a table from the back closet, secured the wobbly legs. Then he arranged the apple juice boxes and plates of pink-frosted sugar cookies. Anne laid out the napkins.

Rhaden next turned to the drawings, displayed in vivid color on the side wall near the stove. Twenty-two pictures total. He took his time judging the exhibit.

"Your favorites?" Revelle came to stand beside him.

"They're all great," he said. "I like *Me and My Shadow*." Done with black and white crayons. "*My Classroom Turtle* has possibilities." A work in Magic Markers. The turtle had to be a snapper with all those teeth.

"*Mom's Fourth Wedding* has merit." He counted four stick men in the picture, drawn in black ink—no doubt the three past husbands and the present groom. A dozen stick kids gathered around the bride, her dress designed in silver glitter. "Huge extended family."

"*My Lunch* is creative." Revelle traced her finger along the crust of a half-eaten sandwich spread with peanut butter and stacked with mini-marshmallows and potato chips.

He tapped his finger on a blank piece of paper. "*My Friend Jack* appears to be invisible—probably an imaginary friend. The artist shows ingenuity or laziness."

She read the student's name. "Christopher Blake. We'll watch for him when the class arrives."

They'd yet to reach a decision on the artwork when the second-grade class clambered through the door. Most of the students were fresh-faced and innocent; a few boys stuck out, lanky and scruffy. Twenty-one kids clustered around Revelle, their excitement high. One boy lagged near the door.

Chris Blake, Rhaden discovered from the teacher, was small and somber until he turned and started talking to thin air. He spoke loud enough for the room to hear his exchange with "Jack." The two of them wanted to get back on the bus. They hated art and field trips.

Rhaden took the initiative. He crossed to the boy, introduced himself. "I'm Rhaden Dunn."

The kid was slow to respond. "Chris."

"Who's your friend?" Rhaden nodded to the space to the left of Chris's shoulder.

"Don't humor me, man." Chris went all adult on Rhaden. "Jack's on my right and he's flipping you off."

"That's not very friendly."

"Jack doesn't take to strangers."

"I'm a guest judge for the art contest," Rhaden explained. "I'm here with Miss Sullivan."

"She's hot."

From the mouth of babes.

"Jack recognized you. He says you play ball."

Rhaden nodded. "I'm with the Rogues."

"Jack says your stats suck."

Insulted by an invisible friend. Rhaden wasn't the best player on the team, but he was a solid hitter and very good fielder. "Everyone has room for improvement. New season, clean slate," he diplomatically replied. "Do you like sports?"

Chris screwed up his face. "I'm the smallest kid in the class. I get knocked down in kickball and trampled in soccer. If it wasn't for Jack, I'd be sod."

"Jack's a big guy?"

"Taller than Tommy Dennison." Chris pointed to a boy who stood several inches above his classmates. "Jack protects me."

Rhaden understood. He'd also started out small, had grown into his hands and feet. He'd been a clumsy kid until he'd hit his teens. Until baseball became his life.

Having an imaginary friend kept Chris from being bullied. No doubt the kids in his class thought him crazy. Yet Chris outsmarted them all. With Jack at his side, he was safe.

"You and Jack can stand by me," Rhaden offered. "If Jack doesn't mind hanging with a ballplayer with bad stats."

"We'll think about it," said Chris.

Rhaden returned to Revelle. She'd been chatting with the kids, discussing their artwork, making each feel special. Soon Chris joined him. Rhaden ruffled his blond head, then attempted to pat Jack's invisible head too.

Several students in the class eyed Rhaden with suspicion. Rhaden just smiled. And Chris stood taller.

There was nothing wrong with having an imaginary friend. Rhaden might create one himself. A friend to help him raise his stats.

He heard Revelle address the children. "The judging has been difficult. The drawings are amazing. You're all so talented."

"Who placed first?" asked the tall kid, Tommy Dennison. His picture, *Sunset in the Desert*, had camels, pyramids, and a fiery sky. The boy drew with the detail of a sixth-grader or he'd had help from his parents.

Revelle looked at Rhaden, but he deferred to her. She

paused to heighten the tension. The kids went wide-eyed and held their breath. "The blue ribbon goes to *My Friend Jack* by Christopher Blake."

"The paper's blank," said a disappointed Tommy.

"Blank to some, visible to others," Revelle said kindly as she placed the ribbon on the sheet of white construction paper.

"I like Jack," a chubby girl with big brown eyes said. "He's never called me fat."

"Jack lets me cut ahead of him in the lunch line," a boy with a buzz cut added. "He and Chris share their French fries."

"Jack has the best voice in chorus," stated another little girl with a frizzy red ponytail. "I bet he'll grow up to be a rock star."

Imaginations were running wild. Rhaden nudged Revelle to move the awards along. She did so. "I have red superstar ribbons for all remaining artists."

In that moment, Rhaden's respect for the woman grew. She'd stopped with first place, allowing Chris to shine as he showcased Jack. With the award of a simple blue ribbon, the small boy turned from an outcast to the center of attention. He was the star for the day.

Revelle pointed toward the table. "Enjoy the juice and cookies."

"Get a juice box for Jack," the girl from chorus said, encouraging Chris. "I'd eat his cookie if he's full from lunch."

Rhaden and Revelle moved off to the side and watched the kids enjoy their snacks. Chris had collected a handful of cookies for Jack. Even Tommy Dennison checked out the empty space beside Chris in an attempt to visualize Jack.

"Does Jack have black hair?" Tommy asked.

"No, he's blond like me," Chris replied.

"Jack and Chris both have blue eyes," said the boy with the buzz cut. "But Jack's a lot taller."

Again, Tommy Dennison squinted into thin air.

"Can I sit by Jack on the bus?" the chubby girl asked Chris as the class moved toward the door. "He can be by the window."

Chris lent Jack to the girl for the ride back to school. He had a dozen offers from other second-graders to sit by one of them. When his teacher suggested he share the front seat with her, Chris jumped at her offer.

Soon the classroom stood quiet. The curator cleared the table and left it standing for Rhaden to put away. He returned it to the closet.

"What will you judge next month?" he asked Revelle.

"Sixth-grade photography," she informed him. "Sonya Garrett from Highland Heights petitioned for an exhibit."

"Tough neighborhood," said Rhaden.

"I've been warned the classes are huge and diversified. The principal is lucky to have a teacher last a year, two at best." She raised a brow. "Are you game?"

It was a guaranteed date to see her again, and he quickly agreed. "I'm in—" short pause. "Are we done for the day?"

"Pretty much so." She leaned against the teacher's desk, a ruler in hand, which she soon set aside for the pointer. Nerves had her next reaching for the dunce cap.

She had long fingers, perfectly manicured nails, and pale hands. He could watch her fidget for hours.

He hated to close out their day.

"Can I catch a ride home?" she finally asked. "I don't live far. You'd be rid of me in twenty minutes."

Maybe he could work it into thirty if he drove slow. "My turn to pick the radio station," he told her. "Hope you like country."

She nodded. "Brad Plaid's one of my favorites."

Rhaden swallowed his laugh. She meant Brad Paisley. He'd take great pleasure introducing her to his music.

Six

Uneasiness had plagued Kason Rhodes's drive home. He sensed something was *off,* the same way he had the day Dayne changed the locks on his trailer.

He'd been delayed by heavy traffic for more than an hour and now he drove faster than normal down the dirt access road. Gravel fired like shrapnel from beneath his tires. He soon slowed his Hummer, within view of his mobile home. Then he stared until his eyes hurt.

What he saw had to be a mirage.

Yet when he blinked, the image held.

Sweet mother, my trailer has laid an aluminum egg.

His nostrils flared and his jaw worked.

His breath stuck in his throat.

The tomboy had trespassed a second time.

His arrival drew Dayne from behind the small metal camper parked behind his double-wide. Cimarron was at her side. She looked different. She was not the same woman who'd claimed squatter's rights to his trailer. She'd dropped her defenses.

She came toward him, wearing a Moody Blues T-shirt, white shorts, and a big smile. She looked animated, carefree, and eager to share her news.

News, Kason was certain, he didn't want to hear.

"You'll never believe what happened today." Her excitement touched him. "I went to the warehouse for boxes to move my stuff. Frank, the owner, said if I moved beyond a bike ride away, he'd lose a good worker. He came up with a solution so I could stay."

Kason knew he'd hate the solution. Hate it a whole hell of a lot.

"Frank and his wife enjoyed camping before they had children," she rushed to tell him. "Now their kids prefer amusement parks to the woods. The camper has sat in storage for years. Frank hauled it out today. It's free rent until I can make other arrangements."

She looked at the camper, happy and proud. "It's a vintage silver Airstream."

"It's a tin can." Twenty feet by ten at best.

"It's my home."

Kason ran one hand down his face. "You parked it here?" There were three trailer parks in Richmond. Any one could accommodate her camper.

She bounced on her toes, swept her hands wide. "Look at all this vacant land. We don't know who owns the acreage. You've trespassed, same as me. Until the owner tosses us off, what he doesn't know won't hurt him."

Kason wasn't trespassing. He legitimately owned the land. Yet he didn't want to share that fact with Dayne. However annoying she might be, a part of him liked being treated like a regular guy.

Appearing down on his luck had its advantages. She believed him a penniless drifter. There weren't any assumptions or pretense between them. She saw him as a man, not a sports star.

"The Airstream's small, but self-contained," she told him. "I've hooked up to your electrical box, and will pay my fair share of the bill. All I have left to do is to set up the exterior shower stall."

That didn't sound good. "No indoor facility?"

"It's me and the great outdoors."

Not his idea of comfort.

"I've moved as much food as possible," she went on to say. "I don't have much shelf space."

"Do you want me to buy what's leftover?" No doubt she could use the cash.

"Or you could just store it for me." She looked hopeful.

Storing meant she would be stopping by his trailer at any hour of the day or night for a can of peaches or a pound of hamburger. She'd remain a constant part of his life, even if she didn't live with him.

Though he'd allow her to camp on his land, he needed to establish boundaries. He'd hold her at arm's length.

"Rules, Dayne." He laid them out. "It's no longer open season on my mobile home. You need to knock before you barge in."

She lifted her chin. "That goes the same for you."

He had no intention of visiting her.

"Maybe we should establish property lines," she said. "I could build a fence."

Property lines? It was his land.

He looked at Cimarron. The Dobie hugged Dayne's side. "Don't forget that Cim's my dog. When I'm home, he's with me."

She chewed her bottom lip, contemplative. "I might get myself a dog. I've never lived where I could have a pet. My camper's too small for a Great Dane or Saint Bernard, but a small dog would be nice. "

A miniature breed, fluffy and yappy. Kason could already hear the dog's high-pitched, irritating bark. Damn, he'd have to invest in earplugs.

Silence brought their conversation to an end. Overhead a light breeze blew clouds over the sun. The air cooled, and it grew so still, a man could hear himself think. Peace descended on the clearing.

Dayne turned in a slow circle, her arms spread wide, as if she embraced the land. The return of the sun streaked her hair more blonde than brown. Her sharp cheekbones slanted to shadowed hollows. Her lips were full and parted.

She inhaled, exhaled, sighed. "I'll be a good neighbor, Kason, quiet as nature."

He'd hold her to that promise.

They retreated to the calm of their own homes.

Cimarron trailed Kason with backward glances and dragging paws. The big dog already missed Dayne.

Thirty minutes later, Kason's peace was shattered by an electric screw gun and the bang of a hammer. He pushed off the couch, crossed to the kitchen window and cranked it wide. He looked out and found Dayne on a short aluminum ladder. Arms raised, she was attempting to install a circular bar off the side of her camper. The bar was centered over the water nozzle, which provided support for the gray plastic shower enclosure.

Tomboy wasn't doing a great job. The bar dipped at two different angles and the ladder wobbled with every shift of her weight. She hadn't locked the hinges. She was an accident waiting to happen.

"Damn," he muttered, knowing he was about to cross property lines. He needed to lend a hand before she broke bones.

Cimarron whipped through the door ahead of him.

The dog took off for Dayne as if shot from a cannon. Cim beat him to the tomboy.

"Need some help?" he called on his approach.

Two screws stuck out the corner of her mouth. "I've got it this time," she mumbled.

He'd stick around and be sure she *got it*. She'd changed into a Pink Floyd T-shirt and faded jeans. A low-slung tool belt wrapped her hips. She'd climbed the ladder with bare feet. Pale peach painted her toenails.

A tiny, lucky silver horseshoe studded her navel. Kason lifted his gaze, caught the soft undersides of her breasts. She was braless again.

His dick saluted her twins.

He shuffled his feet, discreetly shifting his package without a full hand adjustment.

"It's level now." She secured one end of the circular bar and drove in a screw, then leaned back and checked her handiwork. A frown appeared. The rod slanted right.

Kason noticed the dozen holes from her previous attempts. The camper looked riddled with bullets. He blew out a breath, extended his hand. "Give me the screw gun."

She hesitated. "That's neighborly, but I promised not to bother you."

"One time, and one time only."

The ladder wobbled as she climbed down. Kason clasped his hand behind her knee to steady her descent. She was a small woman. His fingers and thumb nearly met over her kneecap.

The space between them seemed to disappear. The scent of peaches wafted from her body, sun-warmed and sexy. With her next step down, his hand rode her thigh.

One more rung and he cupped her ass. Neither one moved for what could have been a single minute or a full five.

Her shiver raised her voice an octave. "Let me down."

He released her, stepped back. Her peaches stayed with him. His hand felt empty. Her bottom had fit his palm. Round, tight, perfect.

"Where'd you get the tool belt?" he asked. Tomboy looked sexy in the thick brown belt with its dozen pouches.

"Frank left it," she told him as she tightened the leather. Even at the last buckle hole, it hung off her hips. The handle of a hammer lay against her thigh. Needle-nose pliers pressed below her navel.

"There's a television antenna in the storage compartment below the Airstream," she added. "It sits on top of the camper. Frank said it gets decent reception. I'll tackle that project tomorrow."

He closed his eyes, worked his jaw, counted to ten. "Do you even have a television?"

"No, but I want to set up the antenna so when I buy one, it's ready to go." Lady had her own logic.

"Don't climb until I get home," he requested. "I'll help you." Neighborly was fast becoming a daily routine.

She bit down on her lower lip. "I appreciate your looking out for me."

"It's no big deal." He didn't want her reading too much into his offer. "I'll hook up the antenna in a tenth of the time it would take you to do it." And he wouldn't get electrocuted in the process. Nor would he slide off the top.

Screw gun in hand, he soon set the shower rod and attached the stall. The enclosure hung a ways off the ground. Dayne stepped inside, turned in a circle. She wasn't fully concealed. Once stripped and showering, she'd bare significant thigh. If she bent over—Kason closed his mind to the imagined flash of her sweet ass.

"How big is the hot water tank?" he asked.

"Good for a two-minute shower. After that, I'll be one big goose bump." She glanced at her watch. "I'm making fried-egg sandwiches shortly. Join me? Dinner in exchange for setting up my shower stall. Cim's invited too."

Tomboy's appreciation showed in food.

Hearing his name, Cimarron barked his acceptance before Kason could agree. The dog wagged his stubby tail and looked at Dayne adoringly. Dinner with the tomboy appealed to the Dobie.

Kason wasn't sure it would be wise to spend more time in her company. Neighborly shouldn't extend beyond a wave as he drove down the road. She wasn't permanent. Yet she touched his life in ways that made him increasingly uneasy.

"Quick sandwich works." He could eat and run.

"One hour—bring your appetite."

Dayne and her sexy tool belt sauntered off.

Fifty-six minutes later, Kason knocked on Dayne Sheridan's door. Her stomach gave an unexpected squeeze. She didn't analyze her reaction, just knew his appearance gave her butterflies.

The Airstream was small and intimate.

He was a big man.

He'd soon be a guest in her new home.

She cracked the door, caught him in profile. Dusk played on his face, sharpening his features. His shaved head was shaped by shadows. His jaw jutted, whiskers dark.

He'd changed his T-shirt, switched white for black. His hands were jammed in the pockets on his jeans. He was a hard man. Uncommunicative and complicated. And set in his ways.

Strangely, she liked him. She even trusted him. He'd bounced her from his trailer, yet allowed her to park the vintage Airstream behind his double-wide. She'd half expected him to hook her camper to his Hummer and haul it down the road. Instead, he'd gone neighborly and let her stay.

Each day, fresh air and sunshine cleared her head. She grew as a person. Strength became her ally. Mick Jakes had broken her heart and bruised her ego. Dumping her on air before a million listeners had been cruel.

Mick had screwed his way to the top. He'd chosen syndication over their marriage.

She'd crawled out of Baltimore, but now walked tall. She'd never again date anyone in the public eye.

Seeing Kason now, she appreciated him as a man.

He was a loner. She liked him low-key.

She took a step back so he could enter. "Welcome."

Cimarron trampled Kason to get inside. The dog turned in two circles, then angled beneath the dining room table, the only place he would fit.

Kason stood inside the door, tall, muscled, and much too large for her camper. He bumped Dayne on the shoulder as he took in her space with a single glance.

She saw what he saw: built-in furniture. The couch was just big enough for one person; the bench behind the table would be a tight squeeze for two. The twin bed was a single step off the kitchen.

"It's a dollhouse," he finally said. "You won't be throwing many parties."

She edged around him, and her hip clipped his thigh. Very tight quarters. "It's my place for now. Temporary, until I get on my feet. With a camper, wherever you go, you're always at home."

"If it works for you, that's all that matters."

It worked for her. The silver Airstream wasn't much bigger than a tin can. Yet she found it cozy. Cleaning would take less than five minutes. Everything in the camper was within arm's reach.

"I thought I'd light candles to save on electricity." She turned toward the table. "Any chance you have matches?"

He fished in his pocket, tossed her a pack. Naughty Monkey matches. The bar was known for its orange neon monkey, stiff drinks, strippers, and lap dances.

Her curiosity got the better of her. "One of your haunts?" she asked.

His expression closed, as if she'd crossed a line. The man didn't share his life.

She averted her gaze. "None of my business, sorry."

Long ticks of silence passed before he said, "Look at me."

When she did, he accounted for the matchbook. "Naughty Monkey hosted a bachelor party for a friend of mine. I snagged the pack to light a cigar."

"You have friends?" The words escaped her. The question bordered on rudeness, yet she'd believed him a man unto himself.

"One or two," he said evasively.

"Did you have a lap dance?" Was he into tassels and G-strings?

"Too many questions off a matchbook." He ended his explanation. "I've known you four days. You're sounding like a wife."

"A wife would have a right to know."

"We're not married, Dayne."

She blushed then, embarrassed by her interest in the man. He didn't do personal. He'd yet to share his last name.

"Dinner." She moved on. "Would you like cheese on your fried-egg sandwiches?"

"Cheese sounds good, and ketchup."

One step, and she lit the three votive candles on the kitchen table. Heather scented the air. She set down the matches, and swore the orange monkey on the cover smirked at her.

Three steps, and she was in the kitchen. She cracked and cooked eggs and stirred lime Kool-Aid.

The fried eggs went on wheat bread. The ketchup came in condiment packets she'd snagged from fast-food restaurants. Her way to cut costs.

She fixed two plates, stacking Kason's with three sandwiches. She and Cimarron would split the remaining two.

She laid out the meal, included a family-size bag of potato chips. Kason scooped half the bag. The man was hungry.

They squeezed together on the single bench. The table was screwed to the floor and pressed their middles. Their thighs touched, their knees bumped, and their elbows knocked. Eating proved difficult, as she was left-handed, and he was right. They leaned into each other with every bite.

Twice Kason knocked food out of her hand. Once Kool-Aid sloshed from her glass onto her T-shirt. He passed her a handful of napkins. She dabbed at the lime drops.

The mishaps seemed minor. Although cramped, the camper was cozy. Dayne had no complaints. Cimarron was content with bites from her sandwich.

Once done with dinner, Kason stretched his arm along the back of the bench. His T-shirt pulled tight across his chest, the symmetry of his six-pack visible. The sleeves bunched over his biceps.

His fingertips tapped her shoulder. "You've fed me three meals," he said. "I've contributed nothing but my appetite. I'll replace your groceries tomorrow."

She cut him a glance. "No repayment necessary until you find work."

"Work?" His brow creased.

"You're unemployed," she said softly, not wanting to hurt his feelings. "I have food for a month. I'll share until you get on your feet."

"On my feet . . ." He shifted, visibly ill at ease.

"I have a couple of job tips," she told him. "Frank at the Food Warehouse is looking for night maintenance men. He pays cash."

A muscle ticked along Kason's jaw.

"Cock-a-Doodle Café at Tri-Corners needs a dishwasher," she continued. "I saw the sign in the window yesterday."

His mouth flattened in a thin line.

"I read in the classifieds that the phone company

needs drivers to deliver directories over the next month. You've got a Hummer, even though it looks like it's on its last legs. That's fast, easy money. Cim could ride along with you."

Kason looked pained. He rested his elbows on the table, eyes downcast. His shoulders were visibly tight. "Look, Dayne . . ." he began.

She cut him off. "These may not be your ideal jobs, but the money would sustain you until you hit on your career choice."

"Solid leads. I appreciate your suggestions," he managed.

"We're neighbors." She patted his arm. "My food is your food. I have tropical rainbow sherbet for dessert."

Kason might have preferred butterscotch pudding, but his two scoops of sherbet went down fast. "I like orange the best," he said of the three flavors.

"I'm partial to pineapple."

Neither favored lemon. It was too tart.

He pushed the bowl aside, then said, "Frank's Warehouse is part-time for you. What do you want to do eventually? Skills, goals, dreams?"

Kason being sociable? His concession stunned Dayne, yet kept her gratified. While her history with Mick Jakes was off-limits, she'd share her future plans.

"Public relations is my field." She missed the customer contact and creative aspects of her job. "I'm a wiz kid at promotions."

"Promotions . . ." He went from relaxed to rigid, then completely closed down.

The candlelight flickered on the severe cut of his features. The soft scent of heather was at odds with the hardened man.

His gaze hit the door. Clearly, his departure was imminent.

His withdrawal frightened Dayne. *Wiz kid? Promotions?* What had she said to offend him? "Kason?" She nudged him with her elbow.

He hefted his big body, moved from the bench to the couch. Only two feet separated them, yet it seemed like a mile. "I'm fine," he said, but he didn't look it. The man was rattled.

"PR and promotions," she repeated. "What put you off?"

"I'm private, and not a fan of publicity."

"I'm not promoting you."

No, she wasn't, Kason Rhodes realized. Her job choice, however, knotted his stomach. "Sorry, gut reaction."

"To *what*?" she pressed.

Tomboy was trying to put her finger on his pulse.

She wanted to know what made him tick.

He didn't want people knowing him.

So he blew her off. "It's nothing." He snapped his fingers, and Cimmaron crawled from beneath the table. "It's late. Cim and I need to call it a night."

"It's six fifteen."

"Nothing wrong with sleeping twelve hours," he said defensively.

"If you're in hibernation."

He pushed to his feet and she slid from behind the table.

They stood leather boot to Converse toe.

She blocked his path to the door, refusing to let him by.

He preferred not to physically lift her out of his way,

so he curled his lip and baited her. "You waiting for a good-night kiss?"

The candlelight captured her blush. "I'm sorry for whatever I said that upset you."

"I'm not upset."

"Yet you're leaving."

"You offered dinner. I ate. I'm gone."

Her expression was of a little girl lost. She looked wounded. Kason's chest gave an unexpected squeeze. He'd have enjoyed hanging out with her, but he didn't want her dependent on him. She needed to make her own happiness.

"Have you bought new batteries for your vibrator?"

Her jaw dropped and her blue eyes went wide. Her nod was a shocked bob of her head.

"Then you've got company."

She turned as red as the candle flame. "Go." She shoved him toward the door.

With his hand on the knob, he asked, "Want Cim to spend the night?"

A small smile replaced her disappointment over his departure. "You don't mind?"

"Dog's happiest in your bed."

"I'll return him in the morning."

"Drop him off with a cup of coffee."

"Deal."

A significant pause while neither moved. While they each took the other in, and any lapse in judgment would start something neither could finish.

He had one foot out the door when she swept the matchbook off the table, tossed it to him. "Don't forget your matches."

Kason fingered the Naughty Monkey matches. He

knew the bachelor party bothered Dayne. When a man didn't come clean, a woman drew her own conclusions. They were often wrong. A part of him needed to clear her misconception.

He'd never explained himself to anyone, so his confession was rusty. "I didn't have a lap dance at Naughty Monkey," he told her. "The bar was loud, the crowd trashed. I prefer dark and quiet corners when I drink. Most times, it's me and a Bud."

She looked at him as if he'd righted the world. The tiny camper worked to his benefit. She came to him with only one step.

Going up on tiptoe, she placed a kiss on his cheek.

Her lips were soft and her breath warmed the corner of his mouth. The urge to turn, take her lips, and touch tongues hit hard. He wanted to show her that he could take things slow. That foreplay was his game. As well as prolonging a woman's pleasure.

That wouldn't happen tonight. Maybe not ever.

They were short-term neighbors. Not lovers.

Control walked him into the night, his footsteps heavy.

The evening closed around him, solitude his silent companion.

Seven

The sound of splashing water followed by a girlie squeal woke Kason from a light sleep. He jackknifed off the bed, went to the back window. A look across the yard, and he located Dayne inside the shower stall. From what he could see of her feet and calves, she was hopping like a rabbit. She'd run out of hot water.

Her last shriek was loud enough to draw the sun's attention. Rays shot from behind a dark gray cloud.

She was not a happy camper.

Cimarron sat outside the enclosure, a drape of white across his shoulders. The tomboy was using his dog as a towel rack. Kason had the urge to whistle, to call the Dobie to him. Which would leave her naked.

A nude Dayne had appeal.

But she'd be furious with him.

He leaned his elbows on the windowsill, watching her jump. She soon shut off the water, stretched her hand toward Cimarron, and snatched the towel off the big dog's back. Once wrapped, she shot from the enclosure.

Kason sucked air. The white terry cloth was more hand towel than bath. Her breasts were peaked, her inner thighs in shadow. The lower curve of her butt cheeks, round and pale.

Her hair hung wet. Her skin damp. She was as slick and slippery as the day he'd first met her. The day he'd tackled her on his mattress and laid her out, spread-eagled before him.

He caught her shiver, a full-body shake. She ran her fingers through her hair, then turned her face to the sun, to air dry. She stood quietly, warming up, and lazily scratched Cim's ear. The dog was totally committed to her.

Dayne would soon bring him coffee. Kason needed to dress.

It was Saturday. Opening Day on Monday pitted the Rogues against the Louisville Colonels. He'd be facing his old teammates. The Colonels were tough. Kason wanted the win.

A trip to James River Stadium was in order today. The players had access to the workout room and batting cages. He planned to spend the morning honing his muscles and his skills.

Later that afternoon he'd erect Dayne's television antenna. His thoughts ran to buying her a small set. She would question where he'd gotten the money. He wasn't ready to admit he could buy her a large plasma with the change in his pocket. He still liked the fact that she thought him poor.

She arrived at his door as he tied on his Nikes. He opened it to find her, his dog, and a hot cup of coffee. She'd dressed for work. Her bike was parked, kickstand down, by his Hummer.

"How was your shower?" he asked with his first sip.

"You saw?" she groaned.

"The enclosure faces my back bedroom window."

"I froze my ass off."

"You need a larger water tank."

"Can't afford one," she said with a sigh. "I'll have to shower faster."

Any quicker, and she'd still have soapsuds in her hair.

"I'm headed into town," he told her. "Want a ride to the warehouse?"

"My bike's fine," she said. "Business is slow and my hours are erratic. I may work two hours, if I'm lucky, four. You wouldn't know when to pick me up."

"Cimarron," he called to the Dobie.

Dayne patted Cim on the head, and the big dog nuzzled her hand. He reluctantly entered the trailer.

"Later." Kason closed the door on Cimarron, crossed to his Hummer.

He left Dayne to pedal down the road.

A short drive, and Kason parked at the stadium. Expectancy walked with him to the workout room. The media had tagged Richmond the ball club to beat. Every National League team would be gunning for the Rogues.

He wasn't the only player there to pump iron. He recognized Psycho McMillan's Dodge Ram and Risk Kincaid's Porsche Cayenne. Risk's sports car of choice was a Lotus, but as soon as he and his wife, Jacy, had decided to start a family, he'd gone SUV. Though Jacy wasn't yet pregnant, Kincaid walked around with a smile on his face. Man was trying hard to be a daddy.

In the locker room, Kason changed into his sweats. He passed Risk in the hallway. The center fielder was headed to the indoor batting cages. In the weight room,

Kason faced off with Psycho and his dumbbells. Neither spoke as Kason chose to bench press.

Both men broke a sweat in a matter of minutes.

On a grunt, Psycho set down the dumbbells, took a break. He pulled up his T-shirt, wiped off his face, then drained a bottle of water.

First baseman Rhaden Dunn joined them, followed by backup center fielder Alex Boxer. Boxer was an arrogant son of a bitch who believed himself invincible and invaluable. Alex had latched onto Risk, gone as far as to imitate his every move. So much so, the guys had started calling him Shadow Boxer.

Tangible energy rolled off the athletes.

They were hyped to start the season.

"Ready to face your old team?" Rhaden called to Kason as he picked up the medicine ball. Rhaden went through a series of slams, holding the ball first over his head, then forcibly throwing it down on the floor. He caught it on the first bounce. Repeated the exercise.

"I want the win." It was all that mattered to Kason.

"We split series with Louisville last year," Boxer put in. "Media's written the opener as a power struggle."

Kason understood. Guy Powers owned the Rogues, his ex-wife Corbin Lily, the Louisville Colonels. Corbin was as beautiful as she was powerful. As the only female owner in Major League Baseball, she brought class and distinction to the old boys' club. She held her own in a man's world.

Though Guy and Corbin were as competitive as any two people could be, the exes remained cordial. Their respect was an invisible bond as they battled through the season.

"It's maturity versus youth," Boxer continued. "Average age of the Colonels is twenty-four."

"Watch this old man knock a ball down some rookie's throat." Rhaden slammed the medicine ball with such force, the floor vibrated.

Psycho snorted. "Veteran, old-timer, who the hell cares? None of us are wearing adult diapers or medical bracelets. Except maybe Rhodes."

Kason ignored him.

"Louisville trash talks," said Boxer.

"We'll let our bats speak for us," answered Rhaden.

The edginess persisted, as the players continued their strength training. Core muscles stretched, burned. Their bodies peaked with explosive power.

Psycho switched on the television mounted on one wall. Saturday morning, and animation dominated the TV. Psycho was a cartoon fanatic. *King of the Hill* soon followed *The Simpsons*.

"Who'd you rather have for a neighbor? Hank or Homer?" Psycho asked as he crossed to the stationary bike.

Kason kept to himself. He already had a neighbor. A tomboy who lived in a tin can.

Boxer worked the lat machine, performing a series of triceps press downs. "With Homer you'd get Bart. I don't need a kid telling me to eat his shorts every damn day."

"Hank's always good for a beer," Rhaden said. "He and his buddies gather on the sidewalk and pop a cold one."

"How about Santa Claus or Frosty the Snowman? Who'd you want next door?" Again from Psycho.

"Santa has presents; Frosty melts." Rhaden judged

logically. "The Easter Bunny might be cool—he has Peeps, a wicked sugar buzz."

The senseless exchange released tension. Similar questions were exchanged in the dugout or bullpen. Men became boys. The absurdities drew chuckles. The more outrageous, the better.

A commercial for Disney Classics flashed, and Boxer's grin broke. "Who'd you date? Snow White or Cinderella?"

Rhaden moved to Russian twists, working his shoulders and hips. "Chick with the glass slipper. Snow White comes with dwarves. I'd never remember their names."

"There's Doc, Dopey, Sleepy, Creepy, Weepy . . ."

Boxer shook his head. "Not even close, Psycho."

"Rhodes?" Psycho baited. "Preference?"

The men stared at Kason. He straddled the weight bench, ready to rise. "I don't do cartoon characters."

"Think hot babes, then," Boxer tossed out. "Blondes or brunettes?"

"Nothing wrong with redheads," said Rhaden.

"Blondes for me," said Psycho. His wife, Keely, had light hair, pale skin, and looked like an angel. Psycho was kin to the prince of darkness.

Dayne and her wild brown hair crossed Kason's mind. Her bangs hung in her eyes; her part was always crooked. She looked forever windblown.

"Nipple or navel rings on your woman?" Boxer asked.

"Definitely nipple," said Rhaden. "Total turn-on."

Kason preferred navel rings. Dayne had a flat belly and smooth skin. He'd like to get a closer look at her horseshoe.

"Tomboy or beauty queen?" Psycho now pedaled with the speed of Lance Armstrong at the Tour de France.

"Tomboy." Kason's gut clutched. He hadn't meant to speak his thoughts aloud.

Psycho's grin was telling. He'd sucked Kason in.

"Tomboy for me too," Rhaden agreed. "Beauty queens are high maintenance. They're always smiling, waving, riding in parades."

Kason wound down. He pushed off the bench, kicked out his legs. His muscles flexed, felt fluid. It was time to hit the batting cages.

"Queen Elizabeth or Queen Latifah?" Psycho caught him at the door. "Who'd you do?"

"Elizabeth, but only if she wore her crown." Kason moved on.

Psycho's choked laughter followed him into the hallway. Kason shook his head. The man was friggin' mental.

He headed for the indoor batting cages. He entered the chain-link enclosure adjacent to Risk Kincaid. He selected a bat, moved to the mat, took several practice swings. He then nodded to the trainer, who'd set up the pitching machine. A machine that threw with the speed and accuracy of a big-league pitcher.

Ninety-mile-an-hour fastballs, nasty sliders, and change-up curveballs readied Kason for competitive play. The nylon netting at the back of the cage strained and stretched with each slam of his bat. The sloped floor automatically fed the baseballs back toward the machine.

"That ball crossed two time zones," Risk complimented after Kason's final hit. The center fielder leaned against the fence, arms crossed over his chest.

"I was thinking Denver," Kason said as he handed his bat to the trainer, ready to leave.

Risk didn't force conversation as the two men headed back to the locker room. Both kept their own thoughts. Opening Day had a way of turning men introspective.

Kason cleaned up, cut out.

Concern once again rode with him down the dirt road home. He hated the feeling of something being *off*. Yet his instincts were right on target. What he saw in the clearing gave him heartburn.

The trailers were multiplying like bunnies. Four now sat on his land. His, Dayne's, and two new ones. He slammed to a stop, shut off the engine, and stared until his eyes burned. A pop-up explorer, expanded at both ends, sat beside a Coachman Mirada the size of a Greyhound bus.

What the fuck?

His steps ate up the distance to Dayne's Airstream. Anger made a man walk fast. He pulled a fist, banging on the door with such force, the uni-wheel rocked. The tin can would blow over in a strong breeze.

Where in God's name was Dayne?

Another round of pounding, and she appeared in pale green pajamas, her hair mussed, her eyes sleepy. A robe hung from her left hand. She yawned at him. And he took her in. Her top hung off one shoulder and the waistband on her pants dipped dangerously low. He caught the horseshoe stud at her navel, turned up for good luck. Concave shadows bracketed her belly.

It was early afternoon. Tomboy was taking a siesta.

He jabbed a finger in the direction of the RVs, his temper ramped up. "Friends of yours?" he ground out.

"Acquaintances," she said as she slipped on her robe. "Don't look so upset—it's all good."

All good, his ass.

"Come in?" She turned to let him enter.

She was way too congenial. He'd allowed her to share his land, and she'd extended invitations to others. It had to end. Right here, right now, with the truth.

He edged past her into the snug space. His elbow brushed her left breast and his hip caught at her waist. She felt soft against him, the scent of peaches ripe on her skin.

He found Cimarron tucked beneath her table, as sleepy-eyed as Dayne. The Dobie flicked his ears, but didn't rise to greet him.

"Second time you've stolen my dog," he accused.

"I only worked one hour," she told him. "Business was slow. I biked home, let Cim out, and he followed me back to my camper."

"Where you both took a nap?"

She stepped into the kitchen, started making coffee. "I didn't sleep well last night," she said slowly. "I was worried about you."

That set him back. "Worried, why?" No one stressed over him. Ever.

"You don't have a job," she went on to say. "You look healthy and employable, but you may have trouble finding work. It's your shaved head. Interviewers judge on appearance. You look hardened, like a man who's spent time in a county facility."

Jail? His jaw went slack. He'd always looked tough. He couldn't change his features. On the plus side, his hair was growing back. "I'll find work," he growled.

"Until then, I have a solution. Hear me out." She hopped onto the lower counter, swung her legs, and smiled. "I met Ben and Brenda Dixon at the warehouse this morning.

They own the smaller pop-up. The couple's from Norton, a town in western Virginia. They were complaining the trailer parks in Richmond are full."

No room at the trailer parks. Kason went still. Acid built in his stomach. This couldn't be good. Surely she hadn't . . .

"The Dixons love baseball," she continued. "They're season-ticket holders, in town to catch the Rogues opener."

Kason sucked air—his privacy was about to go public.

Son of a bitch.

"I told the Dixons they could park their trailer on the empty land." She seemed quite proud of herself. "I'm certain whoever owns the acreage wouldn't mind two more vehicles for three days."

Kason ran one hand down his face. Tomboy was making assumptions. He owned the land, and the invasion set his teeth on edge.

"What about the bus?" His jaw was locked so tight, the words hissed through his teeth.

"The Coachman belongs to Ben's brother-in-law and his wife, Brick and Marge Lawrence. Brick looks just like his name." She chuckled. "Short, solid, and in great shape for a sixty-year-old man.

"The Lawrences have an open-door policy for base-ball fans. Everyone's welcome," she told him. "They packed twenty people in the Coachman for a party last year when the Rogues made the play-offs."

Baseball fanatics, parked fifty feet away.

A nightmare on Rhodes Street.

"The Coachman is huge," she raved. "Brick gave me a tour. Two bedrooms, closet space, and the bathroom has a tub. Both RVs have their own generators and auxiliary batteries. They won't mooch our electricity."

No mooching. Their self-sufficiency didn't cool his temper. Four unknown people now squatted on his land.

Dayne sprang off the counter, opened the silverware drawer. Beneath a stack of plastic forks and spoons, she withdrew a wad of cash. She waved the money beneath his nose. Excitement made her hand tremble.

"I saved the best for last," she beamed. "Six hundred dollars! The couples each paid a hundred dollars a night." She pried open his fingers, stuffed the cash into his clenched fist. "Now you have money until you get a job."

Kason let it all soak in. He stood numb to her generosity. He'd seen red over her renting RV spaces to strangers. But however misguided, she'd done it for him.

So he'd have spending money.

She was giving him the whole amount, when she should have kept half. She needed the cash far more than he.

His anger splintered, and an unidentifiable warmth spread about his heart. The tomboy found him worthy of her consideration. The meaning of her gesture was not lost on Kason.

Her kindness overwhelmed him.

His conscience weighed as heavy as the hundred-dollar bills in his hand. He needed to come clean.

"There's more." She pointed toward her bedroom. "Look on the dresser. A Rogues baseball cap and bobblehead. Gifts from Ben. The cap's yours, if you want it."

Kason owned the official baseball cap. The bobblehead he'd soon whittle to tooth picks. Each Rogue had one made in his likeness, sold as memorabilia at James River Stadium. Apparently Ben was a fan of Psycho Mc-Millan.

"To celebrate your windfall, I made butterscotch pudding," she added.

Pudding crowned the day. He'd skipped lunch, and could eat the whole bowl. She'd been very thoughtful.

He looked at Dayne, and saw hope in her eyes. She cared. Really cared. She wanted to make his life better.

It scared the hell out of him.

There'd be major repercussions once the truth was revealed. She'd believe he'd played her. He could lose her trust. Her friendship. Her respect. All because he'd kept silent about his true identity.

His silence made Dayne uneasy.

She shifted from foot to foot, slapped her hands against her thighs. Bit down on her bottom lip. Then exhaled sharply. Tomboy was a bundle of nerves.

"Does the money offend you?" she finally asked. "I only wanted to boost your spirits. Let me help you now, and you can help me later. Don't be mad—"

"I'm not mad." He set her straight.

She touched his arm. "I've faith in you, Kason. You'll be back on your feet in no time."

Pressure pushed like a palm against his chest. The truth was on the tip of his tongue. "Look," he started, "there—"

"There's Ben and Brenda." Through the window, Dayne caught sight of their SUV pulling in beside the pop-up. She slid past Kason and threw open the door before he could stop her. She waved to catch their attention. "You're antisocial, Kason, but you need to meet them. They're very nice people."

Nice or not, he wasn't ready for an introduction. The meet and greet would not bode well for him.

He tossed the six hundred dollars on her kitchen counter, followed her out. The money belonged to her, no matter the outcome.

The Dixons crossed to Dayne, and Kason stood off to the side. He wasn't invisible, but at least there was distance between them. Maybe they'd concentrate on Dayne and not on him. He could only hope so.

Hope laughed in his face. The couple greeted Dayne, then turned to him. He went stiff, shoulders squared, gut clenched, his stance wide.

Combative and unwelcoming.

The Dixons weren't put off. It was only a moment before recognition dawned. Their expressions soon showed their excitement. A request for his autograph was a heartbeat away.

Shit was about to hit the fan.

"Kason, meet Ben and Brenda Dixon," Dayne said. "Ben's a retired city cop and Brenda once worked at the courthouse in traffic fines."

Ben was as bald as Kason and walked with a slight limp. Brenda stood a half foot taller than her husband. Both wore Rogues jerseys. Ben's jersey was snug. The man needed a larger size.

Silence filled their circle, held everyone in place. A freeze-frame, Kason thought, wishing he could rewind the moment. He'd kill to go back five minutes so he could explain himself to Dayne.

Dayne Sheridan watched Kason turn fierce. He'd gone

all deep scowl and darkly narrowed eyes in a matter of seconds. He looked ready to throw all three of them off the acreage. There wasn't a friendly bone in his body.

She edged toward him, lightly nudged him with her elbow. "They're here for three nights, that's all," she reminded him. "Then they'll—"

"Follow him to Miami," Ben was quick to say.

"Florida?" That made no sense to Dayne. "Kason lives here."

"The boy travels with the Rogues," Brenda informed her. "The team plays one hundred and sixty-two games. He's on the road as often as he's home."

"Rogues?" A major mix-up, Dayne decided. The Dixons had confused Kason with a star athlete. Perhaps there was a resemblance, but that's where it ended. A jock would be rich and famous, whereas Kason was private and poor. She stepped before him now, protective of his feelings. "I'm sorry, you're mistaken," she said to Ben. "Kason—"

"Rhodes is the best left fielder in Major League Baseball," Ben said filling her in. "We were in Tampa in February, caught spring training. I'd know him anywhere. With all due respect, he's one intimidating SOB."

Rhodes. Dayne had learned his last name from strangers. *Spring training.* The reason behind his vacated trailer.

Sideswiped, she drew a steadying breath.

Brenda frowned. "You look confused, sweetie." Her sympathy touched Dayne. "Weren't you aware Kason played ball?"

Her silence was telling. "I had no idea." She hated to

admit it. "We've been neighbors a very short time. I don't follow baseball. The Rogues never came up."

"You know who he is now." Ben beamed. "Maybe you can catch a game this season."

Or maybe not. Kason had played her, and Dayne was no longer a sport. Humiliated, she felt twice the fool and totally pissed.

Angry, she stepped back and looked at him through the Dixons' eyes. She kicked herself for not seeing him clearly.

He stood tall, all broad chest and thick thighs.

His expression was harsh, yet intelligent and intense.

His depth, drive, and decisiveness were evident.

His chest beat with a sportsman's heart.

He dominated in his profession. A lowercase god.

She'd stepped into his life uninvited. Stolen his privacy. Then crowded him with strangers.

Strangers who had provided him with spending money. The six hundred dollars must be laughable to a man who made millions.

Dayne was as mad at herself for not seeing the truth as she was at Kason for hiding it.

"A fan rumor said you were living in the boonies." Brenda raised her hand to protect her eyes from the sun as she scanned the land. "Psycho McMillan once claimed you were raised by wolves."

Kason squared his shoulders, blew out a breath. "You're on my property," he finally admitted. "I own a thousand acres."

The enormity of his statement put Dayne into shock. His land stretched from the double-wide to the main intersection. He owned the dirt road on which she rode her bike, and as far as her eyes could see.

Her face heated, yet her heart felt cold. Hurt lay heavy on her chest. Two strikes took Kason out of her life.

He'd kept his identity a secret.

Worse still, his job played out before thousands of fans. Mick Jakes had soured her to men in the spotlight.

Ben Dixon cleared his throat, then spoke directly to Kason. "We respect your privacy, son. We had no idea this was your land. If you'd like us to hook up and haul our RVs down the road, we're happy to oblige."

"You'll only hear from us at the ballpark," Brenda assured him. "We have seats behind home plate. We'll be cheering you on tomorrow."

Kason ran his hand across the back of his neck, quiet and contemplative. When he spoke, his words surprised them all. "Stay for the three days. Just give me space. My life away from the park is my own."

Definitely his own. Dayne sighed. She'd stepped all over his feet, had trespassed far too long.

Kason shook Ben's hand. "I'll get you a signed team baseball before you leave. And a new jersey."

Ben looked down at his belly. "Too many nachos, hot dogs, and beer at the park," he said ruefully. "Thanks, Rhodes."

Ben and Brenda took their leave. Dayne followed suit. Her legs felt stiff, her footsteps heavy. Her camper seemed a million miles away.

"Breathe in; breathe out; move on," she repeated as she entered her Airstream. She rubbed the *Tomorrow* tattoo at her wrist. There had to be better days ahead.

In a haze, she faced the kitchen, glanced at the clock. In twenty minutes, her life had crashed. Her forward momentum was now slammed in reverse.

She had decisions to make, a future to map.

A headache to treat.

She poured a cup of coffee, took a sip, burned her tongue. She blew, cooled it. Her throat and stomach didn't deserve second-degree burns.

Cimarron crawled from beneath the table, as if he knew she needed him. She absently patted his head.

Hurt and anger warred within her. She didn't know which emotion to release first. She could let the tears fall or she could flop on her bed and punch her pillow.

A knock on the door and her decision was made.

Kason Rhodes entered, uninvited.

Her temper shot through the roof.

The man made a perfect pillow.

Eight

"Get out!" Dayne stood with her hands on her hips, her left foot tapping.

Kason towered over her, a full head taller and ninety pounds heavier. He intimidated with his closeness. No doubt a jock tactic.

"Out!" She shoved at his shoulders.

He was no pillow. There was nothing soft about this man. He met her gaze, attentive yet guarded, and allowed time to stretch out. "I came to install your television antenna," he said at length. "I need a key to the basement."

Basement, the bottom compartment on her camper.

He couldn't be serious or so insensitive. The past twenty minutes had changed everything.

"I don't want your help." Her tone was as ineffective as her thump to his chest. Kason Rhodes was cut from steel.

"I'm here to help," he said. "You have no business on the roof. A slip of the foot and you'll have broken bones."

"My bones to break," she said stubbornly.

One corner of his lip curled. "You're irresponsible."

"You're a liar." Blinded by her own circumstances, she'd assumed he was poor. Yet he hadn't had the decency to tell her otherwise. How convenient for him. How awkward for her.

His expression cooled, closed, and he shrugged. "You believed I was broke the day we met," he said. "You saw my run-down trailer and lack of possessions and took pity on me."

"You never set me straight." She cuffed his bicep. "Damn, Kason, I fed you, felt sorry for you, wanted to help turn your life around."

"I never asked for your assistance."

"But you took it." Her sigh squeezed her chest, compressed her entire body. "I made a fool of myself, and you let me. I came to the woods to heal, and just as I'm feeling grounded again, you hurt me twice over."

She punched him again for good measure—her knuckles to his abdomen. The man was solid, showed not a ripple of pain.

"I feel used. I'm mad, *Rhodes*."

"Your anger's misguided."

Male logic and totally lame.

"I should be pissed you're on my land and that you've launched an RV park. Yet I'm over it."

"I'm not as forgiving," she said. "I was naive, and you took advantage of me. You've had your laugh. Get lost, Kason."

His brow creased and he grew uncomfortable. "You weren't a joke, Dayne." He decided to come clean. "Most days, my life's a fishbowl. I liked that you saw me outside baseball."

"You can't separate who you are from what you do," she said. "Athletes live and breathe their sport."

"I've wanted to tell you." He jammed his hands in his

jeans pockets, his mouth pinched. "I tried today, right before the Dixons arrived."

"You didn't try hard enough."

"You shot out the door."

"And here I thought outfielders were fast," she said, sneering. "You could have blocked my path, caught my arm."

No comeback from Kason. He'd gone quiet. The silence grew strained. He ran one hand across his stomach, and his gaze shifted to the refrigerator. "Guess there won't be pudding."

"You guessed right." She struggled not to slug him again. His thoughts had strayed to food in the middle of their fight. Her stomach was in a knot, and he craved butterscotch pudding. Typical male, and totally aggravating.

He scrubbed his knuckles along his jawline, a sandpaper shadow. His brown eyes darkened with a contemplative heat. "Sex, then?" He tried. "You're damn uptight."

"Fighting isn't foreplay." She ground her words out. "We have no reason to kiss and make up."

"An orgasm gives new perspective to an old problem."

The man was insufferable. A punch to his package . . .

He read her mind, stepped back. "Crippling, Dayne. You'd limit my ability to run. I can't cover the outfield hunched over."

"It would be such a shame to hurt the best left fielder in Major League Baseball." She did sarcasm well.

"I am good," he said without conceit. "I work hard at my profession. I practice my ass off."

"You and your game can leave." They were getting nowhere. "I need time alone."

Cimarron crawled from under the table. He cocked his head in question. Dayne patted his head. "Cim's welcome to stay." The big dog wagged his stub of a tail, adoring and happy.

They'd hit a stalemate, and Kason Rhodes had no more moves. He didn't know how to fight with a woman. In his limited experience, if sex didn't settle an argument, he'd hit the door. He'd never stayed to smooth a rough spot.

Dayne was a different story. Today, tomorrow, next week, he'd right what she considered wrong. She blamed him for keeping his identity a secret, yet he had done so with good reason. He'd wanted her to know him as a man before she saw him as an athlete.

Needless to say, she disliked both sides of him now.

He had the wild urge to pull her close, to hug her, to let her struggle against him until she tired. Judging by her expression, she'd bite, kick, and unman him if he so much as touched her.

He needed his body parts in good working order for Opening Day. If she wanted to be left alone, he'd give her space. He could always come back later.

As the sun was setting, she still refused to answer the door. He knew she was in the camper. She was burning candles and her shadow flickered behind the curtain. Still, she chose to ignore him.

He debated rocking the tin can until she fell out a window. But he didn't want to injure her. And, too, Cimarron was inside. A man didn't hurt his dog.

She cracked the door only after he'd walked away—to return Cim, who didn't want to be sent home. The big dog dragged himself to the double-wide. A handful of Dinkies Dog Biscuits put him in a better mood.

Sunday passed with no sign of Dayne. She'd locked her bike to her camper. Unless she'd taken off on foot, she was still inside. She was taking solitude to an extreme.

Maybe he should cut his losses, insist she relocate. But deep down, Kason knew he'd miss her. She'd driven him insane by taking over his trailer, then camping on his land. Overall it was a good crazy. In one short week, she'd intertwined her life with his, and strangely enough, he no longer cared. She amused him.

He wasn't an easy man to know. Harder yet to like. Somehow they'd become friends and neighbors. The thought of her being his lover left him hard. He liked her tight little tomboy body.

She'd lighten up; he was sure of it.

By dinnertime, he was far less certain.

Brenda Dixon waved him down as he crossed to his Hummer. He'd planned to grab a quick meal at Buckets, a small diner where salad, French fries, hot wings, and blue crab legs came in large aluminum buckets. A lot of food for a low price.

He didn't mind eating out, even though Dayne's food crowded his cupboards. He flat-out refused to take anything more from her.

"Ben told me not to bother you." Brenda wrung her hands together. "I hate to be a busybody. However, I feel responsible for telling Dayne that you were a Rogue when you'd chosen to keep it a secret." She sighed. "She's not a fan, Kason."

Brenda Dixon meddling in his personal life didn't sit well. He didn't know this woman, nor did he want her advice. He widened his stance and his whole body tightened.

She patted his arm, almost motherly. "A great get-out-of-my-face expression, son, but it won't work on me. I raised four boys, all hellions. My youngest could out-mean you."

Kason rolled his shoulders, cut his look in half. He gave her his full attention.

"We gave Dayne a ride to the warehouse this morning," she informed him. "There was no point in her riding her bike."

The tomboy had escaped him. He'd kept one eye on her Airstream, and she hadn't surfaced. She'd no doubt climbed through her bedroom window. It faced the Dixons pop-up, outside his view.

"Ben and I waited while she spoke with her boss and collected boxes." Brenda sighed. "She's packing and plans to pull up stakes by Thursday."

"Thursday?" Only four days away.

"Her moving is based on how quickly she can find a new job," said Brenda, "which, according to Dayne, will be far, far away from the asshole who owns these thousand acres."

"She's not going anywhere." The relief on Brenda's face indicated he'd spoken his thoughts out loud.

He'd never fixed a relationship. He wasn't certain he could. But he was going to try.

"You're a good man, Kason Rhodes." Brenda's impression of him came as a surprise. "You're talented, dedicated, and celebrated when it comes to baseball." She nodded toward Dayne's camper. "Perhaps it's time to step outside the sport to smell the roses."

Or smell the peaches, in Dayne's case. He liked her sun-warmed and earthy scent. "Suggestion noted."

"My husband's an advocate for solitude," she continued. "He had a hunter's cabin in Vermont for many years. He never invited me or our sons to join him, nor did he ever shoot a deer. The man communed with nature. The fresh air cleared his head."

Again, Brenda patted his arm. "Enjoy your evening," she said, then left him to his thoughts.

A short time later, Kason sat in a back booth at Buckets. The diner was dark, the service fast. Dayne remained on his mind through the meal. By the time he'd cracked his second bucket of crab legs and downed his Bohemian beer, he had a plan to ease the tension between them. He'd put it into effect after the season opener.

His mind soon shifted to the game, which demanded his full focus. He was paid big bucks to produce. He refused to let either the team or himself down. In eighteen hours he'd be on the field.

The Rogues wanted a win.

It would set a precedent for the season.

At 1:05 P.M. on Monday, Kason Rhodes looked down the dugout bench. The players had been introduced, the national anthem sung. Richmond's mayor had tossed out the first pitch. Five minutes, and they'd take the field.

The weatherman had forecasted April showers, yet an unexpected heat claimed the day. Under Kason's eyes were greased black to ward off the sun's glare. By the sixth inning, shadows would creep onto the outfield. Fly balls could get lost in the split of light and dark.

The silence intensified as each man went through his

mental ritual. More than one player made the sign of the cross. Several others spat sunflower seeds. Psycho Mc-Millan popped bubble gum. Kason visualized the game ahead.

"Play ball!" The umpire's shout sent the Rogues onto the field. The adrenaline rush was a natural high.

"Three up, three down," Psycho called to pitcher Brek Stryker. "Don't make me apply suntan lotion."

The Louisville batting order proved cocky, mouthy, and willing to swing. Fastball, curveball, slider, the batters aimed for the parking lot without success.

Kason knew the third batter well. Sam "Slam" Janovich had the upper body of a gorilla and was nearly as hairy. Tested weekly for steroids, he could knock a ball into the upper decks with the slightest break of his wrists.

On the second pitch, Sam connected with a changeup. The Colonels fans went wild as the ball shot toward Psycho McMillan in right.

Psycho ran, hit the warning track, and didn't check his stride. All out, he supersized his leap and smacked the wall full force. His downward slide showed the ball in his glove. The Rogues fans stood, stomped, and shouted their approval.

Three outs, and the Rogues grabbed their bats.

"Damn rookie pitcher throws submarines," third baseman Romeo Bellisaro grunted as he moved on-deck.

Kason understood. The pitcher was a sidearm right-hander. His pitches weren't easy to judge. His debut against the Rogues was to showcase him as a star on the rise.

At the plate, Romeo took a fastball for a strike.

He popped a second fastball foul. Strike two.

The third pitch cut high off the right corner, and

creamed his thigh. Romeo dropped the bat, rubbed his leg, glared at the pitcher. Then slowly jogged to first.

"Sub Man's an asshole." Rhaden Dunn pushed to his feet, moved to the dugout fence. "He aimed to maim."

Additional players joined him. All eyes were on the mound. The team protected their own. Hitting Romeo might have been a legitimate mistake, but should Psycho get nailed, the bench would empty.

Kason watched as the pitcher fired low and the ball bit the dirt to the right of home plate. Psycho jumped back, swore. He stomped dust off his cleats.

"Dogfight in the season opener. Can't get much better than that," Alex Boxer said to Kason as both men slid off the bench and gathered at the stairs.

Boxer is an idiot, thought Kason. When adrenaline pumped, cool heads turned hot. In the end, fights delayed play. Eyes were blackened; a jaw or two was sometimes broken. Players got ejected. Richmond needed the force of their starting lineup to beat Louisville.

He was a Rogue now, and if push came to shove, he'd be pitted against his old teammates. He knew who fought dirty, who struck from the back. Who had bitten an opposing player's arm from the bottom of a pileup. Who'd jam his knee into another man's groin.

Kason watched as Psycho dug in, took a practice swing. His game face was carved in a sneer.

A curveball cut sharply, and Psycho sucked air. He tried to pull his hands in, but the ball smashed his wrist. Psycho dropped the bat, clutched his forearm.

The pitcher spread his hands wide, looked worried. Louisville's outfield ran in to back their man on the mound.

The coaches blocked the Rogues' exodus. The trainer

was the only one allowed on the field. Seconds ticked while he checked Psycho's hand.

The trainer pointed toward the locker room—only to have Psycho trot down the first base line. The man was going to play hurt. He showed no weakness.

The Rogues' anger burned. A few started to pace. Many more clustered along the fence. All had strong words for the pitcher.

"Keep it tight," Kason warned. "Don't lose it. The kid's a rookie—it's his first start on the road. He's hyped. Take the body hits; get on base. Walk in the runs. Once he settles in, he'll light up the radar gun."

His words didn't convince every player, but a few backed off. They weren't used to his speaking up. More often than not, they saw him as an antisocial asshole who sat alone at the far end of the dugout bench.

Risk Kincaid batted third.

Kason entered the on-deck circle, batting cleanup. He shouldered two bats, took several practice swings. He then rested one bat against his inner thigh, went on to adjust his batting helmet, straighten his shin guard.

To the fans' disappointment, Risk went down on strikes.

And Kason crossed to the plate.

Equal cheers and boos echoed in his ears before he tuned out the stadium and focused on the pitcher. The media claimed the kid packed an arsenal of surprises.

Psycho and Romeo stretched their leads off first and second, respectively. They stole bases with speed and agility.

Mind games came into play.

The pitcher eyed Kason.

Kason stared the kid down.

The rookie was hard to read. He was low on his fastballs and high on his sliders. Nerves were splintering his game.

Kason took a backdoor slider for strike one. The pitch appeared out of the strike zone, then broke back.

The next fastball fanned his eyebrows. Ball one.

Kason refused to blink. His team, on the other hand, shouted threats. It was the first time his teammates had stood behind him. A unique experience.

A curveball buzzed his balls. That made Kason jump back. His testicles tightened against his body. He might never father children, but he'd like the option left to him and not to a sidearm right-hander.

"Ball two!" called the umpire.

Kason next fouled back a knuckleball. Strike two.

His breath hissed through his teeth and his eyes narrowed. It was time to make a statement.

A slider, and Kason laid his bat on the ball. The ball looped over second for a base hit. The center fielder scooped too soon, and the ball cleared his glove's webbing. He scrambled sideways to retrieve the ball.

Romeo and Psycho scored on the error.

Kason held at first.

To the crowd's dismay, Zen Driscoll and Rhaden Dunn both fell to strikes. The inning closed with a two-run lead.

"Pussy lob," Psycho said to Kason as they collected their gloves.

"My hit brought you home," Kason said.

By the sixth inning, the sun had gone into hiding. Gray clouds gathered, turned black. Rain began to drizzle.

Psycho shook himself like a dog in the dugout. "Anyone got an umbrella?" he asked.

"Screw the umbrella." Kason snagged a towel, wiped his face. "You're more yellow raincoat and matching boots."

Several players chuckled.

Psycho spun on Kason. "Didn't I just hear you performing 'Singing in the Rain' in left?"

"My voice beat your tap dancing on the warning track," said Kason. "You're no Gene Kelly."

Risk Kincaid blew a mouthful of sunflower seeds.

Zen Driscoll spewed water.

The players found the exchange amusing.

Psycho worked his jaw. "Who kissed and woke you up, Sleeping Beauty?" he slammed. "You're damn chatty today. I liked you better muzzled and dull."

"Jackass." Kason swiped his forearms dry.

"Jerk-off." Psycho unwrapped a fresh piece of bubble gum, popped it in his mouth. He then dropped onto the bench between Romeo and Chase.

Three men up, three men down, and the Rogues again took the field. The drizzle was steady, but not bad enough to call the game. The temperature on the field had dropped ten degrees. Kason tugged down the brim on his cap. He rolled his shoulders, shifted his stance, bent his knees. His complete focus was on home plate.

A pop-up to Romeo at third sent the leadoff batter back to the visitors' dugout. A backhanded pickup by Zen Driscoll, quickly fired to first, delivered the second out.

Sam "Slam" Janovich was next to bat.

Janovich blew snot from his nose, spat, scratched. He

dug in, then backed off the plate. All maneuvers to throw off Brek Stryker's momentum.

The drizzle became a steady shower. The grass grew slick, and there was little footing on the field. It would soon be hard as hell to grip the ball. Kason noticed the grounds crew gathering, ready to spread tarps over the infield.

Through the rain, Kason studied Janovich's stance. The man batted right, and could spread the ball around the park, which left every outfielder on edge.

A breaking ball slider, and Janovich crushed it between right and center. Risk ran full-out, called Psycho off; the catch was clearly his. Nearly under the ball, Risk stumbled, pulled up. He threw down his glove and clutched his left thigh.

The ball splashed down, and Psycho recovered. He threw to second, held Janovich to a double.

Time was called as the team physician and trainer shot from the dugout and headed for center. Kason joined his teammates, gathered around Risk.

"Hamstring," Risk self-diagnosed, unable to put weight on his leg. A quick evaluation, and Dr. Provost agreed.

Risk was helped off the field.

Lightning slashed the sky, and thunder kept it company. The umpires clustered and soon ruled a rain-out. The game had gone more than five innings, so the Rogues were awarded the win.

The locker room filled with damp and dirty players. Men stripped and headed for the showers, the mood somber as they awaited word on Kincaid's condition. An hour passed before Dr. Provost emerged from the on-site medical unit.

"Severe hamstring injury," he told those gathered. "Initial ultrasound shows a third-degree rupture of the muscle."

There were moans and groans as every man in the room suffered Kincaid's pain.

"Recovery?" Kason asked.

"Two to three months," the doctor said.

"Son of a bitch." Psycho's curse was echoed by each player's individual expletive.

"Not a great way to start the season," came from Risk as he swung through the locker room door on crutches. Coach Jared Dyson entered in behind him. Dyson was new to the organization. A barrel-chested man whose tough-eyed looks spoke louder than words.

The players circled Risk, all visibly frustrated by their team captain's being out of play. Kincaid nodded to Dyson to deliver the news.

"After talking to the general manager, I've decided Alex Boxer will start in center during Kincaid's rehabilitation," Dyson stated.

"Hot damn." Boxer was too damn happy over Risk's injury. The other players stared the smile right off his face.

"Now, for team captain—" Dyson continued. "Risk won't attend meetings or be at the stadium to give direction and keep the peace."

"My recommendation: cocaptains," said Risk. "Psycho McMillan and Kason Rhodes."

"Rhodes? *Bullshit.*" Psycho's tone was harsh, disbelieving. "He's too new and keeps to himself. Most days I can't remember his name. I'd rather rule alone."

"Cocaptains—take it or leave it." The coach gave Psycho his end-of-discussion squint.

"I'm in," Kason agreed, knowing he and Psycho would clash over the time of day.

"In today, out tomorrow," Psycho predicted.

"Go shoot bird together on your day off," Risk suggested to Psycho. "Bond, bro."

Psycho sneered. "Not wise to put a shotgun in my hand around Rhodes."

"Go home; rest up." Dyson again took control. "Clear skies are forecast for tomorrow. We'll go nine."

"Get off that leg," Kason called to Risk Kincaid as he departed the locker room. Kason felt bad for his teammate, but he had important business to take care of before day's end.

Four o'clock found the waiting area outside player promotions packed with job applicants. More than thirty women sought the assistant's position. Many held resumes and portfolios an inch thick.

The ladies all smiled at Kason. One wiggled her fingers.

Kason gave them a brief nod, then knocked on Revelle Sullivan's office door. He entered before she could request that he wait.

Revelle glanced up at him. "Mr. Rhodes?" She paused in her interview.

He got straight to the point. "Ms. Sullivan, we need to talk."

"I'm going over skills and job experience with Ms. Walker," Revelle told him. "Can't our conversation wait?"

"No, it cannot."

Her color high, she eased back her leather chair and gracefully rose. She then straightened a blue decorative

rose on the lapel of her cream suit jacket. Her agreement
to see him came with an apology to the applicant.

"Please excuse mé, Ms. Walker," she said. "There's
coffee in the conference room down the hall on the left.
I'll get back to you shortly."

Ms. Walker shot Kason a sensuous grin on her
way out.

He had no smile to give back. He closed the door,
leaned against it. He faced Revelle, who was still positioned behind her desk, palms flat on the dark mahogany top.

"Congratulations on your win," she said.

"A win handed to us by the weather."

"My uncle was pleased," she noted. "His ex-wife, not
so much."

"We've a long season ahead." So much for small talk.

She eyed him expectantly. "You barged in and sent
my applicant out for coffee. Why the urgency, Kason?"

"You've started interviews."

"Only the first round. It's a long process. Why the
interest?" she asked. "Are you looking to change jobs?"

"I couldn't work in an office—too shut in," he said. "I
need to breathe."

"I've spoken with forty applicants." She sounded
weary. "And have thirty-five left to see."

"Cancel the remainder of the interviews."

Her lips parted and she blinked at him. "I need to
hire an assistant." She swept her hand toward stacks of
files on the floor. "I'm weeks behind on filing alone."

"I have a person in mind for the job."

"Has she filled out an application?"

He shifted his stance. "I want you to hire her sight
unseen."

Revelle's eyes went wide. "Why would I do that?"

"Because I'm asking you so nicely."

She laughed at him. "You're a hard man, Kason Rhodes, but you apparently have a soft spot for someone."

"Not soft, just righting a wrong."

"This person is qualified?" she pressed.

"It's her dream job."

"Which means no experience?"

Dayne had to know the alphabet. "I'm sure she can file. She might even have computer skills." Kason had no idea what was hidden in Dayne's deep dark past.

"Let me get this straight," Revelle said. "You're asking me to hire a woman with unknown skills when I have a waiting area filled with applicants qualified for the job?"

"Yeah, pretty much so."

"*If* I hire your friend, what's in it for me?" She wanted to know.

"A good assistant."

"More, Kason."

He'd expected a trade-off. He swallowed, sold his soul. "I'll do the commercial for Platinum."

Revelle raised a brow, looked thoughtful. "Why the change of heart? You flat out refused three days ago. Quite rudely, I might add."

"I've reconsidered."

"Major sacrifice?"

Dayne was worth it. "Not so much."

She debated longer than he liked. "Fine. I'll have the contracts drawn up," she finally agreed. "Stop by and sign them later this week."

"Will do." He turned to go.

"By the way," she said, stopping him, "what's my new assistant's name?"

"Dayne." It was all he could give her.

She didn't press. "I'll expect her tomorrow, around nine."

Kason nodded, hoping he'd made the right call. Tomboy had a stubborn streak. She might fight him. He had two additional surprises up his sleeve. One of the three had to bring her around. Sooner rather than later.

Nine

"Open the door, Dayne, or I'll huff and puff and blow this tin can over," Kason Rhodes threatened.

Dayne Sheridan stood at the corner of the window. Dusk chased away the day. It had only been forty-eight hours—she wasn't ready to see him. Yet his continued knocks on the door were wearing her down.

Only moments ago, she'd watched him drive up. She'd seen him unload a box and a covered basket, then disappear inside his double-wide.

On the off chance he'd visit, she'd changed out of her pajamas and into a Bob Dylan T-shirt and black jeans. She'd clipped her hair back and slipped on sneakers. Then stood at the window and waited.

Ten minutes later Kason emerged. He came straight to her. His long strides and determined expression made her heart pound.

She'd missed him, a sad fact to admit. She'd never met a tougher, more inflexible, secretive man in her life. Yet a part of her still liked him. She wasn't certain what that said about her taste in men.

She was no longer angry. Only the hurt lingered. The fact that he hadn't trusted her with his true identity kicked hard. Perhaps he'd had his reasons. She'd tried to see his side of things.

He belonged to the Rogues and their fans. Media stalked him; he was always in the public eye. If she'd followed baseball, she'd have recognized Kason immediately. He was unforgettable and unmistakably hot.

The Dixons had rallied behind him. They'd sworn Kason was one of the best ever to play the game. He was both a Gold Glover and a grand slammer. A shoe-in Hall of Famer.

Dayne, however, had known Kason only as a man living in the woods with his dog. He liked butterscotch pudding. He'd been a good neighbor and set up her outdoor shower stall. He'd appeased her curiosity over his Naughty Monkey matches. She knew better than to call him Kassie.

Most important, he'd allowed her to camp on his land. She knew she was a goner when she found his bald head sexy. His lack of hair sharpened his features. She'd seen his lip curl, but had never seen him smile. He was solid, introverted, and showed no emotion.

No emotion until now. Persistence powered the man outside her door. He growled, knocked even harder, rattling windows and rocking the camper.

Still, she held off from letting him in.

Fully annoyed, he stopped, turned on his heel, and jogged back to his trailer. Only to return seconds later with Cimarron.

Dayne exhaled sharply. Dragging his dog into their argument was cheating. Kason didn't fight fair. She adored Cim. When the Dobie pawed the door and whined, she cracked it, tried to sneak him inside. Kason wasn't far behind.

His broad shoulders blocked the doorway. His wide-legged stance dared her to make a move. She wasn't going anywhere anytime soon.

"Nice to see you too, Dayne" were his first words.

He then narrowed his gaze on the boxes, half-heartedly packed with food, a few pieces of clothing, and an extra blanket. The boxes were not yet sealed.

His jaw worked. "Going someplace?"

She crossed her arms over her chest protectively. "I'm moving. I've overstayed my welcome."

"Isn't that for me to decide?" he asked.

"Not if I'm ready to go."

"Cim won't be happy." A low blow.

"Don't bring your dog into play." She sighed. "This is about you, me, secrets, and trust."

He ran one hand over his bald head. "Damn, Dayne, I can't backtrack and make it better. I did what I needed to do at the time. You assumed too much, but I never meant to hurt you." Same words, different day.

She understood why he'd kept his identity quiet. He was a good-looking guy, and his star status and money would make him even more attractive to women. Though she understood, her feelings were still hurt.

Cimarron dropped to his haunches, nuzzled her hand. She attentively scratched his ears. Anything to distract her from Kason.

He cocked his head. "Are we straight?"

"We're close," she admitted, "but not quite there."

"Would gifts bring you around?" His gaze was sharp as he studied her closely. His caution touched her. He was walking on eggshells, not wanting to make a mistake.

Her heart stuttered. She'd yet to see this side of the

man. Gift giving appeared new to him. Receiving presents was a first for her as well.

Her ex-fiancé, Mick Jakes, had bought her the occasional meal, but never anything special. Not even on her birthday. She'd bought her own cake and ice cream and new pair of shoes.

"You bought me gifts?" All her worries and concerns of the previous days evaporated in the face of his kindness. He was trying to set things right.

"Bribery." He was honest. "Two gifts from me and one from Cimarron."

She studied his hands and pockets—no hidden surprises there.

He noticed her checking him out. "Presents are at my place."

"You're still standing here because . . . ?" she prodded.

"I wasn't sure you'd follow me back."

Breathe in; breathe out; move on, she told herself. She massaged the *Tomorrow* tattoo at her wrist and met him halfway. "I take bribes. I'm on your heels."

A smile twitched his mouth, but didn't fully break. "Let's go."

A companionable silence accompanied them to his double-wide. Cimarron loped in excited circles. If the dog could talk, he'd have spilled the surprises.

Kason held the door for Dayne, and Cim zipped in behind her. The feeling of the trailer was male and familiar. A place she'd missed.

"Have a seat." He motioned toward the sofa.

She dropped down on one end. A spring nudged through the fabric and stabbed her hip. She edged toward the middle.

Kason moved to the kitchen, retrieved a box from the floor. The man dominated left field in baseball, yet at that moment, he seemed ill at ease. Worry creased his brow, his jawline tight.

"This goes with your antenna." He handed her the box. "I'll hook it up tomorrow, should you change your mind and stay."

Dayne's hands trembled. The label on the box read FLAT-SCREEN PLASMA. A small but top-of-the-line color television. The perfect size for her camper.

Emotion warmed her, and she melted inside. Tears flooded her eyes and her nose started to run. She sniffed loudly.

Kason stepped back, his concern evident. He blew out three short breaths, said, "The TV can be exchanged for a stereo."

"The television's perfect," she assured him, her voice watery. She set the box on the coffee table and wiped her eyes with the back of her hand. "These are happy tears, not sad."

He watched her for several seconds, then took her at her word. "Cim can be quite persuasive too." He patted his thigh, and the Dobie crossed to his side. "Give us a minute."

Dayne sat on the couch and collected herself. Kason's gift touched her heart. Seconds later, Cimarron's present stole her soul.

She heard the Dobie's deep bark, followed by a softer yip. In the hallway off the guest bedroom stood Kason, Cimarron, and an extremely thin, wobbly puppy. The pup was the mirror image of Cim, black and rust colored, only tiny. A second yip drew Dayne off the couch.

She dropped to her knees at the corner of the coffee table. The pup scrambled onto her lap. He weighed no more than air.

"His name is Ruckus, and he's an eight-week-old miniature pinscher." Kason stood back and watched as Dayne and the min-pin got acquainted. "He's a rescue dog, same as Cimarron. He's small to begin with, and will only weigh between nine and twelve pounds."

Dayne's throat worked as she gently stroked the min-pin's head, then trailed her fingers along his visible ribs. She straightened the red bow about Ruckus's neck, a crooked ribbon with only one loop, tied by a man with little experience in gift wrapping.

The miniature pinscher fit in the palms of her hands, hyped up and wiggly. Ruckus lived up to his name. He licked her face, nipped at her chin, tugged at the neckline on her T-shirt until he'd loosened a thread. He playfully growled, then went after her hand. The puppy had sharp little teeth.

Kason cleared his throat. "I've scheduled a fence company to come in tomorrow," he said. "I'll install a screen doggie door on your camper. That way Ruckus won't have an accident inside."

The man had thought of everything. He'd put major effort into her gifts. He'd cornered her into staying. A decision she would have made on her own, although a little persuasion never hurt. She'd never felt so spoiled.

"I'm speechless." It was all she could manage as Ruckus wound down. The pup yawned, curled against her chest, and was asleep in a heartbeat.

Cimarron took that moment to join them. He sat before Dayne, eye to eye, his expression reminding her that he came first, no matter the new addition in her life.

"Thanks, Cim." Her voice was soft and appreciative. She stroked the big dog's neck and scratched both ears. She swore the Dobie sighed.

Kason came to her next. From her position on the floor, she saw his boots, then his long legs as she looked up his body. Wide chest, thick neck, granite jaw, and full mouth. His eyes held a heat that did crazy things to her heart.

"I have one more gift." He offered his hand and pulled her to her feet. She clutched Ruckus to her chest. The pup was sound asleep, oblivious to the world around him.

"Last time we had dinner, you mentioned public relations as your dream job." He paused, she nodded, and he continued. "The Rogues have an opening in player promotions that might interest you. An assistant's position."

"You thought of me?" She'd never been more surprised.

"The job's yours if you want it."

She went utterly still. She couldn't speak, couldn't breathe. Could barely think straight. Kason had presented her with a golden opportunity. She wondered who's arm he'd had to twist or break, for that matter.

He snapped his fingers. "You with me, Dayne?"

She nodded. "I'm taking it all in."

"Revelle Sullivan heads Game's On. She's willing to train," he told her. "You can start tomorrow. I'll give you a lift to the stadium until you can find your own transportation. It's too damn far to bike."

"Tomorrow." So soon. Her mind ran to clothes, shoes, a shower. Then on to who would watch Ruckus while she was away.

Kason read her mind. "I've a pet sitter scheduled. Eve McCaffrey, my teammate's wife, will stay with Ruckus and Cim for a few days until the min-pin settles in. Eventually Cimarron will take over as babysitter. He's well trained."

Dayne was instantly relieved.

Kason shifted his stance. "Are we square now?" He needed to know.

"We're fine." Her life was near perfect.

"Good, 'cause I'm out of gifts."

He'd given her more than she'd ever expected. More than she deserved.

Most men showed regret with a card, flowers, or chocolates.

Kason's apology came with a plasma, puppy, and employment.

He'd fixed everything broken in her life.

"I can pay you rent now," she told him.

"The tin can doesn't take up much space."

"Then I'll pay by the foot."

She set the sleeping min-pin on the sofa, and Cimarron stood guard over the pup. Turning back to Kason, she touched his arm. "I won't assume anything about you ever again. As far as the gifts, 'thank you' doesn't seem enough."

She made a move toward him then. There was something incredibly sexy about a hard man showing his soft side. His apology had left her unexpectedly turned on. He'd gifted her with openness, vulnerability, and kindness. Beneath his tough exterior beat a good heart.

She stepped into his body, until their hips met. Her hands curved around his biceps. His scent hinted of rain, woods, and virility. His brown eyes turned black. His jaw was firmly set.

She showed her appreciation with an airbrush kiss to his lips, so light, it might never have happened. A second kiss went deeper, lasted longer, grew suggestive.

Kason held still, in complete control, only taking what she chose to give.

She gave even more. Her intimacy parted his lips, and she tasted him. She caught the moist heat of his mouth on the tip of her tongue, penetrated deeper, withdrew slowly.

Kason let her initiate, then lead. He shifted, but didn't touch her. His arms pressed his sides, as straight and stiff as his body.

Her hands left his arms, soon to flatten against his chest. His body heat was explosive against her palms. The cut and contour of his muscles defined the physical man. He used his body for sport, and maintained the strength and power of an elite athlete.

Men would emulate him.

Women would scheme for his attention.

She clutched the navy cotton of his T-shirt, the urge to strip off his clothes strong. She wanted to snuggle against his chest, kiss the warm crease of his neck, work her way down his body.

Her breathing grew erratic.

His body flexed, his erection in play.

She knew where this was headed when Kason spoke his thoughts out loud. He raised a brow, his expression intense. "Make-up sex?"

He'd asked her before, and he was asking her again. His apology had given them both mental release after their argument. Connecting physically with this man would give her an amazing orgasm. She was close to accepting his last gift. So very close.

Memories of Mick Jakes crowded her mind, and sanity pulled her back. She shook her head. Good sex required the right timing, and their time wasn't now. "We're neighbors, Kason. I don't do friends with benefits."

"Sex could benefit us both," he insisted. "You want me, Dayne."

She damn-sure did. "We're too different," she managed to say. "I like low-key. I just don't want to get involved with someone in the public eye."

That stopped him cold. "Why the hell not? I have a private life."

"Past experience, Kason," she said. "Been there, done that, and won't repeat. End of discussion."

He didn't understand. His expletive told her so.

He did, however, back off, which she appreciated.

Kason Rhodes stared at Dayne. The tomboy had slipped him her tongue, spread her hands over his chest, *felt him.* Yet that's where it ended, with a wild pulse at her throat and him sporting a hard-on.

Taking her to his bed appealed to him. A whole hell of a lot. But he wanted more than a quick screw. That in itself surprised him. Dayne had inserted herself in his life, and he'd moved over and made room for her.

He wasn't about to make a move on her until she jumped his bones. For now, he'd wait for a clear sign that she wanted him. Until then, he'd find physical distraction in longer jogs and lifting weights. He'd go to bed so tired, even his dick would want to sleep.

Ruckus took that moment to open his eyes. The minpin yipped for attention, and Dayne immediately scooped him up. She cuddled the pup, and would spoil him rotten. Kason hoped she wouldn't dress up the small dog. No reason to turn Ruckus into an argyle sweater-vest sissy.

"It's time to tuck in," she finally said.

Cimarron hit the door, ready to go with her.

"Can Cim sleep over?" she asked.

"Why the hell not?" He felt generous.

"Any chance I can use your shower in the morning?" She looked hopeful. "I'd like to wash my hair in warm water. Maybe even get dressed in your guest room. It's more spacious than my camper."

"Set your alarm early, and don't use all the hot water. Be out by seven thirty. We leave for the stadium at eight."

By 7:35 the next morning, Kason figured Dayne had wrapped up her shower. He'd heard her arrive, had listened as she fed Cimarron and Ruckus. She'd then slipped down the hall and into his shower.

He'd lain in bed, his dick saluting the ceiling, as the running water drew pictures of her naked and soapy. He'd enjoyed the fantasy images, then gone on to wish the experience was up close and personal.

He stretched, scratched his belly, then swung his legs over the side of the bed. He'd given her five extra minutes—she knew better than to linger. She should be back in the guest room by now, dressing for work.

He snagged a dark blue towel from the clothes hamper. He'd used it for two showers, but it could go three. It was time to drop his clothes off at the Laundromat, before the hamper overflowed. Wet and Whirl did a quick job, charging by the pound. He'd then be set to go for another week.

Outside his bedroom, the hallway seemed like a sauna. Dayne had splurged on hot water. The aroma of peaches scented the shower steam that had snuck beneath the door. His own skin was damp by the time he twisted the doorknob, only to have it jerked away when the tomboy swung out.

Her head was bent as she shook out her hair. A cream-colored towel hung untucked and loose and exposed much of her body.

Kason took in her high, rounded breasts.

The symmetrical lines of her ribs.

Nipped-in narrow waist.

The sharp curve of her hipbones.

The damp triangle of curls.

And shapely legs.

Her body was tight, hot, and perfect for him.

His testicles tightened, and his dick stood up to get a closer look at her.

Embarrassment burned his neck.

He watched as Dayne swept back her hair, then became shockingly aware both she and he wore nothing but skin. Her watercolor blue eyes went wide. She inhaled so sharply, she started to cough.

Kason thumped her back twice.

Her face flushed as she caught her breath. She quickly overlapped the towel edges and knotted the ends, which helped some, but not a lot. He'd seen her nude, and she remained very visible to him.

She took her sweet time, taking in the morning man

before he'd showered and shaved. She seemed to like what she saw.

"They grow them big in . . ."

She had no idea where he'd grown up. "Missouri," he told her. The Show-Me State. His dick twitched, proud of its size. He pressed the towel over his erection.

"I'd better get ready for work." Her nerves took hold. "I used most of the hot water."

"I figured as much."

"Thank you." Dayne and her towel disappeared into his guest room.

He soon discovered she'd used *all* the hot water. The shower ran icy cold, and actually caused shrinkage.

He dried, dressed, and found Dayne in his kitchen. She was flitting around like a live wire, fully charged.

She stood at the counter. "Toast?" Her voice was as jerky as her movements.

How many slices did she think he could consume? A paper plate hosted an entire loaf of rye, slightly burned and heavily buttered. She'd moved on to the loaf of wheat.

Cimarron and Ruckus sat off to the side, staring up at the counter and the increasing pile of toast.

"Juice?" She poured out four glasses for two people.

Tomboy needed to settle down. Kason stepped before her, brought her flush against him. He wrapped his arms around her, held her for a full minute, until he'd crushed her nerves and she was breathing normally again.

"Breathe, Dayne." He eased back, squeezed her shoulder. "No interview; no worries. You've got the job."

Still, she fidgeted. "What if Revelle doesn't like me?"

"You'll get along fine," he assured her. The Platinum

account guaranteed Revelle would work around any of the tomboy's shortcomings.

She looked down at her outfit and asked, "Am I dressed appropriately?"

A trick question? He reached for a slice of toast, was slow to reply. It was an office job. Her blouse was buttoned; the side-zipper on her skirt was up. Her shoes matched. She'd fluffed her hair soft and curly and inked her lashes with mascara. Her lips, glossed a pale pink, curved full and kissable. He liked her mouth best.

Though Dayne didn't look as uptight and corporate as Revelle, she presented herself well.

"You clean up nice," he told her.

She exhaled. "I'm ready."

He eyed the counter. "The toast?"

She split a slice with Cim and Ruckus, then stuck the remainder in the refrigerator. "I'll make croutons later. We can sprinkle them over a salad at dinner."

Salad—not his idea of man food after nine innings against Louisville. "Sounds good," he agreed. Dayne could chop rabbit food and he'd cook steaks.

Dayne played with the radio all the way to James River Stadium. From the oldies to morning talk shows, she punched buttons, twisted the dial, yet couldn't settle on a station. She tapped into *Mick in the Morning*, syndicated out of Baltimore, and turned ghost white. The DJ's voice was smooth and personable, almost as if a third person rode in the Hummer, chatting amicably.

She hit the Off button so hard, Kason swore his dashboard shook. "Problem?" he asked her.

Pink tinted her pale cheeks. "No need for the radio. I'm happy with my own thoughts."

She didn't look overjoyed. Her features sharpened

and her eyes looked a little wild. She twisted her hands in her lap, stared out the window.

His Hummer was the first vehicle in the players' parking lot. It was four hours until game time. He planned to walk Dayne to Game's On, then grab breakfast at a diner across from the park. His earlier slice of toast wouldn't get him through the day. Afterward, he'd hit the weight room.

"Revelle Sullivan," the head of Game's On greeted Dayne with a smile and genuine warmth. She appeared as relieved to have an assistant as Dayne was to be hired.

"Dayne Sheridan." The tomboy shook her hand.

A corner of his mouth tipped. Kason now knew her last name. After several minutes of getting acquainted, Revelle raised a brow at him, nodding toward the door. His cue to cut out. He waited a bit longer, until Revelle's gaze narrowed and she openly waved him off.

His steps were slow in leaving. He hoped Dayne was a quick study and that Revelle wouldn't have to hold her hand during training. It would make it easier on them both.

After a breakfast of ham and eggs, Kason returned to the stadium. The parking lot had filled with the complete roster of Rogues getting ready for the second game in the series against the Colonels.

By late afternoon, the game had run into extra innings. Power hitting and poor fielding had the score tied 9–9 at the bottom of the twelfth. It seemed as though center fielder Alex Boxer had collected more errors in six innings than the entire team had the previous season. Whether it was bulleted to him or lobbed high, Boxer couldn't catch the ball. The Rogues' manager had finally pulled him from the game, replacing him with yet another rookie.

At bat now, Romeo rocketed a ball over the shortstop's head, ran full-out to first. Psycho batted next, struck out. Back in the dugout, he kicked the end of the bench so hard, the vibration turned the players into bobbleheads.

The center field rookie next went down on strikes.

Kason moved from the on-deck circle to home plate.

"Fate of the free world rests on your hit," Psycho called from the dugout fence. No pressure there.

The crowd was into the game, the stands a thunderous roar. He let the noise roll over him, then completely shut it out. He needed to perform to the high standards of his gargantuan contract. Big bucks for a big hit. It was time to smack the cover off the ball. He owed Guy Powers.

The Colonel's closer lit up the radar gun. His first one-hundred-mile-per-hour fastball blew by Kason, and the second one as well. The third pitch, and Kason didn't just hit the ball, he hammered the son of a bitch. Long and gone. Some lucky kid standing in the parking lot waiting for a home run would have a souvenir.

Kason watched as Romeo rounded the bases, came home. The winning run had scored. His teammates slapped Kason's back, and Psycho punched his arm so hard, his bicep spasmed. Psycho had only wanted an excuse to hit him.

Not one Louisville player approached Kason after the game. He'd not only burned his bridges; he'd bombed them.

"Win tomorrow, and we sweep the series," Psycho said, rallying the players. He then turned to Kason. "We shoot bird on Thursday, our day off." Not a request, but a statement.

Kason sketched directions to his home. If Psycho got lost, Kason didn't much care. He had plenty to do before the team hit the road to play Miami.

Hours spent with Psycho took years off Kason's life.

Ten

Two days later, Psycho stepped from his Dodge Ram, his expression surly. He held up a piece of paper with scribbled directions. "You said to turn left at Tri-Corners, when you meant right. I drove for thirty minutes in the wrong direction."

"Only thirty?" Kason had hoped the man would drive all the way to the Civil War battlefields.

Psycho ignored him, scanned the woods. "Damn, it's quiet. How many acres?"

"A thousand," Kason answered. The Dixons and Lawrences had pulled out late last night, now headed to Miami to catch the Rogues' series against the Marlins. The land sat free and clear of visitors.

Psycho looked toward the double-wide. "Yours?"

Kason nodded. "Construction trailer until I build my home."

"The aluminum egg?" The man was nosy.

"Rental property" was all Kason gave him. He'd purchased the Airstream from Frank at the Food Warehouse. He didn't want the man uprooting Dayne after she'd settled in and seemed happy with her tin can. He would sign over the deed to Dayne shortly.

"Where are the wolves?" Psycho told people Kason was raised in the wild. Some doubted; others debated.

Kason paid no attention. He crossed to the trailer, released the dogs. "Cimarron and Ruckus," he told Psycho. Both animals shot out, wiggly and free.

"Cute little shit." Psycho hunkered down, played with the min-pin. Ruckus's teeth pricked his hand. "Sucker bit me."

"The pup minds well." Kason smirked. "Hope it hurt."

Psycho grunted, pushed to his feet. "Ready to shoot bird?"

"We can set up behind the trailer."

"The noise might bother the dogs," Psycho warned.

"Inside," Kason ordered, and Cimarron obeyed. Ruckus, on the other hand, yipped his disappointment. He ran around Kason's ankles, then shot between his booted feet. A three-pound terror.

Psycho stood back, amused. "Alligator mouth," he finally called out.

The Little League term wasn't lost on Kason. It was the way coaches taught young players to catch a ground ball. The glove would be placed on the ground, and the other hand would be open above the glove, with the heels of the hands fairly close together.

Kason didn't have his glove, but his big hands worked just as well. Ruckus ran right into the reptile's mouth. And Kason closed on him.

"Wish I'd had a camera." Psycho chuckled. "I'd have sent the tape to *America's Funniest Home Videos.*"

Kason wasn't feeling the humor. He gently deposited Ruckus in the double-wide, then turned back to Psycho.

The other man nodded toward his truck. "I'll get the shotguns; you grab the trap."

Kason reached into the flatbed, raised the spring-loaded machine. Sophisticated and fully automated, the trap held six hundred clay pigeons in the magazine. The acoustic system was activated by the shooter's voice. Target speed and trajectories varied.

Psycho shouldered both shotguns. "Ever shoot bird?" he asked as they trudged through the weeds, trampling the low vegetation.

Kason shook his head.

Psycho turned smug. "Good—I'll win. Care to wager?"

"Let me get off a shot before you pick my pocket."

The trap sat on three legs. Psycho programmed in both their voices. "Should I set the flywheel to throw singles or doubles?" he baited.

"Singles, dickhead."

They loaded their shotguns with lead pellets, then stood behind the trap. The sun popped in and out of the clouds.

"Shall I show you how it's done?" Psycho asked.

"Knock yourself out."

"Pull," Psycho's voice triggered the machine, which released a fluorescent orange target. He took aim, shouted "Kason Rhodes" at the top of his lungs, then fired. The inverted saucer shattered. "Kill." He pumped his arm.

Kason cut him a dark look. "You named the bird after me?"

"Damn straight. I've got built-up hostility."

Two could play this game. "Pull." It was Kason's turn. He swung the shotgun in an arc, stayed with the target. "Psycho McMillan," he roared. The pellet winged the bird, but didn't bring it down. The orange saucer soared through the tree branches, flying straight into the woods.

"Not bad," Psycho said. "You nicked me."

"Pull." Kason went again. "Psycho" echoed for a mile. This time he blew the clay pigeon to smithereens.

"You're going out of turn," Psycho said gruffly.

"Screw turns."

"Go again, and I'll shoot a pellet up your ass."

Kason glared at Psycho. "No way in hell."

"Ask Chase Tallan about the scar on the back of his left thigh," Psycho told him. "And he's a friend."

No telling what Psycho would do to an enemy.

Kason kept a close eye on the barrel of Psycho's shotgun. Pellet ass sounded painful.

"Pull." Again from Psycho. "Alex Boxer," he hollered, then proceeded to kill the bird.

"Why Boxer?" Kason asked.

"The punk's doing a crap job in center." Psycho ground the words out. "He's all image, a real arrogant shit."

Kason thought that pretty much described Psycho. "This from a man who's T-shirt reads *Success Swells More than My Head*?"

"Boxer's playing minor league ball," Psycho stated. "I cover right, you cover left, and we'll both need to attend to center. Call Boxer off if you can make the catch."

Kason understood. He'd watched Alex closely. The rookie got distracted. He played, but didn't live the game. Even though the outfield coach drilled Boxer daily, there'd been no improvement. He just couldn't hold on to the ball. But unless the Rogues traded up, Boxer was there to stay.

While the majority of team owners fought against the salary cap, Guy Powers imposed his own. He refused to pad his roster. Powers was banking on Risk Kincaid's return. Until then, every player would have to pick up the slack.

"Pull." Kason squared off for another shot. "Psycho," he called again. He fired, misjudged.

"Bird away," Psycho said. "You missed me."

"Pull, pull, pull," Kason launched three consecutive saucers. "Bat Pack," he yelled. The clay pigeons flew out seconds apart. He nailed all three.

Psycho frowned. "Low, Rhodes," he complained. "Blow Sam Janovich out of the sky."

The man's home run had cost the Rogues a Louisville sweep. The hairy bastard had jacked the ball downtown. Kason mentally painted Janovich's face on the next orange saucer.

"Set the trap for doubles," Kason said. "We'll go at him together."

They fired at Janovich for the next ten minutes.

Until one of the stretch limos in the Rogues' fleet pulled up, parked, and Dayne Sheridan stepped out. Kason and Psycho both stared. The tomboy looked damn hot in her gray pantsuit. The jacket was boxy, the pants slim. The late-afternoon sun played off her silver chain and small hoop earrings. It was an easy style, but she looked sophisticated and sharp.

Revelle had enlisted a limousine for Dayne, a team perk until her assistant could afford her own transportation. Dayne took her lunch hour to run home and check on the dogs. Kason had heard the limo driver was fond of Ruckus, but that he kept on his leather driving gloves to avoid the min-pin's needle teeth.

Revelle had told him that Dayne was smart, innovative, and amazingly productive. Dayne had the same vision for Game's On as Revelle. The tomboy connected to the organization like a puzzle piece. She fit and belonged.

Once Revelle had laid out her duties, Dayne hadn't balked at the enormous workload. She'd been eager to get started and had put in long hours.

The previous evening, Revelle had taken Dayne shopping. Tapping into her expense account, Revelle had updated Dayne's wardrobe. Dayne was now as fashionable as her boss.

Psycho was the first to lower his shotgun. He elbowed Kason. "You get visitors this far out?"

"She's my renter," Kason informed him.

Psycho scratched his jaw. "She looks familiar."

Kason shifted his stance. "She works in player promotions."

"Revelle's new hire—that's where I've seen her."

Kason enjoyed seeing her now. The limo made a sweeping turn and slowly drove off, leaving Dayne standing alone and hesitant to approach him. He waved her over.

"Dayne Sheridan, Psycho McMillan," Kason said introducing the two.

They shook hands, and her gaze homed in on Psycho. "Right fielder, wild man, nudist, daredevil. You're a fan favorite—your bobblehead outsells all the other players'. Your wife's name is Keely, and she's a top interior designer. You've two Newfoundlands and a dachshund. You own Colonel William Lowell's historical Colonial. You promote Dinkies Dog Biscuits." She ran out of breath.

Psycho whistled, impressed. "You've done your home-work, sweetheart."

She smiled. "Revelle brought me up to speed. She gave me basic background on each player."

"What did Revelle say about Rhodes?" Psycho prodded.

Dayne Sheridan looked at Kason. His expression had closed. His stance had widened. He braced a shotgun at his shoulder. He looked intimidating as hell.

"He's private" was all she'd give up.

Psycho grunted. "Nothing new there."

She glanced at the trap, then back at the men. "Shoot-ing clay pigeons?" she asked.

"Releases frustration," Psycho told her.

"Want to take a shot?" Kason offered.

"I wouldn't know how," she confessed.

"I'll stand behind you," Kason offered.

He loaded additional pellets while she slipped off her gray jacket. The short-sleeve silk blouse gave her more movement. Behind her now, he positioned the shotgun. His body heat crept up her back. "How's your hand-eye coordination?" His question fanned her neck.

"We'll see when the pigeon flies and I pull the trig-ger." She wasn't all that confident.

Psycho backed up several steps. "I'm out of range."

"Pull."

Kason's shout made her jump. She jerked the shot-gun, blasted air. The saucer soared south.

"Almost got it," Kason encouraged.

"She missed it by a freakin' mile," Psycho disagreed.

"She was close." Again from Kason.

"Close, my ass."

Dayne caught the dark look Kason turned on Psycho.

Psycho laughed outright.

For a brief few seconds, she studied the men. Both were dark, Kason's own hair growing back fast. Brown-eyed. Tall. Athletic. Kason was thicker in the chest and thighs. Psycho was whipcord lean.

They had an athletic air about them. Swagger, pride, and superiority branded them Rogues. Women would turn, stare, and wish for a night under either man.

Kason wore a get-out-of-my-face expression.

And Psycho had an in-your-face stare.

Each man could back up his look.

Kason was both stubborn and kind.

Psycho's insolence pushed everyone's buttons.

Dayne rolled her shoulders and said, "One more shot."

"Snug up," Psycho suggested to Kason. "Go tight."

Kason took Psycho's advice. He was so close to her now, air couldn't squeeze between them.

His chest hugged her back intimately.

Her bottom nudged his thighs suggestively.

His hands covered hers, and he went as far as to wedge his finger against hers on the trigger. Man was determined she'd get off a good shot.

Once they were in position, Psycho made the call. "Pull."

The sweeping strength of Kason's arms guided the shotgun. With the precise pull of the trigger, lead pelted the target. The clay pigeon spun, broke into pieces.

Kason took back his gun.

Impulse turned her, and she gave him a hug.

He widened his stance, tucked her between his thighs.

Until Psycho cleared his throat. "Sweet appreciation."

Kason eased back, glared at his teammate. "My business."

Psycho's smirk was knowing. "I'm out of here. It's close to dinnertime. My wife's taking a cooking class. Tonight's her second attempt at chicken and dumplings. It's damned hard to digest doughy dumplings." He rubbed his stomach. "Hell, I'd eat dirt if Keely called it mud pie."

Dayne was impressed. The man loved his wife. He'd pop Rolaids so as not to offend her.

Psycho collected the shotguns, and Kason grabbed the trap. They loaded both into the Dodge Ram.

Dayne stood back as the men wound down their day.

"Did we gain any ground?" she heard Psycho ask Kason.

Kason shrugged. "Maybe a yard."

"More like a foot."

"It's going to be a long season."

"We're never going to be friends." Psycho stated the obvious.

"We only need to get along at the park."

"Outside the park you're a dick."

"Douchebag." Kason got in the last word.

Men acting like boys, name-calling and not giving an inch, Dayne mused. Worse than a pissing contest.

Psycho climbed into his truck.

Dayne had the sense to step back.

Psycho gunned the engine and sped off. Dust speckled Kason's T-shirt and forearms.

She moved to his side, brushed him off. "You and Psycho are more similar than different," she observed.

"Never thought you blind, Dayne."

"I see two men with the same goal," she insisted. "Team focus."

"Anything else, coach?"

"How about an early dinner?" she offered. "Hamburgers, but no buns. Hope you don't mind rye bread."

"I'd slap the burgers between paper plates—I'm that hungry."

"You missed lunch?"

"Psycho came out to the woods to settle our dispute."

"No bonding?"

"The man spun his wheels, dusted me." His tone was rueful. "That pretty much says it all."

"I'll feed you, but then it's back to the stadium for the Rogues' Literacy Campaign. One quick photograph—"

"If Psycho's in the picture, it'll take years off everyone's life."

"Not if his wife's dumplings are sitting heavy on his stomach."

Kason nodded. "Good point."

Guy Powers supported the Council for Literacy. He'd handpicked six players to pose for a print ad. The campaign—Flex Your Mental Muscle and Read—would run in major sports, women's, and teen magazines.

"Let's get the dogs." She headed for the double-wide.

At the door, Ruckus flew into her arms. It was a wiggly homecoming. The min-pin was all over Dayne, acting as if months had separated them instead of hours.

Everyone feasted on hamburgers.

Only Kason got butterscotch pudding. Dayne served him the whole bowl.

An hour later, Kason Rhodes was back at James River Stadium. He lived half his life at the park. Once he wrapped up the shoot, he'd drop by his architect's office and pick up the blueprints of his home. The drawings were in the final draft stage, and Kason had one more chance to make any desired changes before they were set in stone.

He thought of Dayne and how he'd left her on the couch, tucked in tight with the dogs, watching TV. He'd set her antenna before Psycho had arrived, and even without cable, she drew in twenty stations. She'd been happily flipping through the comedies, dramas, and reality shows.

By six o'clock, the team photographer had set up in a conference room on the sixth floor. Publicist Catherine Ambrose welcomed each Rogue, then made the decision whether he should sit or stand, as well as the type of book he would be holding.

Those titles would appeal to very different kinds of readers. It was as important for parents to read as it was for their children.

Each ballplayer wore his jersey and navy slacks. Catherine suggested baseball caps for Kason and Psycho. Romeo Bellisaro shouldered a bat and Chase Tallan slipped on his catcher's mask. Zen Driscoll stood in profile. And Alex Boxer shoved front and center.

Catherine Ambrose moved Boxer to the back row and pulled Chase forward. She requested that he hunker down, in position to make a catch. When the books were distributed, some players smiled, others shook their heads as they clutched the volumes in a free hand.

"*The Little Engine that Could,*" Psycho said in a pleased tone.

"A picture book?" Kason laughed.

Chase grinned too—he'd drawn a Western. "If not a ballplayer, I'd have been a cowboy," he said.

Zen palmed a legal thriller.

And Romeo got a romance novel. The guys teased him unmercifully. "You can learn what a woman wants from a female author," he said. "My wife's a fan of Scottish Highlanders."

Psycho said, "Bet you have a kilt."

Romeo didn't miss a beat. "There's freedom under a plaid you don't have with pants."

Laughter broke out, until Alex Boxer grunted. "A self-help book on visual perception and motor skills?"

"If the shoe fits . . ." Psycho stated.

"Shit, I'm playing hard," Alex said defensively.

"Not hard enough," Kason retorted. Boxer's hand-eye coordination needed work.

The publicist handed Kason a young-adult novel on teenage werewolves. Psycho ripped him with, "Your relatives, Rhodes. I knew you were raised by wolves."

Thirty minutes into the shoot, Kason wanted to smack Boxer on the back of the head. The rookie had the attention span of a gnat, and couldn't stand still. When the photographer said "hold it," Alex shifted. He then smiled so big, he looked like a clown.

Once Alex calmed down, Psycho acted up. He made rabbit ears over Boxer's head with each flash. Their childishness had stolen an hour of Kason's life. Dipshits.

"How were the dumplings?" Kason begrudgingly asked Psycho in the parking lot. He stood with the Bat Pack, the last to leave.

Psycho shrugged, was slow to admit, "I ate the chicken

and vegetables and fed the dumplings to the dogs under the table. Keely's moving up to beef stew."

"Gravy can taste like glue," Kason warned.

"If hers does, my organs will stick together." Psycho then cocked his head and asked, "How's your rental property?"

"She's paying rent," was all Kason would say.

The four men ducked into their vehicles and started their engines. Psycho rolled down his window and revved his Ram, an open challenge to race the short distance to the guard gate.

Romeo and Chase gunned their engines too. Kason shook his head. His Hummer was battered and rusty and the odometer showed two hundred thousand miles. It maneuvered like a tank. There was no shit-and-get to his vehicle.

He knew Psycho's Ram had an automatic hemi and went zero to sixty in seven seconds or less. The Dodge was maintained and primed.

Romeo drove a Viper, and Chase a '58 Corvette.

Kason shrugged. What the hell? It was a half-mile drag race to the gate. The lot was deserted as twilight dropped the green flag. He bore down on the accelerator, with no chance of winning. The Hummer lumbered forward, nearly three times heavier than the other vehicles.

Psycho pulled ahead fast in a fishtail of power. Just before the guard station, he whipped the Ram into a NASCAR burnout, rubber and sparks marking his win.

Romeo and Chase rolled to a stop.

Kason kept right on coming. Psycho was too busy celebrating to cross the finish line. The tortoise and the hare came to mind. At forty miles per hour, Kason barreled through the guard gates, the undisputed winner, at least in his mind.

Psycho brought his Ram under control, laid on the horn, and flipped Kason the bird. The man was not a good loser.

Before any of the players could fully clear the grounds, Guy Powers's stretch limousine crawled onto the lot. Sleek and polished, the limo pulled to a stop. Powers worked erratic and long hours. Kason knew the team owner had witnessed their race and would frown on his men acting like boys.

The Bat Pack all slammed on their breaks, backed up. Kason pulled a U-turn.

The men drew up beside the limo and exited their vehicles. They stood by the back-right passenger door as the window rolled down. Guy Powers looked from one to the other, his eyes sharp, his jaw granite, ready to ream them a second one.

"Stupid, dangerous, unacceptable." Powers ground the words out. "The Bat Pack's prone to idiocy. Kason, I thought you had more sense."

"It was all Rhodes's idea," Psycho accused.

Kason set his back teeth, kept silent. In the moments that followed, something inside him shifted, and an odd sense of camaraderie took hold. He'd never felt part of any team, especially the Rogues. The players were as tight as any fraternity. Tonight, he'd raced and gotten caught. He was one of the guys, and about to get ripped by the team owner.

The significance was jarring, but acceptable, and one he refused to analyze further. He'd never be fully comfortable with the Bat Pack, but he was part of the team.

"No more racing." The team owner went on to flash five fingers, his expression stern.

"Cash or check, Guy?" Psycho was the only player on the team to call Powers by his first name.

The window rose, tinted black and ominous, shutting off the owner from his players. The stretch drove off, as silent as the night.

Psycho and Kason stared at each other across two parking spaces. "What's with the five fingers?" Kason asked.

"Powers fined us five hundred for speeding."

Kason was pissed. "You're shitting me."

"We raced, got caught," said Romeo.

Kason narrowed his eyes. "I was doing forty."

"Speed limit's fifteen in the player's lot."

Kason had seen the sign, and always kept within the limit. Until tonight. He'd be paying five hundred for playing with the Bat Pack. He took his stupidity hard.

"Guy's name goes on a clay pigeon when we next shoot bird," said Psycho.

"So does yours." Kason climbed into his Hummer, drove off.

His architect had worked late, and Kason picked up the blueprints. Twenty minutes later, he parked at his trailer. Once inside, he removed the drawings from the long plastic tube and unrolled them. He then smoothed the prints flat with his palms across the dining room table.

Seconds later, someone knocked on his door. It could only be Dayne. He opened to her.

She stood before him in an Aerosmith T-shirt, cut-off gray sweat pants, and red flip-flops. She clutched Ruckus to her chest, and Cimarron leaned against her thigh.

"I'm returning Cim," she told him.

The Dobie looked none too happy.

"Thanks." Kason hesitated to let her in. He'd kept his architectural plans private. The house was his future. He wasn't ready to share the blueprints with anyone, including Dayne.

She looked a little lost, standing on his doorstep. A crease marred her brow before she gave a small shrug. She accepted the fact he didn't want company.

"Good luck against the Marlins," she said as she turned to go.

"Want to see my house?" He'd spoken words best kept to himself. He refused to overanalyze his need to show off the blueprints. But for some strange reason, he wanted her approval.

She returned to him, eyes wide, lips parted. "Show me," she said. Inside, she tucked Ruckus on the couch, and Cim babysat.

Dayne and Kason bumped shoulders and elbows as they hovered over the blueprints and he described every detail. The ranch design fit his needs, styled for a bachelor and his dog. A half hour passed before he eased back and waited for her opinion.

"You don't have a pantry for bulk items" were the first words out of her mouth. "You need to store food for an emergency. Your kitchen's small."

She tapped the drawing with her finger. "You have a guest room, but no children's bedrooms. Don't you want to have kids someday?"

To be honest, no. Any thoughts of extending his family ran to a couple more dogs. Children had never crossed his mind until Dayne sketched the picture.

"You should knock out this wall between the living

room and den and make it an open arch. You'd have more flow."

Kason had liked the separation of rooms.

"And maybe—"

"No *maybes* Dayne." He rolled up the blueprints. "I like the house as it stands."

"You're building a residence for only one person." Her tone was soft and uncertain, flat.

"My house, built for me."

A flicker of sadness, maybe pity, darkened her eyes, but disappeared quickly. "It's a fine house, Kason," she said, but he knew she didn't mean it.

She scooped Ruckus off the couch and crossed to the door. "Safe travels." And she was gone.

Kason stood stiffly. He slapped the architecture tube against his thigh, annoyed but thoughtful. Dayne had no business adding on rooms and knocking down walls. He never should have showed her his home.

He exhaled sharply, pulled the plans from the tube, again spread them on the table. The square footage was moderate yet functional. The architect had modeled the home around Kason's life. The drawings had begun long before Dayne Sheridan and Ruckus entered the picture.

After a hard second look, he traced his finger along the wall that separated the den and living room. An arch might work. Or not.

Though he didn't want Dayne to influence his future, a well-stocked pantry seemed practical. It would save him trips to the grocery.

He scratched his jaw. He'd give it some thought.

Eleven

"Give it some thought, Rhaden." Revelle Sullivan looked at him as if he were her salvation. "You've got four or five minutes."

Rhaden Dunn couldn't wrap his mind around her request. "You want to set me up on a date?" Damn low blow—the very idea twisted his nuts.

"It's for a good cause," Revelle explained. She sat behind her desk in player promotions, dressed in a lavender suit that matched her incredible eyes. She'd steepled her fingers beneath her chin, and now looked at him over the rim of her glasses. "The speed-dating event supports Collage, the historic schoolhouse. Six Rogues participate—each man faces ten women. You'll choose one of your ten and take her to dinner. The ladies pay one thousand dollars for the chance to dine with a professional ballplayer."

Rhaden raised a brow. "They pay, win or lose?"

She nodded. "The participants are wealthy. The women are strong, self-assured, and go after what they want. The donation is a tax write-off. If a participant isn't chosen, she can still enjoy a five-star dinner catered by the hotel."

"Which other Rogues are involved?" He wondered who Revelle had conned into the event.

"The players are all single," she emphasized. "Alex Boxer, James Lawless, Chas Ragan, Rod Brown, and Barry Cameron. Lawless is the only starter—the rest are rookies."

"You thought of me?" His stomach dropped.

"It's painless, Rhaden." She rolled her hip, crossed her legs under her desk. He caught a glance of her suede lavender pumps. "You might get lucky and meet the woman of your dreams."

No one filled his dreams but Revelle. She made nightly visits, sometimes sexy, more often soulful. She'd slip beneath his sheets and snuggle close, her hand placed over his heart. Her presence usually felt so strong, he believed her there.

His palms began to sweat, and he ran them down his khakis-clad thighs. "Give me the details," he requested.

"The event is tonight."

"Short notice, Revelle." The lady had invited him late. Rhaden read her easily. She was desperate, and knew he wouldn't decline. "What if I have plans?"

She bit her bottom lip. "Do you?"

The Rogues had wrapped up a series against Milwaukee. They'd lost two of their three games. He wasn't in the mood to be cordial to ten women vying for his attention.

He'd do this only for Revelle. The schoolhouse was a good cause, and one she favored.

"When and where?" he asked.

"Maximillian Hotel. Seven o'clock."

The finest hotel in Richmond. "How long will the event last?" He dreaded any get-together that cost him more than an hour. He needed a decent night's sleep. The Rogues hit the road tomorrow. Their schedule took them to Atlanta, then on to Washington. The Braves sat atop the National League East. The Rogues wanted to knock them out of first place.

"Plan on three hours," she said.

An entire evening shot to hell.

"The ten women each have six minutes to charm you," she rushed on to say. "Afterward, you select one to wine and dine."

"A restaurant of my choice?"

"No fast food. Please don't hurry dinner."

"What if no woman appeals?"

"Your reputation precedes you." Her shoulders squared. "When you first joined the organization, you were never seen with the same woman twice. I'm sure there'll be some spark of attraction."

His slam-bams had died with Revelle. He hadn't banged anyone for months. He'd flown solo in the shower, hand soap his new best friend.

He'd been waiting for her to give him a sign. Any damn sign that she'd date him. She'd come close several times, only to close the door in his face. He wasn't too proud to beg. Now might be the right time to press his advantage.

"I'll speed date," he slowly agreed, "on one condition: after I take the woman to dinner, you meet me for a drink."

Her hesitation lasted a full minute. He counted the seconds. "Agreed. One cocktail."

"Dress code?" The last hurdle.

"Suit or white shirt and tie." She let him off easy. "I'm not certain Barry Cameron has grown-up clothes."

Away from the stadium, Cameron acted sixteen, a horn dog with a stand-up comic's delivery of dirty jokes.

He had a strong, accurate throwing arm, and would eventually take Psycho McMillan's place in right when Psycho retired.

If Psycho ever retired. The man swore he could cover right in a wheelchair or with a walker and still best Barry Cameron.

The meeting over, Rhaden pushed to his feet. He flattened his palms on Revelle's desk, leaned across the top. They were inches apart, but it could have been miles. Her expression was all business.

Her Chanel teased him, the scent classic and sophisticated. Her red hair had been recently styled, the cut a bit shorter than the last time he'd seen her.

He tried his damnedest to see her several times a week. He'd made up every excuse in the book to knock on her office door. He'd used some twice.

He was on a first-name basis with the florist now. He figured a fresh bouquet on her desk every few days would prod Revelle to think of him. The most recent arrangement, miniature mauve roses in a cranberry vase, softly scented her office. It smelled far better than a spray of Lysol or a room sanitizer.

As he looked into her amazing lavender eyes, he wanted her to see him as the man in her life, not another Rogue on her roster to promote.

"Anything else?" he heard her say.

So much for being special.

He eased back. "I'm gone."

"Thank you, Rhaden." She said it like she meant it. "I'll see you at the hotel. I'm the one timing the speed dating rounds."

He hoped she'd shave a minute off the scheduled six. Five was plenty long.

Rhaden Dunn arrived at the hotel at six fifty-five. He caught sight of Revelle through the etched-glass doors to the ballroom, a gorgeous woman in a little black dress. Her high heels showcased tight calves and great legs.

Her toe was tapping as she looked at her watch. She looked as if she'd assumed he'd stood her up.

"I made it," he told her as he slid in under the wire.

"I wasn't worried." The tension in her face said otherwise. "I always had a plan B."

"Was your backup Kason Rhodes?" he teased her. "He's single."

The mention of Rhodes drew her smile. "Kason was never a possibility. I need a man to talk to the women, not go stone-faced and mute."

She took his arm, walked him down a white marble hallway lined with expensive artwork. Inside the ballroom, chandeliers cast soft light; expensive-looking white orchids were set on the tables. Navy wingback chairs were clustered in twos on the thick Oriental carpet. Fancy octagonal tables allowed for drinks and canapés. Rhaden didn't do finger food. Too damn dainty.

The women turned, looked him over. Some winked, others flicked their tongues. All had hot eyes. Most looked high-maintenance and overindulged. Spray tans darkened soft skin and Botox-smoothed wrinkles.

He nodded to his teammates, already surrounded by speed daters. None of the guys dated anyone seriously. They were easy and available for more than dinner.

Damn, he could use a drink, thought Rhaden. A double scotch would take the edge off. Somehow he would make it through the night. Revelle and a late-night cocktail were in his sights.

She settled him in a far corner of the room, patted

him on the shoulder, sensitive and supportive. "If you need me, scratch your chin."

He narrowed his eyes. "Reason to signal?"

"If a woman gets too amorous," she explained. "A few participants arrived early, and the champagne's been flowing freely."

Intoxicated speed dating—could the night get any better? He leaned one arm over the back of the leather chair, awaiting round one.

"I'm Winter Evans," the first of his ten daters said seconds later. She was sparkly in her silver sequined dress. Running her hands up his arms, she air-kissed both his cheeks.

"I'm thirty-nine," she told him as he seated her. "I've never had plastic surgery and I like to role-play."

Rhaden studied the woman. The cougar was pushing fifty, her smile tight from a nip and a tuck. He wondered whether she shook pompoms or wore a nurse's cap in the bedroom.

He nodded, attentive. "I appreciate your participation and donation to Collage."

"Revelle's schoolhouse." Winter sipped her martini. "History bores me. Meeting you brought me here to-night. I'm a big fan of second base."

Rhaden played first. "You like baseball?" he asked.

"I like the uniforms," she admitted. "The ballplayers look good coming and going."

Definitely a reason to watch the sport. Rhaden discreetly looked at his watch. Only two minutes had passed. It seemed like a lifetime. He made small talk as if his life depended on it.

After several minutes, Winter popped open her silver clutch, slipped him her business card. "I'm hoping you'll pick me tonight, but if not, call anytime. I come with a feather duster, and make a great French maid."

A soft chime echoed across the room. Round two.

Rhaden looked at Revelle. He found her eyes on him, looking thoughtful. He cocked his head, and she flashed nine fingers. She was counting down the speed daters right along with him.

"Angela Spencer." A blue-eyed brunette next greeted him. She perched on the edge of her chair with impeccable posture and pedigree. "I'm an advocate for historical landmarks." Her voice was perfectly modulated. "The earliest Spencers established the Order of First Families of Virginia."

This lady would bring her forefathers to dinner.

"Your favorite restaurant?" he asked.

"Jardinet's or Truffle's." She liked French food.

Rhaden was set on a steak. "Are you a Rogues fan?"

"You're a novelty." At least she was honest. "The men I date are staid, boring, and of my background. I'm looking for—" she hesitated.

"Adventure?" Rhaden filled in the blank. Angela thought him born to be wild, his own heritage beneath her.

"Exactly." She placed her hand over his, squeezed. "I'd like a night to remember before I settle down."

He pitied the woman. Sex ought to enhance a relationship; in his opinion, orgasms were one of God's greatest gifts to mankind. Though Angela might fool around, she'd wed a man with a genealogical tree taller than her own. Her life would be wooden.

The chime sounded and Rhaden pushed back his chair so fast it nearly toppled over. "My pleasure," he said as Angela moved on.

Again, Revelle caught his eye, her expression wistful. Damn, she was beautiful—candle thin with porcelain skin. He wanted to waltz her out of the ballroom without a backward glance. But it wasn't going to happen. Not for forty-eight more minutes.

Round three, and Betina Edwards joined him. "I'm married," she confided on a whisper. "I could, however, be separated in six minutes. Your call."

Lady placed high expectations on speed dating.

Rhaden scratched his chin. Rubbed it hard.

Revelle picked up his signal, and was immediately at his side. She smiled as she asked, "Anything I can do for you?"

"Not at the moment," Rhaden said easily.

She leaned in, lowering her voice for his ears only. "Crying wolf?"

"Merely making sure the signal worked," he returned.

Following round three, Revelle returned with two fingers of scotch and a curious smile. "How's it going?" she asked.

She might not be into him, but he had the childish urge to make her jealous. "First three were hot."

Her expression faltered. "You're enjoying yourself then?"

"I've got ten women vying for my attention."

"Lucky you." Her lips were now pursed.

He watched her return to the center of the ballroom.

Round four delivered Farrah Lane. She was exotic, with long black hair and almond eyes. A deep tan indicated a spray booth or a Florida vacation.

He quickly learned fashion was her passion. Discovering new designers, her mission in life.

Their conversation centered on clothes. "I have three hundred pairs of shoes," she told him.

And only two feet, mused Rhaden. He stifled a yawn.

Belinda Hollister introduced herself for round five. "I have six dogs, four cats, and a ferret," she announced.

That explained the pet hair on her cream-colored blouse.

Belinda drummed her fingers on the coffee table, let him know her biological clock was ticking. Her three-year plan went from dating to birthing twins.

Rhaden hated schedules during the off-season. Belinda wanted to arrange his life when he lived for flexibility and freedom.

He rolled his shoulders, faced round six.

Lux Huntington epitomized sex. Tossed blonde hair, high cheekbones, flawless skin. Her light green eyes matched the slice of lime in her gimlet; her red lips were glossed a shade darker than the tight corset dress that shoved her double-D's in his face.

Lux had sucker-punch impact, until she opened her mouth. "Cocktail frank?" She offered him one from her plate. "Wrapped in a blanket, the weenie looks uncircumcised."

Rhaden's jaw dropped, and Lux took the opportunity to pop the minifrank in his mouth. After her comment, he couldn't bring himself to chew. He snagged the cocktail napkin from under his tumbler and spit it out.

He rubbed his chin.

No immediate rescue from Revelle.

Lux scooted her chair closer. She ran her fingers over his shoulder, down his back, then snuck beneath his suit coat. "Show me your *Who's on First* tattoo?"

Hell, no. The tat was scripted on his groin and only visible to his lovers. Lux wasn't in the running to see it now.

Rhaden pulled back, captured her hands, and secured them on his thigh. She wiggled her fingers, and he tightened his hold. She stuck out her bottom lip, pouted.

Revelle chose that moment to stroll by. She caught what appeared to be an intimate moment between Lux and himself.

Her expression fell, and for an unguarded moment, she looked hurt. Her emotion both surprised and pleased Rhaden. Maybe Revelle had hidden feelings for him, after all. He'd find out over cocktails later that evening.

Lux turned to Revelle. "Can you restart the timer? I'm really into Rhaden. Six minutes is too short."

Rhaden looked at Revelle, shook his head. He had no desire to turn back time. He'd never look at a cocktail frank the same way again. Worse still, he hated fighting off a woman's advances in the ballroom of a five-star hotel.

Revelle forced a smile. "Rhaden has four other ladies to meet. We need to keep the clock running."

Rhaden released her hands, and Lux immediately grabbed his tie. The Windsor knot tightened like a noose as she French-kissed him, deep and hot. She then headed back to the bar.

Revelle passed him a clean cocktail napkin. "Lipstick smear, clown face."

He wiped his mouth clean.

"A night for your diary?" she teased.

"We'll discuss it over cocktails later."

"One drink, remember?"

"Lux nearly sucked my tongue down her throat." He straightened his tie. "I'd say you owe me two."

Four women were yet to come. Rhaden held his breath. He looked around the room, noted his teammates were having the time of their lives. It should have been a great night.

A year ago, he'd have enjoyed himself immensely. Tonight, his feelings for Revelle took him off the market. He didn't want to date anyone but her. In his mind, their relationship was exclusive.

Round seven introduced him to a lady who franchised movie theaters and video stores. She offered him a packet of free tickets, a discount on videos, as well as herself.

Rhaden politely refused all three.

Speed dater eight called him "Curry," because he was hot.

Number nine was quiet and coy. She sent him smoldering looks, letting her eyes speak for her. Rhaden held up his end of the conversation for four minutes, then also went silent. His smile slipped with two minutes to go.

Kara Jordan, the tenth and final dater, shut Rhaden down. She hadn't planned to attend the event, but came in support of her friend, Elizabeth Ellis, who'd wanted to meet Alex Boxer. Kara had no interest in Rhaden whatsoever. She wasn't a sports fan.

Revelle soon ended the round. Most bemoaned the fact it was over. Rhaden, on the other hand, shot from his chair, leaving skid marks.

The Major League ballplayers gathered around Revelle as she thanked everyone for attending the fund-raiser. Many of the women looked blurry eyed and a bit tipsy. All hoped to snag a Rogue.

Revelle called each player's name, then stood back as he selected his dinner companion. There were delighted cheers followed by moans of extreme disappointment.

She left Rhaden for last. Her expression, he noted, was hesitant. Again, he wished he didn't have to go through a four-course meal with another woman to land cocktails with Revelle.

The schoolhouse meant the world to her. She wouldn't bend the rules of the fund-raiser.

"Rhaden Dunn, ladies." Revelle motioned him forward. The whistles and applause made him smile. The fact that other women found him desirable kept him hopeful that Revelle might someday see him as "curry."

"Who's the lucky lady?" Revelle asked him.

He eyed the ten women who'd paid to meet him. He'd felt no attraction or connection with any of them. His gaze lingered on Kara Jordan, held. The wingwoman draped her arm over Elizabeth Ellis's shoulders, a gesture of comfort. Alex Boxer's rejection had devastated her friend.

Rhaden went with his gut. "Kara, will you join me for dinner?" he asked, half expecting her to decline. "I'd like Elizabeth to join us as well, if Revelle will bend the rules."

Kara looked startled; her friend, ecstatic.

Rhaden noticed that Alex Boxer took a second look at Elizabeth. Alex no doubt wondered what Rhaden saw in her, what Alex had missed himself. Curiosity would have Alex calling Elizabeth. Kara's friend would eventually get her date.

"Double your pleasure, Rhaden." Revelle agreed with a smile. "Enjoy your evening."

A round of applause followed the couples from the ballroom. Rhaden hung back, needing to speak to Revelle.

He looked at his watch, said, "Valentino's, ten o'clock. I've reserved a table."

The revolving cocktail lounge sat atop the forty-story hotel, with a panoramic view that showcased the city. Reservations were required, and hard to come by. Rhaden knew the owner, a huge baseball fan. Anthony Valentino took care of his Rogues.

"I'll see you then," she said.

Revelle Sullivan watched Rhaden and his two dinner companions depart the ballroom. Each lady took one of his arms. There was laughing and teasing, but there were no sexual vibes. She was instantly relieved.

Jealousy had pinched during the fund-raiser, and left a bruise. She'd grown unexpectedly anxious, afraid that Rhaden would meet someone special.

The attack of nerves had left her vulnerable.

She fought back emotion, again took control.

The fund-raiser had been an immense success. She had Rhaden and the Rogues to thank. The men had charmed for Collage. The generous donations would keep the schoolhouse open for another year. Creative minds would thrive.

A smile in place, Revelle directed the remaining ladies into the hotel dining room. She decided to join them. A nice meal would wind down the day. Then she'd face Rhaden.

Relaxed and satisfied after Duck à l'Orange and a caramel soufflé, Revelle wished she'd worn control-top pantyhose as she went to meet Rhaden. There was a convention in town, and hotel guests stood six deep at the elevator banks.

At five minutes until ten, she decided to take the outer glass elevators that raced the sides of the world-class hotel like sleek cylindrical bullets. She rode to the thirty-ninth floor, then climbed the wide staircase to the fortieth. Thick black carpeting cushioned her steps. The handrails were polished onyx.

Valentino's opened before her, upscale and intimate, with soft amber lighting to offset the bright city lights. Classic and comfortable combined in the revolving cocktail lounge. Large, plush club chairs circled the floor-to-ceiling windows and booths backed the crescent bar.

Drinks were mixed in the finest crystal. A band of twenty-two-karat gold added a gleaming accent to the barware. Waiters circulated, offering hors d'oeuvres.

The owner of Valentino's approached her, his smile in place. "Do you have a reservation?" he asked.

"She's with me." Rhaden Dunn came up behind her. "Sorry I'm late," he apologized. "Dinner ran long. Kara and Elizabeth enjoyed the full dessert tray."

Revelle turned slightly, took him in. He was one handsome man with his light brown hair brushed back off his face, revealing strong, angular features. Amusement darkened his green gaze, and the upturned corner of his mouth indicated he liked her eyes on him.

His suit, black and tailored to his broad shoulders, fit him perfectly. His tie was patterned in deep blue and burgundy. His dress pants were sharply creased. A man in wingtips showed his style. Rhaden looked amazing.

"This way, Mr. Dunn." Anthony Valentino led them

to a table banked by gray leather chairs. "Cognac?" he asked.

Their host knew Rhaden well. Revelle wondered how many women the first baseman had brought to the lounge.

Rhaden looked at her. "Courvoisier?"

She nodded, her focus on the city below. The slow, fifty-minute rotation of the top floor was barely noticeable. The view on this crystal clear night was spectacular.

Rhaden leaned in close, pointed east. "James River Stadium."

"The Monroe Building and the capitol," she named two additional landmarks. The lights from surrounding skyscrapers reflected on the James River, its path glossy and winding.

Their cognac arrived in cobalt blue balloon snifters. They both passed on the canapés.

Rhaden swirled the Courvoisier, took a sip, then introduced himself as if they were speed dating. "I'm Rhaden Dunn. I was born and raised in Phoenix, Arizona, and attended college at the University of Southern California."

"Revelle Sullivan." She played along, remarkably comfortable with this man. "I grew up in Chicago, cheered for the White Sox."

"American League—kill me now," Rhaden said with a groan.

"I've since gone Rogue."

He looked relieved. "Do you come here often?"

A typical pick-up line. "A first for me."

"A Valentino virgin. I like that." His voice was deep

and sexy, intriguing. His gaze touched her face, as tangible as fingertips.

"How about you?" She took a sip of her cognac. "Are your dates impressed by the view?"

"No dates, just me." His words surprised her. "This is where I escape life. The night, the lights, all work for me. Anthony Valentino lets me sit, enjoy a drink and fifty minutes of downtime. I leave a new man."

"I understand the need to put the day behind you," she said. "I stop off at Double-Dip, south of the stadium. I sit at the end of the counter and enjoy two scoops of butter pecan in a waffle cone."

Rhaden looked thoughtful. "My hometown had an old-fashioned ice-cream parlor, owned by the widow Baker. I'd go in, a cocky senior in high school, and ask for samples. She'd pile the flavors in a Styrofoam cup and never charge me a dime."

"Sounds like a nice lady."

He grinned. "She was young when her husband died, in her late twenties, and I'd just turned eighteen."

A hotshot high school jock and an older woman with sexual needs. Revelle knew where the story was headed. "She turned you into a sundae?"

"Topped with pineapple and gummies. I had to tweeze the sprinkles from my chest hair."

"The gummies?"

"Stuck in places best not discussed."

Revelle grinned. Rhaden Dunn had vast sexual experience. She couldn't be jealous of his past. There was humor in his story.

"Tell me more about your childhood," she encouraged, curious about the boy behind the man.

He stretched out his legs, settled fully into his club

chair. "My dad was a mechanic, he ran his own garage. I lived and breathed engines until I discovered girls." He winked at her. "That's when I learned the importance of a big backseat."

Another sip of Courvoisier and he said, "I haven't gotten all the grease from under my nails. In my spare time I restore antique cars."

"Sports cars, vans, station wagons?" she asked, interested in his off hours.

"Muscle cars, sweetheart." There was pride in his voice. "I'm working on two now. My favorite's a 1957 red Thunderbird, the first of the restyles with the hardtop and grille dropped down into the front bumper."

She nodded, took it all in.

"I also have a 1966 GTO Sport Coupe," he told her, "Fontaine blue and kick-ass. Neither car is ready for the road, but when one is, I might offer you a ride."

"I might accept," she said lightly.

"Tell me something about you as a child," he asked. "Something no one else knows. A secret."

She'd had a private hobby. "I bought beanbag birds with my allowance," she said, a little embarrassed about the nerdy collection. "They were educational toys. You'd squeeze the beanbag and it made an authentic bird sound."

Rhaden had difficulty keeping a straight face. She swore he was fighting back a smile. She thought about kicking him in the shin, but decided that wasn't ladylike.

"Laugh if you want," she said on a sigh.

"I'd rather *caw*." He chuckled.

She ignored him. "I still have the snowy owl, toucan, and Canadian goose."

"I thought this was a kid's hobby."

"That doesn't mean I can't enjoy them as an adult."

Amusement creased the corners of his eyes. "Do you have the beanbag birds on display in your home?"

She didn't miss a beat. "The toucan and owl are displayed in large, gold cages in the living room. The goose roosts on the edge of an indoor fountain in the entrance hallway."

No smile now. He'd shifted, grown uncomfortable.

Revelle poked his arm. "Got you."

He threw back his head, laughed deeply. "Anything else I should know about you?" he asked.

"I like beading." She held up her bracelet, a circlet of sterling silver with Swarovski crystals. "I make jewelry in my spare time."

"I'm impressed." He took her hand, twisted the bracelet and admired her work, then laced their fingers together.

His hold was loose but with a hint of possession. He ran his thumb under the circlet, then over her fingers. The calloused brush tightened her nipples, and pleasure slipped inside her panties.

Desire made her vulnerable. A mere stroke of his thumb and she'd gone damp for this man. Heat started low and crept into her cheeks. She dipped her head, unable to look at him.

Her tension eased when he admitted, "My mom signed me up for ballroom dance when I was twelve. I was lanky as a kid, uncoordinated, not great at sports. I wasn't a natural like Kason Rhodes or the Bat Pack. It took years to grow into my body. My mother wanted to help me with movement. She also paid for ballet, but I skipped every class. Too damn girlie."

"Do you waltz, cha-cha, samba?"

"I took honors in two-step. I liked slow dancing."

"Me too," slipped out. The thought of being tucked against Rhaden's body, moving slowly and touching in all the right places, turned her on. Thank goodness there was no music to dance to. Sitting and staring at the man was all she could handle for one night.

She ran one finger around the rim of the balloon snifter, asked, "Were you a good student in school?"

"I got As in kindergarten. You?"

"I loved to learn, but had to really study for good grades."

"My college baseball coach set me up with a tutor my sophomore year," he told her. "A cute little blonde who introduced me to great literature and library sex."

The man had scored with a lot of women.

"How's the Cora Dora campaign going?" she asked.

"I just shot a television commercial," he said. "I'm sitting at a kitchen table with three pies: pecan, cherry, and apple. The close-ups are on the pies, not on me. I make a few hand gestures, shrug, unable to decide which pie to slice. My one line: 'Dessert, a three-course meal,' is delivered as I cut into each one."

"When does the ad air?" She'd tape the commercial and watch it over and over again.

"Next month."

He squeezed her hand. "We're good at speed dating. It's easy with you."

She felt the same way. "Would you have picked me over the other participants?" A gutsy question.

"A toss-up between you and the cougar."

A waiter stopped by their table with a tray of decorative fortune cookies, chocolate-dipped and drizzled with coconut and lemon frosting. Rhaden selected two, and handed her one.

She broke open her cookie. "A feminist quote." She read, "'Some of us are becoming the men we wanted to marry.'"

Rhaden went serious on her. "You're a strong woman, Revelle, self-assured, innovative, driven. Do you ever plan to marry?"

She folded her fortune, set it aside. "A woman makes room for the right man," she said slowly. "I've been wrapped up in establishing myself in a man's world." So busy, in fact, a part of her life felt barren. "Someday I'd like to be both a wife and mother, as well as keep my finger on the pulse of player promotions."

"Multitasking isn't easy," he said.

"It is with partner support."

"My fortune now." He cracked the cookie in half, pulled out the message. "General, but accurate: 'You're about to embark on a journey.'" He covered his yawn with one hand. "Rogues play three series out of town."

Revelle's eyes went wide. She glanced at her watch, realized it was long after midnight. The cocktail lounge was on its third rotation. "Your flight leaves at seven," she said recalling the players' schedule. "It's late—you won't get much sleep."

"It's been time well spent."

She brought the balloon snifter to her lips, took one last sip of cognac. She and Rhaden then stood, and he released her hand. She instantly missed the contact.

"I run a tab," he told her. "No bill to pay until the end of the month." He tipped a twenty, then added another ten. "I take care of the people who take care of me," he told her on their way out.

They rode down in the glass elevator, slowed their steps as they crossed the lobby. The canopied entrance stood vacant except for the valet, who called for both their vehicles. Revelle wished she'd had more time with Rhaden.

The moment turned awkward, and neither made a move. A handshake, a hug, a kiss?

Rhaden tucked his hands into his pants pockets, said, "You never followed up on the photography contest at Collage. Did you find a better judge?"

She'd never leave him out of the loop. "It's not for another two weeks," she said. "The photographs have been taken and once the students frame their pictures, they'll go on display."

"The Rogues return in twelve days," he said. "Set the judging for my day off."

"I will," she promised. Seconds later, she was captured in the headlights of her BMW. The valet waited patiently, holding her car door wide. Still, she stood on the sidewalk, unable to leave. The cool night air made her shiver.

Rhaden immediately slipped off his suit jacket, secured it over her shoulders before she got goose bumps. His warmth and scent seduced her—she felt wrapped in the man.

"Better?" he asked.

She nodded. His jacket gave off a lot of heat.

He flattened his hand on her back, guided her around the hood of the bimmer. He tipped the valet, and the man returned to his station.

She'd lingered too long, Revelle realized. She had given Rhaden fifteen minutes to kiss her, and he'd let them tick by.

"Night," she managed, and hoped only she heard the disappointment in her voice. "I'll see you soon. Your suit coat—"

"I'm not concerned about my jacket." She caught the indecision in his eyes, edged by desire.

Wanting her won. He clutched the lapels just above her breasts and lifted her on tiptoe. If she'd thought his suit coat warm, it had nothing on his body. The man was all heat and strength as he drew her close.

His kiss was one of warmth yet reserve. The tangible tightening of his body left her liquid. She initiated, led him where she wanted to go.

Nipping his lower lip, she increased the intimacy.

She freed one hand from between their bodies and traced his sculpted chest, then trickled her fingers down his side.

He responded with tongue and a firmer grip on the lapels. She'd never felt so taken by a kiss.

Headlights broke them apart as the valet delivered Rhaden's vehicle. In those unaccountable moments, she'd forgotten they were lingering on the street. He loosened his grip on the sport coat, and she slid down his body. The soles of her feet hit cold pavement.

She looked down on her stocking feet. Wiggled her toes. Rhaden Dunn had kissed her shoes off.

Twelve

The Rogues kicked Cub ass in Chicago, and had a three-game streak going. Against Houston, they battled until noses and uniforms were bloodied. A fight emptied the benches against the Astros on a bad call by the third base umpire. Tempers lit, exploded, and fists flew.

Kason and Psycho both got punched as they pulled their teammates off the opposing players. It sucked being cocaptain. Kason was forced to set an example and remain the voice of reason. But when the Rogues won the series justice was served.

Philadelphia had been rough—the Rogues lost another player to injury. Infielder James Lawless had hunkered tight, anticipating the runner at first to steal second.

The Phillies player dove toward the base, and his shoulder slammed into Lawless's shin. The sound of breaking bone and James's fall to his knees silenced the stadium.

Lawless would be in an air cast for eight weeks; then he'd face rehab. With Risk Kincaid out as well, there was a huge hole down the middle. Rookie Rod Brown now played second, and Alex Boxer remained in center. The veterans would need to keep a sharp eye on both men. The team couldn't afford miscalculations or errors.

Thunderstorms and tornado warnings delayed their flight out of Philly, so they'd spent the night. The ballplayers celebrated as a team, and all were restless to return home.

Kason was on a high—the Rogues had won their last nine games. They'd risen to second in the National League East standings. The opportunity to knock the Mets out of first arrived with their next series. They played New York at home that weekend.

Once the plane landed, he collected his Hummer and drove home to check on the dogs. At Dayne's camper, he found Cimarron babysitting Ruckus. He noticed the min-pin had chewed through one leg on the small dining room table. Apparently the wood proved more fascinating than his dozen dog toys.

Kason played with the pups, only to have Dayne crowd his downtime once again. She'd snagged his attention thirty-two times in three hours. He'd kept track. He'd never been turned on by the mere thought of a woman, yet Dayne did it for him.

Outside in the sun, he threw tennis balls to give Cimarron exercise. Ruckus chased after Cim for all of ten feet, then took off after a butterfly.

A half hour passed, and he decided to run by the stadium. He'd hit the batting cages, keep his shoulder loose and his timing tight. Afterward, he'd look in on Dayne. He'd gotten her the job. He had every right to check on her.

"Home," Kason called to Cim, and the big dog trotted to the double-wide, ready to settle in.

Ruckus didn't mind well. The min-pin ran in circles,

a dizzy dog with more yap than sense. Kason again hinged his palms into a gator's mouth and captured the pup, who spun like a top. Ruckus bit his fingers, damn hard for such a small mouth.

So much for obedience school. Dayne had given her evenings to taking Ruckus to a beginner's class. Apparently nothing had soaked into his puppy brain. The only things that could hold his attention were butterflies. He went nuts over lightning bugs.

Once back in the Hummer, Kason headed for James River Stadium. He found Alex Boxer and Rhaden Dunn in the workout room. The men kept to themselves, until Boxer asked Kason to toss the medicine ball with him. Though Kason would have preferred to pump iron, he agreed to a few passes. He was cocaptain now, and needed to put forth effort with the players.

They started with sideways catches. The men faced each other, then twisted right or left, and released the twelve-pound ball. The conditioning provided core balance.

Two passes and Alex turned talkative. "Either of you guys have a history on the new hire in promotions?" he asked between throws. "The brunette with super tits."

Kason went still, was slow in releasing the medicine ball. He didn't like Boxer's description of Dayne nor the rookie's disrespect.

"Dayne Sheridan," from Rhaden. "She's Revelle's new assistant."

"I'd like a piece—ugh!" Alex grunted with Kason's next toss, the twelve pounds aimed hard, square, and nutcracker low.

"Dude, watch my boys." Alex bent over, caught his breath. "What's your fuckin' problem?"

"Show some respect for my neighbor," Kason said. "Don't dick around with Dayne. She doesn't need the distraction."

"Don't call me off her." Alex adjusted himself. "Unless you're going down on her."

Kason stared at Boxer, burned a hole through the man.

Alex finally shrugged. "Fine, I'll ask Revelle out instead."

Kason noticed Rhaden's sudden glare, and wondered whether the first baseman had his sights set on the redhead.

"Your turn to play catch with Alex," Kason said to Rhaden.

Rhaden pushed off the gym mat, two hundred sit-ups behind him. He approached Alex with a dangerous glint in his eye. The rookie was about to take another hit to his groin.

After batting cages and a shower, Kason took the elevator to the sixth floor of Powers Tower. His excuse to see Dayne centered on the Platinum account. He planned to ask her the date of the shoot.

He found her office door cracked open, heard her phone ring. He decided to let her finish the call before entering.

Dayne sat at her desk, files piled to her eyebrows. Her computer screen was barely visible over the mounds of mail that needed to be read and sorted. The hundreds of envelopes held franchise, major corporation, and private company requests for Rogue promotions.

She and Revelle would evaluate each petition, then decide which opportunity best suited each ballplayer.

She smiled to herself over the many appeals. She wondered which man might consider a campaign for sundried prunes or who would apply male makeup.

At present, catcher Chase Tallan was considering an endorsement for an all-utility work boot. And shortstop Zen Driscoll had been approached to be the spokesperson for a global financial firm. Driscoll was the Einstein of stocks, bonds, and securities. Many Rogues turned to Zen for investment advice.

Queen's "We Are the Champions" sounded, her new cells ring tone. She hit the button for speakerphone, answered, "Dayne Sheridan, player promotions."

"Hey, babe." Mick Jakes's voice spooked her.

She pressed a hand to her diaphragm, forced herself to breathe. "How did you find me?" she managed.

"Violet Flannery from Rogues personnel called WBT, checking your references." His tone was cocky. "The station manager informed me of your relocation."

No one could keep a secret, especially Willow Clarke, Mick's boss and lover. Dayne had asked Violet to make the inquiry as discreet as possible. No doubt Willow had run straight to Mick with the news that Dayne now resided in Richmond.

She swiveled her chair right, ready to disconnect. "I'm hanging up," she warned.

"Two minutes," he pleaded. "You still there?"

"Not for long."

"I've proposed to Willow." His words were rushed. "She wants me involved in the wedding. We need the name of your planner."

Mick was getting married. Dayne waited for the pain to slam her into tomorrow, but she felt little more than disgust for the man. During their engagement, Mick hadn't cared whether they got married in a church or a community center. That was before he dumped her on air.

"Walk your fingers through the Yellow Pages," she said, her best offer of advice.

She heard his sigh of frustration. "Willow won't get off my back until I get the name."

"Your problem, Mick, not mine."

"What can I do to change your mind?"

"Never call me again."

Short pause. "End of the road, Dayne. I promise. A name and I'm gone."

"Vivian Bates at Walk Down the Aisle." The white lie rolled off her tongue. Payback tasted incredibly sweet.

Vivian had been the first planner Dayne hired, then turned around and fired in the same week. Viv was loud and pushy and tried to talk over Dayne. The planner had designed the wedding of her own dreams, and disregarded Dayne's ideas and suggestions.

Let Willow Clarke face off with Vivian. "Don't mention my name," she said to Mick. "Viv wasn't happy I called off the wedding. She only received half her commission."

Mick's voice had a slight hitch when he next asked, "I'm curious, babe—where would we have gotten married?"

At the church at Creighton Bend. A small, historic redbrick church with a mosaic sanctuary in downtown Baltimore. She'd planned a late-afternoon wedding, when the sun patterned the tiles, and the church felt warm and blessed.

Instead she said, "At Livingston Park, down by the lake."

Mick coughed. "The lake's overrun with black ducks. There's poop along the banks."

"We'd have watched where we stepped or perhaps worn rubber boots."

"Rubbers with a tux?" His tone was incredulous. "The quacking would have drowned out the ceremony."

"An outdoor wedding in the crisp autumn air would have been perfect," she persisted. "I found gold tuxedo shirts to match the cummerbunds and the changing leaves."

"Gold, huh?" No excitement there. "Not my color."

Of which she was aware. Mick was the only man she knew to have his colors done. He favored blues and greens. Gold made him look ten years older, drawn out and tired. The way she imagined him now.

Silence, before he braved, "What about the reception?"

She'd reserved a banquet room at the Baltimore Harbor Hotel. She'd scrimped and saved for six months, and when she'd canceled, hadn't gotten her deposit back.

"The Fairmont Community Center basement." She could lie with the best of them.

"The Center smells like old-folks bingo."

"Fairmont rented by the hour."

"Bar?" He sounded like he could use a drink.

A champagne fountain would have flowed at their reception. "No liquor on county-maintained property."

"Damn." Long pause. "Music?"

Harpist and string quartet. Classy and romantic. "Poco Loco." She forced back a smile.

"The mariachi band that performs on the street corner before J. Pepe's?" The man was stunned.

"Very nice guys and they came cheap."

"Cake?" His tone hinted at fear of her answer.

A traditional white cake with white frosting, decorated with fresh pink roses. "Chocolate raspberry."

"I'm allergic to raspberries."

"I know."

"Bitch."

"Plan your own wedding, Mick."

She disconnected their call. Mick Jakes was a jackass. He'd broken her heart and she'd healed, moved on. No man would ever wrap her around his finger again.

She gently rubbed the *Tomorrow* tattoo at her wrist. *Breathe in; breathe out; move on.*

Dayne swiveled her chair, found Kason Rhodes leaning negligently against the doorjamb. She almost jumped out of her skin; she was so startled, she bumped her elbow on the desk. Her funny bone laughed loudly. She massaged the pain that shot to her shoulder.

How long had he been standing in the doorway? How much of her conversation had he heard? Laid-back, his arms crossed his chest, he lounged with one leg bent at the knee. His expression gave nothing away. His casualness could be deceiving. She hoped he'd just arrived.

"Congratulations on your winning streak," she said, initiating.

"Thanks." Nothing more.

"Did you stop by the trailer to see the dogs?" She was making small talk, and they both knew it.

He looked down at his hands. "Your boy's a biter."

She cut her glance to the framed Polaroid of Cimarron and Ruckus she kept on the corner of her desk. Cim had lain down for the photo, patient as Dayne posed him. Ruckus had seen the big dog's ears as chew toys.

Cimarron cooperated for three photos before he'd stood and nudged Ruckus aside with his nose.

"Ruckus didn't fair well at obedience school." Heat crept into her cheeks over her inability to control the min-pin. "He was very social with the other puppies, but wouldn't follow a single command. He flunked sit-come-stay. The trainer found him immature. He thought Ruckus might take the training more seriously at twelve weeks."

"Maybe Ruckus should take lessons from Cimarron."

"Good idea." Kason's suggestion had merit. The miniature pinscher adored the older Dobie. He'd already picked up many of Cim's good habits. Unfortunately he'd developed equally as many bad ones on his own.

An uneasy silence filled the office. "Can I help you with something?" Kason lived his life with purpose. There would be a solid reason behind his visit.

"Has the Platinum shoot been scheduled?" he asked.

She turned to her computer, typed in Kason's name and the jewelry account. "It's set for next Wednesday, May seventh. All five segments will be shot on the same day for continuity. Barnaby's East will provide wardrobe for you and the model."

"Why would I need wardrobe?" He pushed off the jamb, approached her. His look was dark, bordering on mutinous.

She knew him too well to feel threatened, and ignored his scowl. She went on to explain, "The series of ads is supposed to occur over several months. Different day, different outfit. You and your love interest meet five times at Platinum. You'll need to change clothes. Barnaby's is high-end."

"Son of a bitch," he said, low in his throat, but the words reached her ears. "Not what I signed up for."

"Then why did you agree to the contract?" she questioned. "Revelle said you were difficult to begin with, but that you eventually came around."

He stood before her desk now, a tower of man, thick chested and totally ripped. The gold standard for fitness.

Revelle chose that moment to make an appearance. Sleek and professional in a pewter skirt suit, she looked from Kason to Dayne, asked, "Problem?"

"We were discussing the Platinum account," Dayne explained.

Revelle remained cool, collected. "You're not backing out, are you? We have an agreement."

Something in Kason's eyes told Dayne that he had sold his soul when he'd signed the contract. He was a public figure at the park, a private man outside the stadium. There was some mystery behind his agreeing to do the promotion. She wondered what had pushed him to sign.

Revelle slipped Dayne a dozen phone messages. "Return these calls for me, please. Schedule lunch meetings or cocktails with the presidents of the companies. Mark the times and dates on my calendar. Appreciate it."

Dayne nodded, and Revelle departed.

She set aside the messages, looked up, and was hit by Kason's stare, so intense, her blood warmed and every cell was electrified. The current made her toes curl.

She licked her lips, asked, "Anything else?"

He raised one brow, narrowed both eyes. "Know a good wedding planner?"

Her heart jarred, and she nearly slid off her swivel chair. Kason had overheard her conversation with Mick Jakes. No doubt the whole damn call. That would teach her to stay off speakerphone.

Heat streaked her cheekbones, and her composure flatlined. She'd planned to tell Kason about Mick and her broken engagement someday—just not today.

"*You* may need a planner after the Platinum shoot." She sidestepped. "The storyline is very romantic. And I was with Revelle when she interviewed the models. The women are all gorgeous. You get to pick your favorite for the ad. Who knows, you may fall madly in love with her."

"Back up, Dayne," he directed. His jaw was set so tight, a muscle twitched. He was seeking an explanation on a topic she couldn't fully address at work. But he was stubborn, and wouldn't leave until satisfied.

She gave him the fastest accounting possible, and hoped he'd let it go. "Baltimore, engaged to a DJ who dumped me on air. Broken heart, moved to Richmond."

He kept his eyes on her, his forehead creased. "Your ex was an ass." He turned then, a man of few words, and walked out.

Relief left her light-headed. She'd given Kason the abbreviated version of her love life, and he'd cursed Mick Jakes. A million radio listeners had thought her a loser. Yet Kason had taken her side. She was grateful.

She'd fill in the blanks that evening, just to clear the air. It wasn't easy confessing to being dumped. She practiced what she planned to say on the limousine ride home.

Twilight lent the day thirty extra minutes. Their dinner ended just as the sun set. Discussion came with candlelight and hot fudge sundaes at her tiny dining room table

"I worked in radio promotions at WBT in Baltimore." She scooped vanilla ice cream, let it melt on her tongue. "I got involved with Mick Jakes—"

"Mick in the Morning?"

"One and the same." She dipped her head, fingered the hem on her Joan Jett T-shirt. "He'd do on-site promos, and I'd be his sidekick. I've been costumed as a pickle, a taco, a newspaper, a coffee mug, a mattress—"

"Lady with a bed on her back?"

She looked up, caught the humor in his eyes. "Not funny, Kason."

"I'm sympathetic."

"I wore a coconut bra and grass hula skirt in the dead of winter as I welcomed customers into Pacific Travel. My nipples got frostbite. Mick drew names for free cruises and I bestowed Hawaiian leis on the winners.

"The travel agent slipped Mick a round-trip plane ticket to Maui. I got to keep the wilted orchids in my hair."

No comment from Kason as he finished off his sundae.

"Mick and I got engaged on New Year's Eve."

"Was he drunk?"

"A little tipsy, maybe."

"You should have waited until he sobered up to accept."

Maybe she should have. "We were going to wait until fall. I hired a wedding planner and put together the perfect ceremony."

"A lake, rubber boots, and duck poop—definitely ideal."

"I lied to Mick."

"I figured as much. A woman in love doesn't dress a man in a gold dress shirt and have him dancing to Poco Loco."

"Loco is a lively street band."

"If you're a Mexican jumping bean."

She scraped the bottom of the ice-cream bowl, licked the spoon. "Mick wanted fame. Willow Clarke, our station manager, traded syndication for sex and now marriage."

"Blonde, big breasts?" he asked.

"She'd named them Thelma and Louise."

"Men get twisted by Ds."

"Even you?" Her words were soft.

"I'm a butt and leg man."

Dayne craned her neck, checked herself out. She wanted to see her backside as Kason viewed her. Vanity shot heat up her spine, scorched her cheeks. Could she feel any more foolish? Her sweatpants bagged, making her butt look enormous.

She settled back to finish her story. "Mick didn't have the guts to break up with me face-to-face. He announced it on air. He froze our joint bank account and changed the locks on the condo. I left Baltimore beaten down. Richmond was a great place to heal my heart."

Kason narrowed his gaze on her. "Are you healed, ready to move on?"

"Soon, very soon."

"What's the holdup?"

"Final closure," she told him. "I need to burn my wedding file to remove Mick from my life forever."

Kason patted his pocket. "I've got Naughty Monkey matches."

Her heart squeezed. "You'd help me?"

"Very selfish motive," he admitted. "We torch the file, then I take you to bed."

His thought drew a warm sexual heat from her.

Her nipples tightened.

Her v-zone tingled.

Backed by a pitch-dark sky, a metal garbage can soon blazed, and the file burned. A rather short burn in comparison to the long months that had gone into planning her life with Mick Jakes.

Kason pulled her back against him, his hands flat on her belly. His fingers tucked beneath the waistband on her sweats, the calloused tips rough against her softer contours.

The heat from the fire warmed her front, his body her back. His strength shored up her vulnerability, and a private, tangible connection grew between them. For the first time in her life, she felt safe and protected.

He held her until the fire died, until her past was a pile of ashes. Afterward, he turned her to him, pulled her close. The feel of his body calmed her on a deep level.

He stroked the tension from her brow, soothed and removed all conflict. Threading his fingers through her hair, he sifted the strands with an unhurried touch. He massaged the back of her neck, the curve of her shoulders, then ran his big hands up and down her arms, as if restoring circulation. The warmth was welcome.

"We lost a great opportunity to roast marshmallows." Her voice was muffled against his chest.

"I'm not hungry for marshmallows."

She let him take her hand and lead her back to her camper. Cimarron and Ruckus slept like the dead. Sidestepping the dogs, they moved quietly into her bedroom.

She lit two candles, then stood before him in the doorway, mere inches away. The scent of heather softened the air, a contrast to the imposing physical presence that was Kason Rhodes. Anticipation touched them both, a sensual stirring. His intense gaze aroused her completely. She went liquid, ached for the man.

"Are you ready for me?" he asked.

The time was now. "Make it good, Rhodes."

"You have no idea. . . ." The words were a low growl from his throat.

Sex thickened the air.

He wanted her.

She needed him.

Within the stillness of the night, they came together, taking their time. Foreplay turned as arousing as a climax.

Teasingly slow, he ran his thumb along her jaw, drawing her closer, so near that the scent of his skin taunted her with musk and masculinity. His touch was timeless as he cupped her head and captured her mouth.

Her arms circled his waist, and her hands smoothed down his spine. She melted into him, turning soft and yielding, wanting the oneness only lovers experience.

His eyes shut with their contact. They kissed for a very long time. His deeper kisses drugged, stole her breath and soul. Her mouth felt bruised, swollen, his.

Still, she wanted more. More of his mouth. More of his hands. More of his body. She grew increasingly restless. Heat pooled deep and low and urgency quickened her pulse. She wanted to sift into his skin.

Kason sensed her need and played to it. He wanted

her totally into him before he laid her bare. The deep score of her nails along his sides signaled her readiness. He lifted her T-shirt, then thumbed down her sweats. Her flip-flops evaporated to bare feet.

Braless, she stood before him in abbreviated tanga bikini briefs, so sheer, she could have been naked. She soon was.

He stared, eyes hot and narrowed, as candlelight tipped her nipples and shadowed her thighs. His breathing came quick and his nostrils flared wide. The man was turned on by the very sight of her.

She wanted to appreciate him as well. Off came his shirt, and she made fast work of his jeans. His boxers caught on the head of his penis. He kicked off his boots, toed off his socks, and stood unself-consciously nude in the flickering light.

His body should have been illegal. He was all chiseled cheekbones and square-cut jaw. His sculpted shoulders and killer abs were supported by strong hips and thick thighs.

His erection was long and hard.

He shamed her porno vibrator.

He was that impressive.

"Protection." He turned his jean pockets inside out. A wallet, quarter and dime, and four latex condoms fell onto his hand.

He ripped one packet open, sheathed himself.

Kason was on her in a heartbeat. He kissed from the curve of her throat to her inner thigh, seduced each hollow and pulse. Her senses became supersensitive, and her entire body sparked.

He took her down to the mattress, eased her onto cool white cotton sheets. He lay on his side; she was flat on her back. His rough hands slid all over her body. Her muscles felt liquid as he palmed her breasts and brought her nipples to button hardness. His fingers trailed to the slit of her navel, then followed the curve of her thighs into the shadows between her legs, lingered there, then coaxed her wet.

He rolled over her, braced on his elbows. She loved the hard, heavy feel of him. He parted her thighs with his knee. She wrapped her legs about his hips.

Slowly, very, very slowly, he entered her. He strained, controlled, until she could fully accept him.

His eyes slitted on his second thrust.

Hers widened with pleasure.

The sensation was indescribable, impossibly intense.

The bed was small and meant for one person. The walls closed around them. He bumped his shoulder, and she jammed her elbow. His knees slipped, and he banged her hip.

Through it all, the friction of their bodies was raw and primitive. They went at it, hot and greedy. Desperate.

His breath came hard and fast against her ear.

Hers broke sharp and jerky at his shoulder.

The muscles in his chest contracted.

Heat licked and seared her senses.

Tension spiraled, and they strained to reach completion. The air seemed to crackle as helpless spasms claimed them. They climaxed together.

Kason groaned, deep and guttural.

Dayne's own release came on a soul-shattering sigh. She flew loose and free, and a sense of destiny settled bone deep.

A slow meltdown followed.

They lay sated, skin brushing naked skin, fingers twined and thighs wedged, their bodies now slick with perspiration and sex. Even in his relaxed state, Kason looked powerfully male, all ripped and semierect.

She kissed his chest close to his heart and felt it pound under her lips, steady and strong. Vital.

His expession softened, and to her surprise, a smile touched his mouth, small yet significant.

His first smile for her, slow, sexy, and ready to seduce her a second time.

Suddenly, nothing was the same anymore.

Thirteen

Two weeks later, Dayne Sheridan and Revelle Sullivan walked into the Platinum shoot at nine sharp. Kason Rhodes strolled in at 9:20. His expression held everyone at bay. The Rogues had faired poorly on the road against St. Louis and Milwaukee, and his scowl would not photograph well. This was the first time Dayne had seen him since their night together. An image of him naked, hard, and inside her demanded a repeat performance.

Kason had yet to look her way. She hoped for the sake of the campaign, one of the models would lighten his mood, put a smile on his face.

Gayle de Milo approached them, a statuesque sixty with gray hair and eyes, and a warmth that could melt the hardest heart. She embraced everyone, including Kason, with sincerity and heartfelt words. Kason showed no emotion at all.

Dayne watched him as he took in Platinum. The jewelry store was exquisite. Wallpaper in silver and gold paisley foil defined elegance. The dove gray carpet was so thick that her feet sank an inch deep into the pile. In the shape of a giant star, the jeweler's showcase angled to five points. Set with pale amber glass, each arm displayed unique pieces from de Milo's new cosmopolitan line.

Kason took over one corner of the room. He leaned against the wall, viewing all that went on. The camera crew set up and checked the lighting. Albie from Barnaby's East came at Kason with a tape measure, only to back away and do a mental measurement.

"Definitely not preppie." The haberdasher with the spiked hair and thin eyebrows tapped his toe, debating out loud. "He's more rugged adventurer with a criminal edge. Does anyone have a razor?"

"Kason doesn't need to shave." Dayne heard Gayle de Milo veto the idea. "I want him edgy."

Albie tsk-tsked. "You need a male model that draws people into Platinum, not a jock who scares business away."

"He'll loosen up," Gayle insisted.

"I'll take that bet," Albie shot over his shoulder as he returned to the long racks of wardrobe.

Dayne hung back as Revelle next introduced the three models to Kason. Courtney, Bay, and Becca were all blonde and blue-eyed, a pleasing contrast to his dark looks.

A twinge of jealousy forced Dayne to look away. The women were all over Kason, chatting him up one side and stroking him down the other. Each vied to be his love interest in the national campaign.

Gayle de Milo wanted sexual chemistry in the shoot. She suggested a test run with the models. One by one, each would stand by the jewelry counter, pretending to look at earrings. Kason would then walk through the door, his purpose to buy a pair for Mother's Day. He'd check out the store, his gaze slowly settling on the beautiful customer.

The two male actors brought in as extras would be staged at opposite ends of the jewelry case in muted light, casual and browsing. The extras would keep their heads down, and not look up for the camera. Gayle wanted viewer concentration on Kason, the female model, and their love connection.

Dayne noticed Kason's face tighten at the jeweler's words. He shifted his stance, stood taller, and the models all stepped back. The women were wary of him.

Gayle clapped her hands, directed, "Let's make the model selection, then work with wardrobe."

Courtney took her place at the circular center of the star showcase, where the earrings were displayed. Dayne thought her slender and striking with her shiny shoulder-length hair.

"Work *the* look," Gayle called from off camera. "Check each other out—get hot."

Kason walked from the door to the counter. His gaze swept the two customers, then hit on Courtney. The model went coy, dipping her head and lowering her lashes. Kason did no more than stare at her, totally indifferent.

"Not a spark," Gayle whispered to Revelle and Dayne. "Next," she called out.

Bay moved in, wafer thin, all poise and perfection. The tallest of the three, she added another four inches to her height with stilettos. She stood eye level with Kason when he crossed to her.

The model's eyes dilated and her nostrils flared, she was turned on, but Kason didn't warm to her. Bay put a lot of effort into arousing him. She ran her hand up his arm, stroked his jaw, massaged the back of his neck.

Dayne could almost see Kason's blood run cold.

"Maybe Becca can get a rise." Gayle kept her voice low as she motioned the third model forward.

Becca was so beautiful, no man could resist her. Her fragility offset Kason's immense strength. They made a good-looking couple, so complementary, Dayne could barely breathe.

Dayne did her best to separate business from the pleasure she'd known with Kason. It was darn hard to see him with another woman when images of them horizontal on a mattress crowded out thoughts of the campaign.

She fought her feelings, took the high road. She wanted only the best for the Platinum commercial. She hoped Becca would engage his full attention. They were out of models.

Off to the side, the camera crew and wardrobe advisor grew antsy. Gayle de Milo wanted the segments wrapped by six sharp. There'd be no break for lunch. It was going to be a very long day.

Gayle turned to Revelle, and said loud enough that Dayne could also hear, "No heat with Becca. The man's healthy, red-blooded, and not gay. I want him to strip a woman with his eyes."

"Maybe you have the wrong man," Revelle softly suggested.

"Kason's perfect," Gayle asserted. "He's tough, unapproachable, but with the right woman, he'll soften. That's the side of him I want for my ad."

Dayne edged back, dropped out of their conversation. Kason now stood alone behind the circular counter, looking badass and ornery in the dim light. The models clustered by wardrobe, all chatting with Albie and checking out the clothes.

Dayne took a deep, steadying breath and approached him. "You're not a jewelry kind of guy," she said. "How can I make the shoot easier for you?"

"I could take you on the counter."

Color heated her cheeks. "No sex tapes."

He half smiled, shook his head. "This whole campaign makes me uneasy. I'd never walk into Platinum on my own. The last Mother's Day gift I gave was a pop-top necklace in the third grade." He cut his glance toward the models. "Breathing mannequins—too thin, too plastic, not my type."

Her lips twitched. "You prefer a woman who claims squatter's rights and confiscates your trailer. Then hauls a camper onto your land."

"I like your tin can." His confession was deep and intimate, his gaze hot with memory. "I'm a big fan of tight places and single mattresses."

His words were a physical caress.

Her entire body blushed.

Kason edged closer, crowded her. She swore he sniffed her hair. "Fourteen days, and I can still feel you, Dayne—soft, morning-warm, and open to me."

A man of few words, Kason said it all. Her body burned even hotter. His scent drove her crazy: raw, sexual, with an interplay of sunshine and deep woods.

Hidden behind the counter, his denim knee pressed between the pleats on her navy skirt. His Wranglers rode rough against her smooth thighs. Her nipples puckered and her panties grew damp. She was ten seconds to panting.

She'd sell her soul for a private moment with this man. She wanted to tuck into his neck, nip his whiskered chin, kiss the underside of his jaw, then work her way down his body, slowly, lazily arousing him with her mouth, in the same manner he'd pleasured her.

Kason's thoughts joined with hers. His look was hungry, knowing, and utterly sinful. The lines of his mouth had relaxed, and his breath felt hot against her brow. Discreetly, he took her hand and rubbed his calloused thumb across the pulse at her wrist. Her heart raced for him.

Her sigh was almost a moan. If they weren't at Platinum—

"That's the look!" Gayle de Milo's shout and applause drew everyone's attention to the center of the star. "Kason and your assistant," she said to Revelle. "That's the match."

Dayne's nerves were hot-wired, and she stepped back so fast she knocked into the jewelry case.

Kason grabbed her arm, steadied her.

"Hmm, might work." Revelle studied them both. "He stripped her with his eyes."

Dayne raised her hands, desperately tried to explain away the heat of their moment. "You're wrong; you've misread the situation. We were just talking—"

"Some conversation," said Gayle, her smile now wide. "Trust me, honey—you were naked."

Dayne couldn't breathe, couldn't swallow, couldn't meet anyone's eye. Kason rubbed his palm low on her spine, a reassuring gesture that didn't fully calm her.

She didn't want to be in the spotlight. Yet Gayle had targeted her for the shoot. She wished the idea away.

"We have *the look*." Gayle was elated. "Let's get them

in wardrobe and shoot the first promo, see how it shakes out."

Gayle went on to dismiss the models, then motioned to Albie. "Wardrobe, please. I want the first outfits to be casual—we'll build to the wedding gown."

Dayne's knees gave out. Had Kason not had her back, she'd have hit the floor. "Wedding gown?" She'd been out of the room when they'd inserted that segment.

"The exchange of vows is crucial," Gayle told her. "We'll work through Mother's Day, additional gifts, then showcase my infinity wedding bands in the final segment."

Gayle clapped her hands. "On task—let's go."

Dayne couldn't move. Her knees had locked and her feet felt like cement blocks. She looked to Kason for support, only to find him looking inordinately pleased. The corners of his mouth curved into a semblance of a grin.

He looked freakin' happy.

She raised a brow. "You're enjoying this?"

"Damn straight," he admitted. "Misery loves company. You'll see what it's like living in the spotlight, and value your privacy ten times over."

"Breathe in; breathe out; move on," Dayne chanted, but the air seemed stuck in her lungs, and she found it difficult to exhale.

Albie was on them in a heartbeat, clothes on hangers in hand. "Solid colors work best." He draped a mauve blouse over Dayne's shoulder, pressed a pair of gray tailored slacks to her waist. "Perfect. Low-heeled pumps and we're good to go. No jewelry in the first shoot."

"For the bruiser—" He looked at Kason. "Gayle wants you dark and untouchable." He pursed his lips, said, "We go all black with mirrored aviators. That's how

Dayne's image will first be captured, as a reflection in your lenses."

Once everyone was outfitted, the extras took their places at the star points, and Dayne was positioned in the middle. Someone had laid out a selection of earrings on a square, gray velvet cushion, from diamond studs to tiered chandeliers. She stood in profile, her hair loose and styled to shadow her face.

"Relax," Gayle called to her. "Keep your eyes on the jewelry until Kason approaches. Then it's all about first looks and immediate attraction."

The jeweler paused, her mind working. "During the thirty-second ad, you're going to help him select the perfect Mother's Day gift. At twenty-five seconds, the camera will close in on the double-hoop drop pearl earrings inlaid with tiny diamond hearts. There's no dialogue, so we'll run a full description in the final narration."

"Shouldn't we rehearse at least once?" Dayne was a bundle of nerves.

Gayle shook her head. "The more natural, the better."

The store grew quiet, the spotlights warm. Angled away from the door, Dayne couldn't see Kason's entrance, yet she could feel him. His presence filled the room, larger than life. In a tick of seconds, he was beside her.

He flattened his hands on the showcase, peered down. That's when Dayne chanced a glance. He sensed her stare, and turned slightly. She caught her reflection in his mirrored shades, and didn't recognize herself. Her eyes were wide and her lips parted. The shift in her breathing couldn't be faked—Kason had that effect on her. She'd gone visibly soft for the man.

He removed his aviators and hit her with a smoldering once-over, his dark brown eyes unholy. He looked ready to lift her onto the showcase and slide home. She hoped her blush wouldn't clash with her mauve blouse.

The seconds swept by as they brushed wrists, touched fingers, and both admired the same pair of earrings. Kason laid the gold double hoops on his wide palm. The contrast of pearls and diamonds against his work-hardened calluses made the earrings appear twice as delicate. The camera zoomed in, and the jewelry stole the show.

Gayle de Milo applauded them. "Absolutely perfect," she praised. "The gold hoops set the stage for the next spot. The narration will indicate that Kason bought a pair for both his mother and the mystery lady who's captured his interest. Dayne will wear those earrings in the next four spots."

Under Gayle's direction, the campaign flowed smoothly. Albie updated their wardrobe as Kason and Dayne next returned to Platinum to celebrate their one-week anniversary. Kason rolled his eyes, scowled, but Dayne claimed the occasion sweet.

It was here that he presented her with a long strand of turquoise and green tourmaline. Simple and elegant, the beautiful necklace seemed to glow on the pale skin of her cleavage.

Shoot three brought the two of them into the jewelers for a one-month gift. A sterling heart bracelet announced they were a couple. Dayne liked the idea of belonging to him.

In the fourth segment, Albie forced Kason into a sport coat. Kason's muscles went taut, his expression pained. The seams stretched, and the front hung open. The buttons wouldn't close over his chest. Kason was a big man.

Dayne slipped into a pencil skirt with a cream blouse and military-style jacket. With her hair twisted into a French braid, her face was fully exposed. A hint of color sharpened her cheekbones. She looked elegant, different, in this sophisticated attire.

The brooch Kason attached to her lapel made her sigh. The oval amethyst in an antique setting had a timeless beauty. A woman would hand down the piece to her daughter. The brooch would stay in the family for generations to come.

The day came to a close with only one spot left to shoot. The wedding scene.

Decorations—white tissue paper bells and two silver foil gift boxes—were spread across the jewelry counter, along with an imitation wedding cake. The moment was surreal. In this single day she'd gone from being Kason's neighbor to his bride.

But a promotional campaign didn't constitute a relationship. She needed to slow her heart, reset reality.

Albie hovered like the mother of the bride as he fitted her gown. The column of ivory satin seduced with its simple elegance. The focus would be on the exchange of wedding bands, not on her imaginary walk down the aisle.

Albie led her to Kason, and Dayne took in his latest look. Kason was not a man born for a tux, but in this case, no one could fault the formal fit. The dark stubble at his jaw contrasted with the cream of his dress shirt. There was an insolence to the man that said he'd never conform, that he'd always live by his own rules. Yet he'd meet the right woman halfway as they walked down the aisle.

Kason stared at Dayne as if seeing her for the first

time. Gayle de Milo gave them precious minutes to adjust to the formality of the moment. Crystal flutes sparkled with champagne. The couple would make a toast in the final seconds, followed by a camera close-up on their rings.

It was twenty minutes to six; time was short, and there could be no mistakes in the final segment.

Gayle made a few suggestions. "Fall hard, fall fast. Let your emotions show. Don't hold back."

The roll of the camera set them in motion. In those initial seconds, Kason focused only on Dayne. He skimmed his knuckles down her cheek, then gently cupped her jaw. Time ceased to exist as he slanted his mouth over hers.

He kissed her as a groom would his bride. Drawn into his body, she clutched his forearms, and her nails scored his tux sleeves. They stood so close, she could feel the beat of his heart in her own breast.

He slowly lifted his head and they looked into each other's eyes. Kason could act; he appeared a man humbled by his woman's love.

Emotion broke in her chest and sentiment left her vulnerable. Tears glistened in her eyes. She'd fallen fast for Kason Rhodes, and was heart-deep in love with the man.

Rainbow sparks from the diamond band shot across the showcase as he slipped the ring on the fourth finger of her left hand. The gold was weighted with the promise of forever.

Her hands shook so bad, she couldn't fit the wide gold band, inset with diamond chips, onto his finger. Kason covered her hand, steadied her. Together, they slid the ring over his knuckles.

They raised their crystal flutes in a toast, and the cameraman locked on their wedding rings. "Wrap," he called to the room, which had been bound in silence.

"Incendiary." Gayle released her breath. "You really worked it. I felt you growing as a couple. That last spot could win an Oscar. I'm one happy jeweler."

Gayle requested their bands, wanting to return them to the office safe. Physical pain gripped Dayne in the absence of the ring. She felt exposed and unsettled as the campaign came to a close.

Albie was quick to help her out of the wedding dress. Her casual clothes brought her down to earth. Today she'd played a woman in love. What scared her most was that she hadn't been acting. She cherished Kason Rhodes.

Back in the showroom, she met with Revelle. "You did a great job," her boss praised. "Gayle plans to pay you for your time. A check will be delivered to the stadium in the morning."

Player promotions. Tomorrow she'd face a deskload of work. Tonight she'd drift on the day's memories. Thoughts of Kason warmed her heart, made her mellow. She couldn't allow her feelings for him to shape her future. He was a man who guarded his privacy, was distant and alone.

She was more into him than he was into her.

"Want to honeymoon?" Kason came up behind her, his voice low and suggestive.

She couldn't help herself. "Your trailer or mine?"

"Let's go double-wide."

Big man, bigger bed, biggest night of her life ahead.

Fourteen

Rhaden Dunn parked in the back lot behind the historic schoolhouse. He turned off the truck's engine and cracked his window. The sky stretched clear and blue, hinting at a hot summer ahead. The sun played across his face, making him sleepy. He'd slept little in the past two weeks. All because he'd kissed Revelle Sullivan.

Memories of her amazing mouth kept him up at night. She'd given him more than a good-night tease on the sidewalk outside the Maximillian Hotel. She'd initiated, tasted, and sucked on his tongue. He still wanted her so much that he suffered blue balls.

Revelle was the type of woman who made a man's hands sweat, his pulse pound. A stray impulse would have him tattooing her name over his heart.

He'd held off sending her flowers this week, on the off chance she'd miss the delivery. He loved spoiling her, but he also needed her to think of him without the reminder of a vase of roses.

Today they'd judge a sixth-grade photography exhibit together. Then he planned to kidnap her and take her off-roading. They'd drive to Hiker Hills and explore bumpy back trails, deep valleys, river crossings, and, if he got lucky, each other.

Catching sight of the Rogues stretch limo made his

heart thump. Revelle as she exited was worth the wait. Her skirt hitched at midthigh, and Rhaden had a nice long look at her legs.

He hopped out of his Ford pickup, crossed to her. Her soft pink skirt suit was less severe than her usual black. A spritz of Chanel scented her throat. Her lavender eyes were soft and her smile tentative. His gaze lit on her mouth and she self-consciously licked her lips. They both remembered their kiss. The memory clearly made her apprehensive.

He quelled her nerves. Tipping up her chin, he kissed her. The kiss was as playful as it was intimate, and one that was difficult to break.

The limo driver raised his brow and a man skirting them on the sidewalk winked at Rhaden. One of those male bonding winks that complimented Rhaden on his taste in women and stated he was one lucky bastard.

He didn't feel all that fortunate. Revelle wasn't officially his. Rhaden had never analyzed his time with any woman. Women came; women went. He never second-guessed himself.

Revelle, however, was special. He damn sure hoped he wasn't reading more into their situation than was warranted.

"Ready to judge the photography?" she asked.

"I've looked forward to the sixth-grade exhibit." His anticipation had run high at seeing her again.

"Me too." He thought her enthusiasm matched his.

She took his arm, and they moved as one into the schoolhouse. He liked the way she felt at his side.

Some women brushed against him, crowded his space. With Revelle, he wanted her close. Their hips pressed and her full skirt flirted with his thigh. The pale pink fabric snuck around his leg, teasing and inviting.

Men were visual animals, and sex entered their minds every six seconds. He'd like a second look at her lacy thigh-high stockings should the opportunity arise. Long, shapely legs did it for him.

Curator Anne Malone met them just inside the door. Garbed in period clothing, she wore a matching expression, schoolmarmish and severe. She nodded to Revelle, but spoke directly to Rhaden. "Nice to see you again, Mr. Dunn. Ms. Sullivan must feel confident in your judging skills. No other Rogue has had the honor of a return visit."

Revelle blushed, and Rhaden enjoyed the color in her cheeks. Good old Annie had let the cat out of the bag. He now knew that more than his assessment of the art-work had prompted Revelle's invitation. Their kiss had sealed round two.

Anne nodded toward the photography. "Some photos are risqué," she informed them with a frown. "I'm of an older generation, but I'd swear these kids' hormones have already kicked in. Sonya Garrett's sixth graders have sex on the brain."

Rhaden was certain she was right. Statistics showed increased pregnancies in the projects. Babies were born to babies, and girls as young as twelve were now moth-ers. Beset by violence, low incomes, cramped housing, and single parenthood, families barely held together.

Cops were posted on the elementary campus to keep the peace. Eight-year-olds had been busted for guns. Ten-year-olds arrested for selling drugs.

"Sonya petitioned for the exhibit," Revelle told the

curator. "Collage donated the disposable cameras. While the photographs may not seem age-appropriate to you, kids grow up fast these days. What I knew at sixteen, most children learn by seven. I have a thirteen-year-old nephew whose Christmas list included condoms and a subscription to *Playboy*."

The curator sighed. "I do feel old and out of touch. Are the sixth graders too big for juice boxes and sugar cookies? Do we even offer snacks?"

Revelle tapped a finger on her chin. "Sonya's class is huge, close to forty students. Let's go with popcorn in plastic bowls and canned soda."

"I'll start popping," said Anne as she headed to the storeroom that shelved supplies, a small refrigerator, and a microwave.

Rhaden wandered over to the wall with the framed black-and-white photographs. The pictures were a lesson in contrasts. A succession of shots caught his attention and he soon shook his head, amazed by the audacity of twelve-year-old photographer Samson Banks at a local mall.

Sam-boy had crouched off to the side at the bottom of an escalator near a massive potted plant. Ficus leaves edged the photographs and neon signs from the food court lit up the background.

Hunkered low, Samson had captured customers as they'd ridden down. He'd snapped six quick shots, then set up his framed prints so the viewer could feel the descent of the escalator.

It was an intriguing concept, if a person could get around the subject matter. Looking up, Samson had gotten *under* those he filmed. He'd captured three teenage girls in miniskirts, as well as a flash of their panties.

Samson had snapped a man adjusting himself. And a grandma with one side of her dress tucked into her pantyhose. Last, came a snapshot of a middle-aged woman with her hand down the front of her blouse, scratching her breast.

The kid had guts to shoot those photos, Rhaden thought. Where was mall security when Samson was sneaking off shots?

He closed in on Revelle, who was studying a photograph of a window display at Satin Dreams, a sexy lingerie store. A jeweled bustier, a collection of lacy thongs, and thigh-high nylons with decorative back seams stimulated wet dreams. The two female mannequins were both naked and extremely well endowed.

Whether posed or accidentally positioned, one of the mannequin's hands cupped the other's mound. The photo was startling, even disgusting, yet it made Rhaden smile. Men would find humor in the shot. Revelle, on the other hand, wasn't quite certain what to make of the picture.

"Sixth-grade boys are sexually inquisitive," he told her. "Guys giggle like girls over nudity, even if it's storefront mannequins."

Her brow creased. "They must have laughed themselves silly. The second-grade exhibit was much easier to judge. Although this photography is expressive, I much prefer crayons and charcoal."

"How about *H Street*?" Rhaden pointed to a photograph of a street corner backed by brick walls and plastered with graffiti. A trash can had been overturned near the stoplight, garbage everywhere. The camera captured two women at twilight, eyeing the traffic. Prostitutes, Rhaden figured, given their skimpy outfits, dangling cigarettes, and defeated expressions.

They reviewed all forty photographs, most of which dealt with the students' community. Rhaden caught the slump in Revelle's shoulders as she took on the weight of Highland Heights. The photos revealed the harsh reality of the children's lives. Revelle was deeply touched and sympathetic. She felt their struggle.

Seconds before the school bus arrived, they came to a decision. First prize would go to *The Playground*, a photograph that featured the class at recess. The girls were clustered by a broken swing set, the boys by a bent and twisted chain-link fence. All postured, trying to act cool, yet in that single moment, their eyes betrayed the bitterness of life and their inner need for acceptance.

The sixth graders soon arrived, all loud and undisciplined. There was horseplay, some profanity, and total disrespect. Each student held a disposable camera. They took pictures of one another, the flashes blindingly bright. Then they staggered around like zombies, bumping into the desks and bouncing off the walls.

Sonya Garrett blew a whistle, so loud and sharp, she couldn't be ignored. The kids gave her five minutes.

Rhaden studied the boys, a diversified group—black, white, and Hispanic. Dressed for their one and only outing that year, they all wore the same blue T-shirts with the school logo; the guys had cut off the sleeves. Baggy jeans flashed boxers and one young plumber's crack.

The girls shirts were red. Cut off at the waist, the cotton T's became belly shirts. Most wore tight jeans, a few denim miniskirts. The visible elastic on their thongs was as much a statement of who they were as their heavily made-up faces.

Several girls showed off birth-control patches on the high curve of their hips. A sixth-grade status symbol.

There was belching and farting.

Someone in the crowd needed a shower, bad.

They're twelve, Rhaden forced himself to remember. These kids weren't yet teenagers, yet life had aged them fast. They were street-corner tough.

"The field trip from hell," Sonya Garrett said under her breath when Revelle introduced her to Rhaden. "Samson Banks tried to escape through the emergency exit of the bus and set off the alarm. A police car pulled us over. My students hung out the windows and called them pigs."

Rhaden easily picked Samson out of the group. He was the leader of the pack. Gangly with slicked-back hair, he had a piercing stare and a fuck-you curl to his lip. He had the badass attitude that made it easy to lead kids astray.

After a second blow on her whistle, Sonya introduced the students to Rhaden and Revelle. The boys showed momentary interest in him as a ballplayer before their gazes locked on Revelle. The guys found her hot; the girls felt jealous.

"Let's give out the awards," the teacher requested. "The sooner we return to school, the better."

The kid Rhaden now knew as Samson was shifty. Camera in hand, the boy cut behind Revelle and attempted a snapshot of her butt as she bent over the teacher's desk to retrieve the first-place ribbon.

Rhaden was quick. He covered the camera lens with his hand, and Samson's click captured Rhaden's palm.

"Busted," he said to the sixth grader.

Samson cocked his head, showed no remorse. For a twelve-year-old, the kid had balls. He whipped up his camera and shot Rhaden dead in the eyes. The flash exploded, and Rhaden saw stars. He blinked until his eyes watered. When his vision cleared, he found Samson chatting up Revelle.

He's a sixth grader, Rhaden repeated to himself. Twelve going on twenty. Rhaden had been hot for older chicks at that age too. Revelle was sophisticated, sexy, and would inspire adolescent erections. Adult ones too, judging by his constant state of arousal.

He caught her eye and she smiled at him. A crook of her finger and he crossed to her. "You can announce the winner." She handed him the ribbon.

Rhaden led with, "All the photographs were great. The blue ribbon goes to Herita Suarez for *The Playground.*"

"Stupid-ass picture," said Samson, which prompted the other boys to boo as well.

Herita flipped Samson the bird and claimed her ribbon.

"Everyone else gets an honorable mention." Revelle went on to pass out the red ribbons. Most ribbons ended up on the floor. Only a handful found pockets.

Revelle was a saint, Rhaden decided. She didn't criticize or demand manners from the kids. Instead, she said, "How about popcorn and a soda?"

Sonya Garrett blocked the stampede to the table where the curator had laid out the snacks. "No," she stated with the authority of a drill sergeant. "You lost your snack privileges last Friday when you trashed the classroom with cake and ice cream brought in for Herita's birthday. We leave Collage the way we came: no food fight, no messes."

Samson called Miss Garrett a very bad name. The other kids smirked their agreement.

"Back to the bus," the teacher ordered.

More pushing, shoving, and jostling ensued as they all tried to fit through the door at once. Only Samson Banks remained. He circled toward the snack table, scooped a handful of popcorn, stuffed his mouth. He then inched along the chalkboard, swiped something off the lip, and pocketed it.

Rhaden wasn't the kid's teacher and held no authority over him, yet he called the boy out. "Samson?"

The sixth grader had one foot out the door. "What'd I do?" Popcorn sprayed and his defenses went up.

"You tell me." Rhaden cut his gaze to the chalkboard.

Samson gave him a fuck-you glare. "Christ, the chalk?"

Rhaden nodded. "Put it back."

The boy jammed one hand in his baggy jeans pocket, produced the short white stick. "It's chalk, asshole—a stupid piece of chalk."

"It's stealing," Rhaden stated. "Chalk today, a car tomorrow."

"My dad and uncle got busted for hot-wiring, then carjacking." Samson didn't seem fazed. "They're both at Arstole State."

A maximum-security prison. Samson's petty theft could lead to felonies, and six years down the road, he would be charged as an adult. He could join his relatives behind bars.

Rhaden pulled out his wallet, removed a business card. "Ever hear of First Base?" he asked.

Samson nodded. "One of my cousins got invited."

Rhaden had founded the facility for at-risk boys. Sports, tutoring, and counseling taught the eight- to fourteen-year-olds to exercise both their minds and bodies. Maybe, just maybe, a few would rise above gangs, drugs, and violence.

Rhaden flipped Samson the card. "You're welcome to join."

"Not interested." Samson blew him off. "First Base is across town from where I live. My mom don't have a car. I ain't walking."

Rhaden pointed to two phone numbers on the card. "Call for a ride. Someone will pick you up."

Samson sniffed before he stuck the card under the elastic band on his boxers. "I'll jam on it." He then passed Rhaden what he'd stolen. "You got a thing for chalk?"

"The chalk belongs to Collage, and Ms. Sullivan takes pride in the schoolhouse," Rhaden told him.

Samson was quick. "You got the burn for her?"

"She's a friend" was all Rhaden gave up.

The kid smirked. "Yeah, right, and I don't smoke pot."

"The bus, Samson." His teacher pointed to the door. "Keep your window up on the ride back to school and no spitting on passing cars."

"Or what, detention?" Samson snorted.

"Out-of-school suspension," Sonya Garrett threatened.

Rhaden caught the look in Samson's eyes—the boy liked the second option. He could hang out with no hassles. Mindless shit would get him nowhere.

Rhaden had offered First Base, yet he never pushed a kid to comply. He hoped Samson would smarten up, that he'd call the club, get a bead on life outside the projects.

"A wild group today," Revelle commented as she came to stand beside him. She looked weary.

He ran one hand along the back of his neck. "Few boundaries, little discipline, *Lord of the Flies* chaos."

She smiled her agreement.

"Popcorn, anyone?" Anne Malone called from the snack table.

"Keep some for yourself, and Ziploc the rest," Rhaden suggested on the spur of the moment. "We'd like two sodas to go as well."

Revelle lifted a brow. "Shouldn't you return to the park?"

He shook his head. "I spent time at the stadium this morning. Tomorrow we face Ottawa." His grin curved. "This afternoon, you're mine. I'm not above kidnapping."

She licked her lips. "I'll go willingly."

The curator delivered their snacks and they were off. His hands itched to help Revelle onto the front seat of his jacked-up truck, but she surprised him. One hop, and she pulled herself up and in. Her full skirt flared, flashed the back of her thighs. The lady had damn fine legs.

Revelle Sullivan strapped herself into the cab of the truck. Her heart beat as wildly as the revved-up engine. She'd never played hooky from work. She was a driven woman, professional and successful. Game's On was attached to the Rogues organization. It meant everything to her.

Rhaden Dunn meant more.

She had phone calls to return and a dinner meeting to attend, yet all commitments blurred next to this man. Rumor had him between women. She hoped to slide into his life and find the perfect fit.

She withdrew her BlackBerry from her brown suede

purse and sent a text message to Dayne Sheridan. She requested that her appointments be rescheduled for another day.

Dayne was competent and would hold the office together in her absence. Someday, if all went well, Dayne could become her partner. Revelle had that much faith in her.

Dayne's future was linked to Kason Rhodes; of that, Revelle was certain. The left fielder had stripped Dayne with his eyes at the Platinum shoot. The sexual smolder made a woman feel desired and cherished. And all his.

Revelle hoped Rhaden would soon be turning that look on her. Hiker Hills would certainly give him ample opportunity.

West of Richmond, the hills were a squatty second cousin to the majestic Blue Ridge Mountains. The entire area was a great place to hike, dirt bike, and go off-roading.

The scenery was phenomenal. Spring renewed nature after a rough winter. The back trail angled, wound, and drew them higher up the hill. Revelle cracked her window and let the wind blow over her face and through her hair. She felt free of responsibility. An absolute first for her.

"There's no road!" Her eyes went wide when Rhaden cut the wheel and the truck shot between two spruce trees. The low-hanging branches slapped the windshield, pivoted the outside mirrors. He shifted into four-wheel drive and traction gripped the rough terrain.

The road less traveled cut into the hillside and snaked its way along the slope in a steady climb. The truck bumped, bounced, and jarred her back fillings.

The Ford picked up speed beyond the halfway marker.

There was a moment of clear-cut driving along a grassy knoll before the road continued into the brush.

Several more miles, and Rhaden cut the engine at a creek crossing. The hills formed a valley, green and lush. The sunlight was thick, golden, and cast a sheen on a small pond banked by long gray slabs and enormous boulders.

Their approach sent geese into flight, and the idyllic setting was left to them alone.

Clean air and wide-open spaces. Revelle had the sudden urge to go barefoot, to feel the grass under her feet. She wanted to dip her toes into the pond, perhaps wade up to her knees.

She slipped off her pumps and rolled down her stockings. She curled her toes, felt rooted to the earth.

"This meadow is beautiful," she said to Rhaden.

"So are you." He was staring at her, his expression one of intense interest. He'd kicked off his loafers, rolled up his pant legs, untucked his blue button-down. His masculinity was both casual and sexy.

"Take a walk?" He offered his hand.

She liked the athletic roughness of his palm as they laced fingers. His body heat caressed her side. His scent was as clean as the starch on his shirt collar. His five-o'clock shadow arrived at three.

They strolled along tire tracks from previous visitors. All imprints stopped at the pond. "High school kids come here to skinny dip and make out," he told her. "Mother Nature keeps their secret."

They moved to a boulder, only wide enough for one person. Before she could protest, Rhaden pulled her down on his lap.

He folded his hands beneath her breasts.

She rested her cheek against his chest.

The muscles in his legs tightened, his arousal now evident. She suddenly ached for the man.

She didn't dip her head, nor did she blush.

His desire made her bold. She rolled her hips against him, discovered he was nicely sized.

"You didn't send flowers this week." Her voice was no more than a whisper.

"Did you miss them?" The warmth of his breath teased her throat.

She swallowed. "My desk seemed empty."

She'd hoped for a delivery, had gone as far as to clear a spot on her desk in case an arrangement arrived. Friday came and went, and no roses. She'd worried Rhaden had lost interest.

"It's time you think of me beyond a weekly bouquet."

She turned slightly. "You're on my mind constantly, ever since you were injured against the Pirates."

She caught his surprise. "That was last September."

She touched the bump on his nose. "I caught the game from the owner's box. I watched the runner slide into first, saw you take that batting helmet to the face. My nose hurt as much as yours."

A groove deepened in his cheek as he grinned. "Damn, I never knew."

"You do now," she said on a sigh. "We work together, Rhaden. My uncle frowns on in-house fraternization. I've never dated a ballplayer. People talk. I don't want to go public. I'm honestly not certain—"

He took her mouth and erased all doubt.

Her pulse quickened as she poured seven months of wanting him into her kiss.

She twisted in his lap and her skirt hiked high. A tug on her hem, and she fully straddled him.

His maleness bound her before he'd even touched her.

Secluded within the slabs of granite, she worked his shirt, undoing the buttons, sneaking her hands inside. His chest was solid, all virile strength and strong muscle. His arms were hard sinew.

She undid his belt, unzipped his pants. Her hands shook as she pressed her palms to his bare stomach. When she dipped under his waistband, his dick made her acquaintance.

All the while, Rhaden kissed her, hot and French, deep and drugging. She was out of her head as she took him into her heart.

Her blazer came off, then her thin camisole. He stared openly at her breasts. Her nipples made hard points in the center of each ivory cup. His green eyes darkened a shade.

A competent flick of his thumbnail and the front clasp parted. Her breasts spilled into his palms. He stroked the undersides, paid equal attention to her sensitive nipples. He traced her cleavage, then arrowed to her navel.

His hand snuck under her skirt and he fingered her thong. She barely sensed him lifting her or snatching away the lacy floss.

There were more mind-numbing kisses, more caresses. Her lower body ached, and her core sought him. She wrapped her legs about his waist, made a low sound when he stroked her inner thigh.

They went at it, slick tongues, seeking hands, and spiraling need. His fingers slid between their bodies, rubbed her sex. She grew restless, felt wild.

Condom. The thought struck them both.

"Pocket," he forced out, subtly shifting so she could score the packet.

His erection was long and throbbing and stretched the latex. She moved over him, lowered slowly, and he pulsed inside her like a heartbeat.

His eyes half closed, Rhaden groaned. He rocked, deepened his thrusts, drove her beyond herself.

Her body drew tight, took on a life of its own. Beneath the lazy, late-afternoon sunshine, the unflappable, always collected Revelle Sullivan rode Rhaden Dunn's thighs in breathless pleasure.

A low moan blended with the breeze.

Maybe his. Maybe hers.

Maybe theirs.

They were both panting, both straining, as they shook and dissolved in helpless spasms, seemingly endless orgasms.

As they subsided in exhaustion, his hand settled on her cheek. She drew a shaky breath, felt him pull out of her. She moved off his legs, gave him room to clean up.

A breeze blew up her skirt, dried the dampness between her thighs. She bent to locate her thong.

Her toes touched a vine she hadn't noticed on their arrival. Straggling over the ground, it climbed the sides of the boulder. At first glance, she thought it Virginia Creeper. On closer inspection, she knew better. She'd been a Girl Scout, and had excelled at nature hikes.

She counted the leaves. *If it's three, let it be.*

"Hot shower, Rhaden!" Her voice hit a high note. "We just had sex on poison ivy."

Fifteen

"Dude, you got crabs?" Psycho McMillan caught Rhaden Dunn scratching his groin. *Really* scratching it, as if his pubes were alive.

Kason Rhodes looked down the dugout bench where Dunn stood. Ten minutes until game time, and the man had definite problems. He couldn't sit still. If he rubbed his abdomen and thighs much harder, he'd tear a hole in his uniform pants.

"Not crabs," Alex Boxer put in. "Poison ivy. Dunn's covered in a red rash. There's a dozen bottles of calamine lotion in his locker."

Heat stained Rhaden's neck. He looked pissed as hell over Boxer's comment, however true.

"Hands down, man, or hit the tunnel," Kason ordered. "Media will film you playing with yourself."

Rhaden moved into the shadows, beyond view of the cameras. He rubbed his back and butt against the cement wall.

Boxer looked smug. "Guess who else has an itch she can't scratch?"

Every player on the bench turned for his answer. "Revelle Sullivan in player promotions. I was in her office before the game. She was twitching, had red blotches on her hands and—"

"Shut the fuck up." Dunn came out of the tunnel and shoved Boxer hard.

Boxer raised his hands, backed off. "Facts, Dunn. There was a pair of oven mitts on her desk to keep her from scratching. Has to be hard to type—"

Dunn again lunged at Boxer, and Kason stepped between them. "Take your tempers to the field. Direct your anger toward Ottawa. Raptors are on a streak. We're down two in the series and need this win."

The second week in May, and the Rogues sat sixth in the National League East. The team had been inconsistent. They needed to bring it today.

"Which comic book character would you do?" Boxer continued to needle Rhaden. The game had yet to start; the men were downright restless. "Harley Quinn or Poison Ivy?"

Beats of silence before Psycho took the bait. "Both hang with the Joker. On a good day, they could kick Batman's ass."

"I'd do Wonder Woman." Boxer chose good over evil. "She's got the Laro of Truth and a bullet-deflecting bracelet."

Kason grunted. "You into female action figures?"

"I have five sisters," Boxer said defensively.

"Bet you'd do Barbie," Psycho razzed.

"She's got Ken," Alex said a little too quickly.

The players laughed him down the bench.

The game started, and by the bottom of the third, another Rogue was lost to injury. Zen Driscoll's hustle caused him to roll his ankle, and it didn't roll back. The bone protruded at a ninety-degree angle. Supported by both the trainer and the physician, he hobbled off the field.

Two innings later, a cup check stopped the game. Catcher Chase Tallen had taken a foul tip to his groin. The time-out took him to the locker room. The diagnosis came quickly: the foul had broken his athletic cup and ruptured a testicle.

Every player cringed, felt Chase's pain.

The team was now down four starters. The coach assigned rookie Chas Ragan to short and brought in Kyle Lake to catch.

Kason exhaled sharply. Alex Boxer was an All-Star compared to Ragan and Lake.

The season wasn't looking pretty.

Psycho threw his glove across the dugout. "Son of a bitch. We're cursed with injuries."

Kason didn't believe in superstition. He did, however, stare down Boxer. "Any recent breakups?" he pressed. "Any old girlfriends into evil spells or voodoo curses?"

Boxer spat sunflower seeds. "I'm into kink, not high priestesses and witches."

That was strangely reassuring. Kason took a deep breath, focused on the players he had, not on those he'd lost. "We're down by three." He raised his voice to be heard. "You rookies need to bat like veterans. We need to be a patient team against an impatient stadium. Our fans don't believe we'll earn back the runs. Trust yourself, and don't overcompensate."

"And Boxer," Psycho added, "don't be the centerpiece for an underachieving team. It sucks being cellar dwellers in our division."

The Rogues went on to bat. The order had shifted with the injuries. Boxer led off. He swung at a fastball before it even crossed the plate. He connected with a slider, only to have it go foul and nail the Raptors' mascot near the visitors' dugout. The ball smacked Rappy on the back of his head. He was one angry bird.

The Raptor ignored the umpire's warning to back off. He charged home, kicked dirt onto the plate with his big, yellow plastic feet, then wing-slapped Boxer. Twice.

"Oh, hell," Kason muttered as Boxer poked the bird with the end of his bat. His next swing hooked Rappy's beak. Stupid-ass rookie.

The Ottawa fans went apeshit. Their mascot was sacred. It didn't matter if the bird instigated, provoked, or landed in more fights than any major league player. The Raptor was held in high esteem.

The Rogues lined the dugout fence, watching as the umpire called time and both coaches stepped between Boxer and the bird.

"Game's going south," Psycho said to Kason.

Kason's mouth flattened against his teeth. "We'll turn it around."

In a surprise performance, Boxer grounded to right. A solid base runner, he busted out of the box, turning a single into a double.

Psycho made it to first with a roller between short and third. Boxer held at second.

Kason next moved to the plate. Adrenaline rushed through him at the chance to tie the score. He looked at the sky, caught the end of a contrail. With the right pitch, he could comet the ball over the center field wall.

The time was now. . . .

"Let's close up shop and catch the end of the game," Revelle Sullivan suggested to Dayne from the doorway of her office. She dangled a key from her red-blotched fingers, clutching her purse under her arm. "My uncle's in the owner's box. We can watch from his suite. Guy has a sixty-inch plasma."

Dayne shut down her computer, pushed off her swivel chair. She'd yet to see Kason play, and she was suddenly nervous.

They rode the elevator to the twelfth floor, walked the mile-long carpet to the penthouse. Once behind thick oak double doors, Dayne could only stare.

Deep burgundy walls showcased ultramodern furniture, a massive bookcase, and an impressive collection of wooden masks. An S-shaped bar twisted between the formal living and dining rooms. The extensive selection of liquor bottles indicated Powers entertained often and well.

Photographs covered an entire wall, pictures of both the Rogues and other major league owners and players, as well as celebrities and politicians seated in the stands.

"Guy lives here during the season, but also has a house away from the stadium," Revelle told Dayne. "He crashes here when he works late and doesn't want to disturb one of the limo drivers. His getaway condo in Louisville positions him near Corbin Lily."

It sounded as if Guy still had feelings for his ex-wife. Maybe they found common ground after the World Series and before spring training. A most interesting thought.

"Chai tea?" Revelle offered from the kitchen.

Dayne accepted a tall iced glass.

Revelle steered her toward the den, and they dropped onto overstuffed chairs before the TV. Revelle tapped the remote with a manicured nail, and Kason Rhodes filled the screen, larger than life. Dayne's eyes went wide and she forced a breath.

Big-league field.

Big-league athletes.

There was something about a hard-faced batter staring right through the pitcher that was highly unsettling. The term total badass was too mild for Rhodes.

The fans were on their feet and the stadium rocked.

"Bottom of the fifth, no outs, Rogues trail by three." Revelle quickly brought her up to speed.

The condensation on the glass, along with the sweat from her palms, forced Dayne to locate a coaster. She set her tea on a tiered side table.

"Slam it, Rhodes!" the articulate, always poised Revelle shouted at the TV.

Dayne smiled to see that her boss could cut loose and enjoy the game. According to the announcer, Kason had spoiled his first pitch by hitting it foul.

As the pitcher prepared to throw, Dayne was on the edge of her seat. A slider, and Kason didn't just hit the ball; he hammered it. He laid down a triple.

"Rogues don't just run the bases; they own them," Revelle said with admiration as Boxer and Psycho scored easily.

The camera honed in on Kason, who held at third. Dayne knew him as her neighbor and lover, but not as an elite athlete. His game face intimidated the hell out of her.

Rhaden Dunn now stood in the batter's box. He shifted, adjusted himself, ran his hands down his thighs, went on to scratch his butt.

"Is Rhaden always so twitchy?" Dayne turned to

Revelle, only to find her boss rapidly rubbing her hands together.

"He's played better" was all Revelle would say.

Rhaden's timing was off—*way off*. He swung before and after the ball, went down on strikes.

On a sigh, Revelle pulled a bottle of calamine lotion from her purse and quickly slathered her skin pink. In her hurry, she splashed lotion on the front of her apple green blazer, as well as dotting the hem of her skirt.

The head of Game's On looked frustrated, embarrassed, and still quite itchy. "Anything I can do?" Dayne offered.

"Remind me never to—" Revelle cut herself off, blushed, further comment lost to the game.

"Don't go for being a hero, Chas Ragan." Revelle knew the lineup well. "Get on base; let Romeo bring both you and Rhodes in."

Ragan didn't heed her warning. He tried to kill the ball, only to murder his chance to get on base.

A camera close-up of Kason returning to the dugout for his glove showed one angry man. He'd wanted to score—*needed* to score. Ragan had pissed away the tie.

Another hour brought the bottom of the ninth. The Rogues remained down by one.

"Pressure's on." Revelle stopped scratching, held her breath. "Two outs, and it's all up to Kason."

The pressure rose beyond reason as the Richmond fans demanded a hit. The network panned to the stands. Dayne caught a close-up of Ben and Brenda Dixon behind home, madly waving rally towels.

Dayne started to shake, and hugged herself. Her heart threatened to beat out of her chest.

The moment blurred. Through it all, Kason didn't go

quietly; he rallied. He searched for the big hit, and at full count, crushed the ball over the center field wall.

Dayne jerked with the smack of his bat.

The crowd went wild, and Kason rounded the bases at a dead run. Execution and speed—he had it all.

Game over. Rogues 4, Raptors 3.

Dayne was so light-headed, she nearly lost consciousness. Her ten-hour-a-day job seemed a breeze compared to the nervous energy she'd expended during the last innings of the game.

She fell back in the chair, utterly exhausted.

Several commercials ran prior to the on-field and locker-room interviews. She was caught completely off guard when the first of the Platinum ads aired. She'd forgotten Mother's Day was coming up fast.

The first advertisement was for a tire company; the second featured Kason Rhodes entering the jewelry store. He appeared a diamond in the rough, and incredibly masculine.

Goose bumps skittered over every inch of her skin. From the sweep of his gaze, his approach, to the startling way they looked at each other, the ad was a perfect blend of the intriguing and sensual.

There was minimal narration that noted Gayle de Milo's launch of her cosmopolitan line of jewelry. The store itself conveyed a feeling of elegance.

The majority of the ad centered on *the look*. Kason's intense interest made Dayne squirm on her chair. No one could deny their heat or keep from wondering: would the boy get the girl?

They were a couple for the campaign, but weren't together in real life. Dayne had to pull back, separate the fantasy from reality. She found it incredibly hard.

"Some ad," Revelle commented as she sipped the last of her tea. "Platinum will draw in customers buying jewelry and looking for love."

Dayne had yet to deposit the ten-thousand-dollar check the jeweler had written for the shoot. It was clipped to the front of her refrigerator, where she enjoyed seeing it first thing in the morning and right before bed.

Security, she thought. She could buy a car, put a down payment on a home—she had so many options. She had money for the first time in her life, and it felt good.

"Back to work?" Dayne looked at Revelle.

Her boss shook her head. "I'm not scratching my way back to the office. Cover for me, please?"

Dayne nodded. "Take care of that rash." She left Revelle to her oven mitts and calamine lotion.

The second she stepped onto the sixth floor, whistles sounded from all sides. Women poked their heads from accounting and public relations, most wearing big smiles, a few looking downright envious.

"We caught the Platinum ad," one of the accountants told her. "Sizzling, Dayne. The chemistry made my heart race. Are you and Rhodes officially a couple?"

A couple? Dayne froze, softly asked, "Why the interest?"

"Curiosity runs high," the number cruncher answered. "Kason's a Rogue, a real hard-ass. Richmond fans will be glad he's settled in and fallen for someone. You'll be the couple of the season."

How utterly frightening. "It was a commercial," Dayne reminded all those gathered.

"Honey, it reached beyond advertising. You brought heat to the moment, restored my belief in love at first sight." The accountant sighed. "No man's ever looked at me the way Rhodes gazed on you. Not even my husband."

"I want that look too," a publicist agreed.

"It was *pretend*." Dayne wanted that clear.

"Women can fake orgasms, but no man can fake that look," the woman from public relations responded. "He had you naked in thirty seconds flat."

Kason had seen her bare and beneath him. He'd had little to imagine at the shoot. She pressed her hand to her abdomen, breathed deeply. The ad had taken on a life of its own. That scared her silly.

She was met with similiar reactions at the post office and grocery store. People turned, stared, smiled. One woman asked for her autograph.

Dayne shouldn't have been surprised. The world watched television. The Platinum ad had been perfectly timed, thrust between the game and the interviews. Somehow she now stood in the spotlight as Kason's woman.

That night, Kason didn't seemed fazed by the ad. He looked at her from across his dining room table, wearing a cobalt blue polo, jeans, and a grin.

His mouth was meant for smiling, Dayne thought. The curve softened the hardness of his face, made him twice as handsome. Although he didn't smile much, he did on occasion for her. His biggest grin came after sex, as if she'd pleased him greatly.

"Congratulations on your win," she said between bites of tuna casserole. "I watched the end of the game with Revelle from Guy Powers's suite. You nearly gave me a heart attack."

A lift to his brow. "Why's that?"

"The noise, the pressure, your need to perform." She met his gaze. "I took it to heart and nearly fainted."

He buttered a crescent roll, set down his knife. "All in a day's work."

"You have nerves of steel."

"I have fight, Dayne." His voice deepened. "The need to succeed came at an early age. I was good at baseball and drove myself into a major league contract."

"Your parents must be proud."

Kason's teeth clamped down and a muscle ticked at his jaw. He pushed aside his plate, jammed his elbows on the table. His stare hit just beyond her shoulder, shadowed yet unprotected, as memories overwhelmed him.

Dayne watched him struggle. She sensed the ugliness of his youth. He'd closed down, and she wanted him back. "Talk to me, Kason," she softly encouraged.

Long minutes passed before he palmed his eyes and again focused on her. "I never knew my real dad, Joe Rhodes," he finally said. "Joe was military. He had sex with his brother Ray's girlfriend before his deployment. Nine months later, I was born. Joe was killed overseas, and never knew he'd fathered a child. I was raised by Ray, and he was one mean son of a bitch."

Time ticked, and Kason released his childhood. He shared memories of T-ball, of having his head shaved, of being called Kassie. Through the years, he'd refused to let anyone into his life, up until the day she'd claimed squatter's rights and he'd allowed her to stay.

"You're crying." Apprehensive, Kason leaned across the table, wiped the moisture from her cheek with his thumb.

"I feel for you," said Dayne. "Not pity or sadness, only

optimism from the fact that you became such a good man. You made it, Kason, on your own. I think you're remarkable."

He let her words soak in, and soon exhaled. All tension left his neck and shoulders. He kicked back in his chair, crossing his arms over his chest. "You think I'm remarkable?"

He wasn't searching for ego munchies, only a bit of reassurance. His pride wouldn't let him accept a compliment that wasn't deserved.

She gave him what he needed. "You're amazing at the stadium, with Cimarron and Ruckus, and, most of all, in bed."

"Speaking of which . . ." he said, initiating.

"I have butterscotch pudding," she offered, before she gave of herself.

His gaze went wickedly dark. "Whipped cream too?"

She nodded. "As well as maraschino cherries."

"Licking pudding off skin is a win-win."

Dayne went wet at his suggestion.

While the dogs camped on his couch, Kason drew Dayne to the kitchen. He handed her the toppings and took the bowl for himself.

"I'm hungry, woman." His look said he could eat her alive.

Her craving was equally as strong.

Kason Rhodes smiled four times that night.

Morning sun split the slats on the window shade. Dayne protested at the invasion. She slung her forearm over her eyes, peeked at Kason from beneath her elbow.

The big man had showered, toweled, and now stood in burgundy boxers. Seven weeks, and his hair had returned, military short. He looked strong, confident, capable.

His duffel bag lay unzipped at the foot of the bed, his clothes stacked to pack. Dayne dreaded his departure. Sixteen days on the road seemed like forever.

The team would catch a flight at noon, travel west.

They'd play the Diamondbacks, Padres, and Giants, then stop over in St. Louis to play the Colonels.

Kason claimed the schedule was grueling.

Dayne knew that as cocaptains, Psycho and he babysat the rookies, corralling them for dinner, limiting liquor, and imposing curfews. No Rogue played with a hangover.

Their pep talks both encouraged and disciplined.

Psycho and he had found common ground.

"I'll miss you," she softly told him.

He folded a black pullover, looked up. "It's good to be missed."

Ruckus took that moment to steal one of his Nikes from the floor. The min-pin grabbed a shoelace, growled, and inched backward out the door.

Seconds later, Cimarron returned it.

"Your boy's out of control," Kason stated.

"I see him as free-spirited."

"He needs a few commands."

"*Come,* Ruckus." Dayne patted the bed.

The tiny pup charged into the bedroom, stood on his back paws, and bounced until she lifted him onto the mattress. Ruckus tucked into her side. "He listens," she said defensively.

"Get him to stop biting the sheet," Kason said. "I don't have any more clean ones."

They'd smudged two sets the previous night. She just hoped pudding didn't stain. Butterscotch had never tasted so good as when licked off a man's abdomen. Kason had stuck, then sucked maraschino cherries from her navel. He'd drizzled cherry juice over her tummy, laved every drop. He'd been fascinated by her horseshoe belly stud, turning it up for luck.

Dropping onto the edge of the bed, he tapped her nose, ran his finger down her Beatles T-shirt, then slipped a finger beneath her flesh-toned tanga panties.

"Ruckus," she reminded him.

Kason grunted. "Shut down by a dog."

"I'm, uh, also a bit sore." She hated to admit it. "You're a big man, Kason Rhodes."

He looked more proud than sympathetic. "You should have stopped me at three."

"The fourth let me ride astride," she said. "I loved watching you come."

He'd been all hot eyes and sexy smile. "That's the advantage of being on top."

The sex had been phenomenal. Kason was a total turn-on—his heavy breathing, the tightness in his abdomen and thighs, the wildness in his eyes, and the tenseness in his jaw. All were released when he came, leaving him one satisfied man.

Afterward, she'd stretched full-length, blanketed him with her body. His heat rose, covering her with his scent, his strength, his virility.

Had he taken her again, she wouldn't have walked for days. Even now her thigh muscles ached, cramped. She needed a hot shower, maybe a massage.

He squeezed her knee. "You need to get ready for work."

She agreed. "Revelle may take the day off—bad case of poison ivy."

"Rhaden Dunn's scratching his ass off," Kason told her. "Man smeared on so much calamine lotion it bled through his uniform, looked like he had his period."

Dayne came up on one elbow, kissed him hard. "See you in sixteen days."

"Make plenty of pudding and be ready to go five."

Sixteen

MARRY HER, RHODES!

"Look at all those signs, posters, and banners." Revelle Sullivan pointed to the television in the employees' lounge, tuned to the game. "You're an instant celebrity, Dayne Sheridan."

Several corporate staffers had gathered for lunch, and all looked from the TV to Dayne and back again. Three of the five Platinum ads had now aired, causing quite a stir. Fanatical fans lived the love connection. Dayne had gone from obscure to mobbed as the crowd took the fantasy campaign to heart, believing it real.

Fans gone wild, thought Dayne. The phenomena had turned her life upside down. She was a walking bundle of nerves. Her stomach ached and she could barely swallow.

Through it all, jeweler Gayle de Milo rejoiced. Her cosmopolitan line sold out the first week. She had a long waiting list for upcoming designs.

"You're looking pale," Revelle told her.

Dayne patted color back into her cheeks, then took a seat at a table beside Revelle, who'd recovered from her poison ivy, with the exception of several blisters on her hands. She'd confided to Dayne that the blemishes were the hazards of back roads and dating Rhaden Dunn.

It appeared the very reserved Revelle had fallen for the rugged first baseman. A dozen bouquets now scented her office. Rhaden seemed equally smitten.

Guy Powers had bent his corporate/player rule and given them his blessing. Wedding bells were in their future.

Dayne looked at her own life, and her time with Kason. The road trip had been tough. Romeo Bellisaro had fallen to injury in Los Angeles. The third baseman had fractured his hip sliding home.

Only four starters now shored up the team.

Rhaden held his own at first.

Brek Stryker pitched his ass off.

Psycho played right, backing both second and center.

Kason staked left, picked up the slack behind third and short. The three positions strained him both mentally and physically.

The five rookies had the mobility of cement statues.

Unbalanced, conflicted, the Rogues had dropped to last place in the NL East. Tempers burned, fingers pointed, and no one shouldered the blame.

Revelle had told Dayne that Kason and Psycho had verbally punched the crap out of the team. The cocaptains' lectures were long, intense, demanding.

Kason refused to see the team crumble.

Psycho had his back.

At 1:10, the team took the field, hell-bent on beating the Marlins. By four thirty, nine innings had left them with a nasty loss.

No Rogue had crossed home plate.

Dayne heard the final score on the radio in the limo on her ride home. Revelle had recognized the long hours she'd recently worked and released her early. She knew Kason would need more than sex and pudding to right his world.

"Go mindless," she encouraged him when the sun set and he showed up on her doorstep. It was her turn to spoil him.

She settled him on the small sofa, handed him a Beck's, then slid *Blade Runner* into the DVD player.

"How'd you know I liked that movie?" he asked.

"Rogues Fun Facts."

He grunted, took a long pull on his beer.

She made BLT sandwiches, served him in silence. She held back, let him unwind.

Raiders of the Lost Arc came next, followed by *The Notebook* and popcorn. He lifted a brow, but didn't object to the romance. They watched movies till midnight.

She let the dogs out, then came back in.

"Should I leave?" His voice was low, weary.

"I want you to stay."

She took his hand, and he shoved off the sofa. She led him to her single mattress, undressed him. He lay face-down, and she straddled his lower back. Their connection moved beyond sexual as she massaged the tension from his neck, shoulders, and spine.

Thirty minutes later, his body went slack.

He'd fallen asleep beneath her hands.

She quietly rose, slipped out of her jeans, got into bed in her Duran Duran T-shirt and bikini panties. She kept an inch between them as she covered them both.

Come morning, she woke to find him inside her, and slowly thrusting. His gaze was hooded, lazy. His smile sexy. His body fully aroused.

Wet and turned on, she caught his rhythm. Gentleness built to a delicious torment. They climaxed three minutes before the alarm.

"Nice way to start the day." Kason kissed her forehead, pushed to his feet, flushed his condom.

His shower was quick, and Dayne knew he was saving her hot water. She fed Ruckus and Cimarron, made coffee.

Saturday loomed ahead, and she had no plans until Kason offered, "Would you like to attend the game? Ben Dixon reached me at the stadium yesterday, offered you a ticket. Apparently his brother-in-law has bronchitis, and he hated to see the seat go to waste."

She hesitated. Watching Kason play would be exciting if she could work past her nerves. She wanted him to do well, and hated the fact the team had recently crashed and burned.

"I'd like that," she finally agreed.

Kason flicked open his cell phone, dialed. After a thirty-second chat, it was agreed the Dixons would swing by the camper and drive Dayne to the game.

"The Dixons have seats behind home plate," Kason told her. "Best view in the park."

Kason Rhodes arrived at James River Stadium three hours prior to game time. He had a ritual of warming up, and he kept to it. Psycho McMillan was the only man in the workout room, which opened the door for a private conversation.

"I have an idea," he told Psycho.

"Figured as much," Psycho returned. "The lightbulb over your head's flashing like a blue-light special."

"At least I think on occasion."

Both men stood, arms folded over their chests. Hard looks passed between them, not so much for each other, but for the seriousness of the situation.

"The rookies depend on us to carry the team," Kason began. "We can't shoulder all the positions. We're not supermen."

"Speak for yourself."

"We've had a streak of rookie strike-outs and outfield errors. We need to scare them straight."

"I can do scary."

"Can you lie?" asked Kason.

"Does a priest pray?"

Kason continued. "What's a major leaguer's worst fear?"

"Impotence."

"Second worst fear?"

"Getting traded to the American League."

"Christ, Psycho, third worst?"

"Being sent back to the minors."

"Exactly," Kason agreed. "We need to start a rumor meant for the rookies, one that will put the fear of God into their souls."

"A rumor they'll be sent to the minors?"

Kason nodded. "We lead them to believe that two will be asked to clear their lockers after today's game and that Powers is already looking into midseason trades."

Psycho's lip curled. "Rogues got you last July, and we weren't happy."

"Neither was I—you guys were all assholes."

"If the coaches, general manager, or Powers hear the gossip, we'll be fined."

"I just paid for racing in the parking lot," Kason growled. "What's another five hundred? The rumor's to our benefit."

"You think it will work?"

"Maybe, maybe not."

"I think the rookies care more about themselves than they do about the game," Psycho bluntly stated. "Alex Boxer spends as much time in front of the mirror as he does in center field."

Psycho shifted his stance, squinted at him. "Let's wager. All the Rogues have tattoos but you. If your idea blows, you get a tat—my design."

Kason flexed his jaw. "No Tweety Bird, hula dancer, or red heart with *Mom* in the middle."

"You'll wish for those once I've chosen."

"If the rumor strikes fear and the rookies play hard?"

"I streak through the locker room naked."

"You do that every damn day already."

"Pick my poison."

"A month of manual labor," Kason pitched. "I start building my house once the season ends. I'll need someone to lay cinder block."

"Hire a damn contractor."

"I'll be subbing out work, but I want to do most of it myself."

Psycho pulled a face. "Agreed, as long as that little biter dog's not on-site."

"Ruckus has lost most of his baby teeth," Kason told him. "He's more into stealing shoes than gnawing hands."

"Plan made and laid," from Psycho.

Game on.

* * *

One o'clock, and introductions of the team took place. Kason's teammates got an ovation, while he received a roar. Banners waved, whistles shrilled, and feet stomped.

MARRY HER, RHODES was every damn where. He didn't need the distraction. Reporters asked him as many questions about Dayne as they did about his stats.

Psycho punched his arm, harder than was necessary. "Platinum's turned you into a household name."

Dayne's popularity had grown as well. She'd been mobbed by fans, all asking whether they'd set a wedding date. Everyone's nose was in their business. It was damn intrusive.

The fourth and fifth ads would air over the next two weeks. The frenzy would only increase as the Rogues played at home. Kason had caught Dayne looking at him differently of late, as if she too had caught fan fever.

The shoot bent reality. He and Dayne were friends and lovers, but he wasn't marriage-minded.

Two minutes and counting. Kason and Psycho moved to opposite ends of the dugout bench, where each spoke to one rookie. Kason's choice was Alex Boxer.

"You shittin' me?" Boxer's voice broke and all color drained from his face. "Two will be booted after the game?"

"You haven't done jack to stay."

Boxer gagged, and Kason passed him a paper cup of Gatorade. "Redeem yourself" were his final words.

He knew Boxer would pass the rumor. Soon fear and adrenaline would drive their play.

"Play ball!" called the umpire.

On defense, Brek Stryker pitched a World Series–

caliber inning. Stryke had made a statement, and Kason hoped the offense would respond in kind.

The lineup continued to shift; the batting coach had yet to find a winning combination.

Psycho led off, landed a double.

Alex Boxer's bunt rolled like a golf putt straight to the pitcher. Easy out. His poor performance took him to the locker room, where he puked his guts out.

Nerves sent Rod Brown and Chas Ragan down on strikes.

"Fairies tattooed on each hip," Psycho shot at Kason as they left the dugout. "Maybe Tinker Bell."

Kason flipped him off inside his glove.

Brek Stryker ruled the mound. Three up, three down, he again brought the Rogues to bat.

"Anyone here to play ball?" Kason shouted along the bench. The rookies dipped their heads.

"Sign them up for Ping-Pong," Psycho spat.

Kyle Lake led off, and Kason stood on deck. He'd spotted Dayne earlier, during the national anthem. He cut her a glance again now.

She sat in a Rogues T-shirt bearing his number. Her elbows rested on her knees and her hands were steepled, as if in prayer. She sought a higher power to support their win.

Kason impressed her with a triple, only to be stranded at third when the next two rookie batters failed to bring him home.

"Tattoo," Psycho taunted at the dugout steps. "A monkey bending over so his asshole's at your navel."

No fuckin' way. The image was disturbing.

Despite Brek Stryker's efforts, the Marlins scored twice in the third inning. Kason's gut tightened.

Psycho went ballistic in the dugout. "I'm sick of losing." He thumped the giant Igloo cooler so hard, the lid tipped and orange Gatorade sprayed everywhere.

Kason waved good-bye to Boxer as the rookie swung two bats in the on-deck circle. Boxer tripped over his own feet on his walk to home plate.

Boxer went full count before he squeezed a slider between second and short. Slow out of the box, he was nearly tagged out.

Rod Brown dug in next. Kason got whiplash from all his foul balls. Brown finally connected on a fastball, arrowed it over the shortstop's head. The fans were so stunned, eyes popped and jaws dropped.

The cheering soon started, and the noise was deafening. Rally towels waved and foam fingers pointed to the scoreboard. The fans were in it for the Rogues to win it.

The rumor had reached Chas Ragan, who also proved his worth. He made it to first on a hopper down the third-base line.

The fans were beside themselves.

The bases were loaded with rookies.

Rhaden Dunn got hit by a pitch, which walked Alex Boxer across home plate. The crowd couldn't stop screaming.

"Construction," Kason said to Psycho as he strapped on his shin guard. "You'll need a hard hat and steel-toed boots."

"I have a wheelbarrow."

"We're not planting a garden."

Psycho looked him in the eye. "I'll invest two months of labor if you put the game away."

Kason wanted the win as badly as Psycho. He waited . . . and waited for the right pitch, then airmailed it to Maryland.

Grand slam.

The Rogues broke out of their slump, rode the momentum. Singles became doubles. Doubles turned to triples. Nine innings, and they beat the Marlins 8–2.

Kason looked toward Dayne before he ducked into the tunnel. He caught her eye, winked. She waved. Lady looked sunburned and wilted. She'd worked hard through the game, shouting, stomping, supporting her team. At least she had Ben and Brenda to see her home.

Beer sprayed like champagne in the locker room. The guys were celebrating a win that had been long in coming. Not until Coach Dyson called for quiet did the players settle. Dyson praised the team, pressed them to stay focused.

A weighty silence held until Rod Brown swallowed hard and asked, "Who's to pack, coach?"

"Pack?" Dyson looked puzzled. "We play at home again tomorrow."

Brown cleared his throat. "Two rookies were to be sent back to the minors tonight."

"No one's going anywhere," the coach stated. "Who told you that?"

"Alex Boxer," Brown said.

Dyson hit Boxer with a look, and Boxer gave up his source. "Came from Kason."

"I heard it from Psycho," Kason passed the buck.

"I heard voices." Psycho drew everyone's chuckle.

"False rumor," Dyson told the team.

The rookies pumped their arms, relieved.

"Anyone hear anything else?" Dyson wanted to clear the air.

"That Kason Rhodes was gay," said Chas Ragan.

Kason glared at Psycho.

Psycho grinned.

The rookies headed to the showers.

Dyson turned to the cocaptains, shook his head. "You motivated them with a rumor?"

"A means to an end—we won." Kason had no regrets.

Dyson jabbed his thumb toward the door. "Hallway—interviews. Play nice with the press."

Kason and Psycho stood shoulder to shoulder against the swarm of reporters.

"Talk about your grand slam." A reporter stuck a microphone in Kason's face.

"The guys got on base and I brought them home. Total team effort. We played hard, made statements."

"What lit a fire under the rookies today?" a member of the press asked.

The fear of the minors. "We finally came together, hit our stride," stated Kason.

"You're sitting sixth." The same reporter said.

"Give us a month; I'm predicting second," answered Psycho.

"Platinum," a female reporter shouted from the back. "When are you getting married, Rhodes?"

"Yeah, dude, give us a date." Psycho put Kason on the spot.

"The day I ask Psycho to be my best man is the day I walk down the aisle." Kason's sarcasm shut down the press.

Everyone knew the men barely tolerated being on the same team. They butted heads, were outright combative.

A dozen more questions, and the men ended the press conference. They backed through the locker room doors.

"Major dig on the best man." Psycho stripped for his shower.

"I've no intention of getting married."

"Does your renter feel the same?"

"Dayne has no expectations."

"Be sure, dude. Be very, very sure."

Dayne Sheridan caught Kason Rhodes's interview in her camper shortly after the game. She'd passed on dinner with the Dixons, needing to exhale from the strain of the day.

She'd turned on the TV, curled up on the couch. Ruckus had cuddled on her lap, with Cimarron stretched by her feet. The sports network had recounted the highlights of the game.

Kason's grand slam had made the headlines, as well as talk of the team's comeback. Praise for the Rogues was at an all-time high.

Kason's statement on marriage bent Dayne low. He hadn't even paused to consider the reporter's question. He'd curled his lip, looking cocky and uninterested, the image of a single jock.

She liked Richmond, loved working with Revelle. But the Platinum promotion had opened her eyes to how little Kason felt for her. He'd acted in the ads, a man with a hot look and sexy presence. In the end, she was no more than a reflection in his aviators.

Her heart caught a chill. She'd been blown off again
in public.

She pulled a plaid blanket about her shoulders, snuggled deeper on the small sofa. It was six o'clock, but she
had no appetite. The Rogues would celebrate their win.
Kason wouldn't find his way home for several hours.

Dayne rested her head against the back of the couch,
closed her eyes and dreamed. . . .

Somewhere between light sleep and waking fantasy,
she was being kissed. Deeply kissed awake. A warm
male mouth knew what she liked and gave it. The kiss
went on and on, growing hungrier and more demanding.

She moaned, aroused, as the man drew her outside
herself and into him. He tasted faintly of beer and a
breath mint. He kissed like Kason. . . .

She sighed, left the fantasy behind, and opened her
eyes. She found him now seated beside her. He wore a
tan T-shirt and Wranglers. A cigar stuck out of his shirt
pocket.

"We won, Dayne." He breathed against her mouth.
"Today we beat the odds."

Kason was a hell of a ballplayer on his own, yet he'd
instilled new energy into a team on a downhill slide. She
was proud of him.

He brushed back the strands of hair that caught at the
corner of her mouth, ran his thumb over her cheekbone.
"All it took was a rumor of the minors to get the rookies
back on track."

She gave him a soft smile. "You are my hero. I'm glad
you were successful."

He put the back of his hand to his mouth, yawned. "I

could use a good night's sleep. Do you mind if I take Cim and head out?" He departed before she could reply.

The interview at the park came to mind, and she hardened her heart. She wouldn't beg him to stay. Tonight she'd go it alone.

"I don't understand all the attention I'm getting," Dayne said to Revelle as they ate lunch the next day at a health-food store near the stadium.

Cucumber's combined sage-and-wheat checkerboard tiles with lemon yellow leather booths. The owner had a motto: "Feed the customer, but don't fatten him up." Portions were moderate, organic, and healthy.

Revelle added more sprouts to her veggie burger. "The popularity of the Platinum ads is unprecedented. We live in a society where people love the idea of love. The campaign captures the magic of a hot look that carries a man and woman to happily ever after."

Dayne pushed a Greek salad around on her plate, but couldn't stomach a bite. "I'm not happy. I can't cross a street without someone asking about Kason and me."

"Kason's a very private person. The campaign wasn't easy for him either," Revelle reminded her.

"But he agreed to it, I got roped in."

Revelle touched a napkin to the corner of her mouth, looked at Dayne strangely. "You don't know, do you?"

Dayne blinked. "Know what?"

"I'm not certain it's my place to tell you."

"You're my boss; we work together."

Still Revelle hesitated. She finished half her veggie burger before admitting, "Kason did the shoot for you."

Dayne didn't believe her. "He did the ad for a hundred grand." She'd seen the check.

Revelle fingered the edge of her place mat. "Kason's not about money. He signed his check over to Rhaden last week in support of First Base. Rhaden's had a lot of rough kids join the center lately, including a hellion named Samson Banks. He's spent a lot of time with the kid."

Revelle paused while a waiter refilled her glass with sparkling mineral water. "As far as Kason," she continued, "he flat turned me down when I first approached him. I'd every intention of hounding him again, but he came to me shortly afterward, on Opening Day, right as I'd started to interview applicants for the assistant's position. Kason said he had someone in mind for the job and asked me to hire her sight unseen.

"He was determined you got the job, and I gave in. At that moment, he owed me. I cornered him, asked what he'd give in return. He agreed to the Platinum account. He'd never have done the shoot had it not been for you."

Dayne stared at the other woman, her emotions in a whirl. Kason had *gifted* her with the job. It had been one of three presents in his attempt to smooth over their earlier disagreement. He despised publicity, hated the spotlight, yet he'd sold his soul for her.

Still, he couldn't commit. He hadn't stopped at her camper that morning to say good-bye. She'd heard the crunch of his tires on the dirt road as he'd headed to the airport.

"Platinum took on a life of its own," Revelle said. "No one could have predicted the city would fall in love with you as a couple. Gayle de Milo was right. The bigger the man, the harder his fall for the right woman. The ads said it all."

"The shoot was fanciful," Dayne reminded not only Revelle, but herself. She'd lived it, believed it, only to have reality slap her in the face.

"Your heart was in those ads, and Kason gave you the look."

"The *look* meant nothing. He contradicted the campaign in his interview after the game yesterday."

"If Psycho's going to be his best man, I don't think the wedding will happen anytime soon," Revelle said, forced to agree.

"I'm in love with him."

"I know." Revelle's gaze was sympathetic. She sipped her sparkling water, turned thoughtful. "I may have a solution to bring the man around."

"No coercion, no tricks."

"Let me lay it out. . . ."

Seventeen

Kason Rhodes strode down the hallway to Revelle Sullivan's office. It was after eight P.M. when Rhaden Dunn had mentioned she was working late. Kason needed to see her. Revelle was his only connection to Dayne.

Her door stood open, and he walked in. "Where's Dayne?" he demanded. "She left a note, said she'd gone out of town."

Revelle took her sweet time in replying. She removed her glasses, rubbed the dark circles under her eyes. "Dayne's on loan to Corbin Lily Powers. Corbin's franchising player promotions."

"You traded Dayne to Louisville?"

"For a three-month stay, unless Corbin hires her away from me."

Kason's jaw set and his entire body tightened. "She left the dogs." He'd come home to find Eve McCaffrey babysitting Cim and Ruckus.

"Corbin set Dayne up in an apartment—no pets allowed. She hated to leave the dogs, but plans to send for Ruckus if the job pans out."

Send for Ruckus? He saw red. "No way in hell."

Revelle pushed to her feet, her voice soft with concern. "Dayne needed a breather from the frenzy of Platinum. We had fanatics seeking her out in the elevators and private corporate offices, and had to hire extra security. For some reason, people chose to believe you were a couple. The ads got out of hand."

Her mouth pinched. "Worse still, you told the media there would never be a wedding."

Kason jammed his hands in his jeans pockets. "The female reporter got personal and I got pissed. I mentioned Psycho as my best man to get her off my back. The media knows we hate each other's guts. My full concentration was on the team, turning the season around, making a comeback. Baseball is my job."

"Dayne's your woman. Your comment embarrassed her, Kason. You shot her down."

His gut burned. "I never meant to hurt her."

"She cares for you."

"She left me." The words tasted bitter on his tongue.

"You've two days between series. Bring her home."

"Corbin Lily will be one ticked team owner."

"I'll deal with my aunt."

Kason Rhodes debated flying. In the end, he decided to drive to Louisville, Kentucky. That way, the dogs could ride along. He shoved a change of clothes into his duffel, grabbed a bag of dog food and a water bowl, and he was set to roll.

Ruckus fought his carrier, and found his way onto Kason's lap for the entire trip. Cimarron rode shotgun.

After driving 460 miles west, Kason skirted Louisville. He'd sorted out his feelings for Dayne, and knew he wanted her in his life. More than wanted; he needed her.

He'd taken to her from their first meeting. He'd never forget the sight of the wet tomboy wrapped in a towel, claiming squatter's rights. While she'd frustrated the hell out of him, she'd also seen through his facade to the real man. She'd appreciated and cared for him. She'd set his interests ahead of her own. It was time he gave back.

Kason knew Louisville like the back of his hand. He drove straight to the stadium. After a ten-minute struggle, he coerced Ruckus into his carrier. Well-mannered Cimarron accepted his leash. They entered the corporate building as a team.

Unease walked with him to the receptionist's desk, where he was immediately recognized and welcomed.

"Good to see you, Mr. Rhodes." Tara, the receptionist, smiled warmly. She'd been with the organization during Kason's seven years with the Colonels. She looked first at the dog carrier, then at the big Dobie on the leash. "Sorry, sir; no pets in the building."

Kason refused to return them to his Hummer. They played a big part in his negotiations with Dayne. "This is a pet-friendly building," Kason stated. "The team owner allows her two bulldogs total freedom."

"Corbin Lily *owns* the building."

"Corbin's not here now." The owner traveled with her team, and the Colonels were in Florida for a four-game series. "I need to see Dayne Sheridan in player promotions. Thirty minutes max and we're gone."

Tara pulled up a site map. "The second and third floors are under renovation, and it's a maze." She placed a red X on a small conference room that backed the elevators. Lowering her voice, she whispered, "No dog doody."

Offended by her comment, Ruckus bared his teeth and growled. He'd taken care of business by the flagpole to the left of the front door. The azaleas were now fertilized.

Bypassing staff, Kason took the emergency exit stairs to the third floor. The alarms had been dismantled for the crew to work. The sound of hammering and buzz saws came from the floor below. The hallway ahead stretched long and quiet. He could hear himself breathe.

He maneuvered around sawhorses, scaffolding, and tarps, then paused outside Dayne's office. He sucked air. There was no guarantee she'd return with him to Richmond. Caveman tactics were always an option—he had no qualms about tossing her over his shoulder. Cim and Ruckus would support him.

He dropped to one knee on the dust-covered floor and unhitched the door on the dog carrier. Freedom rang, and the min-pin darted out.

Ruckus sniffed the air as if picking up Dayne's scent. He then charged into the conference room, his yip ear-piercingly shrill. Kason and Cim followed Ruckus inside. Kason unhooked the leash, let Cimarron also rush her.

Kason crossed his arms over his chest, leaned against the far wall. He kept his distance, let the dogs soften her heart.

Dayne's unguarded expression told him all he needed to know. He caught her wonder, deep emotion, and extreme happiness. Her hand over her heart, she slid off her desk chair and went down on her knees. She scooped up Ruckus, buried her face against his skinny, wiggling body. Then she hugged the stuffing out of Cimmaron.

"How'd you guys get here?" She was so choked up, she could barely breathe. "Where's Kason?" Her words were muffled in Cim's neck.

A shifting shadow on the back wall caught her eye. Dayne Sheridan looked up and her heart skipped two beats. Kason Rhodes, pressed against the back wall, was as tall and as intimidating as the day she'd met him.

A muscle ticked in his jaw; his gaze was threateningly dark. He had badass down to a science. His gray T-shirt and jeans were wrinkled and he looked damn mad.

Her legs shook as she pushed to her feet, Ruckus still clutched to her chest. She dusted off the knees of her navy slacks, straightened her cream silk blouse. "What brings you to Louisville?" she asked, forcing her voice to remain steady.

"You."

The one word stole her breath. "Now that you've found me . . . ?" she dared to ask.

"Come home with me. With us."

Home. That sounded like family, but she had to be sure. She needed to have him say he wanted her forever. "We make good friends and neighbors." Her throat tightened around the words. "Give me more, Kason."

"I want us to live together in my trailer."

"What about my Airstream?"

"I bought the camper from Frank at the warehouse several weeks ago, to give you security," he finally told her. "I'll sign the deed over to you. We can use it to store bulk food."

Still she hesitated, and Ruckus started to squirm. She set him on the floor and he chased his shadow. The min-pin was easily entertained. "I'm not certain I can return to Richmond," she said. The city had taken a toll on her.

"Platinum did a number on us both," Kason said. "My comment to the reporter was no reflection on you. I wanted to shift the focus off my personal life and back on the team."

She understood. The promo had taken over her life too. She hadn't caught her breath for weeks. *What now?* she wondered. Where would they go from here?

"I love you, Dayne Sheridan." His words reached across the room, touched her heart.

Breathe in; breathe out; move on. She rubbed her *Tomorrow* tattoo, knew what she had to do.

She turned to her desk, located a blank piece of paper. Nerves shook her hand as she wrote him a message. Emotion clogged her throat and tears filled her eyes as she held up her sign for him to read.

MARRY ME, RHODES.

Kason was on her in a heartbeat. He hugged her so hard, she was certain they were now joined at the hip. Long minutes passed as they absorbed each other's heat, heartbeat, and commitment.

"Wedding planner?" He eased back an inch, let her breathe. "Church, reception?"

"No planner." This time she wanted quick and simple. "I want to get married in the woods at sunset. I'll ask Revelle to be my maid of honor."

"Psycho will be my best man."

"The press will love it."

"Psycho will hate it."

Two months later

It was mid-July, and Mr. and Mrs. Kason Rhodes sat on low beach chairs beside their pool—a kiddie pool Dayne had dragged between the trailers for fun in the sun. Kason still couldn't believe he'd agreed to join her, but seeing his wife in a red string bikini planted his ass beside her.

Plus he had a cooler of beer.

She'd put him in charge of the coconut suntan oil, which he spread every twenty minutes over her tight little body. He kept her well protected from the UV rays.

Cimarron lay with his head on the rim of the pool. More water ran out than remained in. Dayne kept the hose running.

The pool was deep enough for Ruckus to swim. He wore a puppy life vest and gave a whole new meaning to dog paddle. Dayne splashed her feet, and the min-pin bobbed like a cork.

Kason shucked his T-shirt, put his arms over his head, and stretched his legs out straight. Bleached white cut-offs hung low on his hips, and his tattoo caught the sun-light.

Sliding Home was scripted in black ink.

His teammates saw the tat as a commentary on his stats: he'd scored more winning runs than any other player in the National League.

In truth, the tattoo had a more significant meaning, one shared only with his wife. Sex with Dayne was like sliding home forever. She was his rush and emotion. His peace and clarity. His grace and greatest pleasure.

She totally did it for him.

He reached into the cooler, popped a cold one. "We should add an indoor pool to the architectural plans."

Dayne slid her sunglasses down her nose, met his gaze. "You've made a dozen changes already."

He shrugged. "What's one more? I liked your ideas of

a pantry, an arch between the living room and den, and the addition of four children's bedrooms."

"Think we can handle four kids?"

"Could they be any worse than Ruckus?" Ruckus had bobbed over to Cimarron and now licked the big dog's face. "He can be sweet."

"Tell that to Psycho."

Dayne chuckled. "The wedding photo of Ruckus attacking Psycho's wingtip is my favorite."

Kason had to agree. He could still see Psycho's pained expression as his best man tried to detach Ruckus from the heel of his formal dress shoe during the wedding ceremony.

Ruckus had yelped, fought, clenched his teeth on the leather. Psycho had picked up the min-pin and handed him to Kason for disciplinary action during the ring exchange.

Kason had settled the pup in the crook of his arm and Ruckus had quieted. He'd only wanted attention.

Gayle de Milo had designed Dayne's ring. The one-of-a-kind princess-cut chocolate diamond set amid a circlet of pink diamond chips was as unique and beautiful as his bride.

Dayne and he had kept the wedding casual. She'd worn a white sundress and he'd gone with a black-and-white striped shirt and black slacks.

They'd invited Rhaden, and Psycho had brought his wife, Keely. The Dixons had shown up for the outdoor reception, as had his teammates. The celebration had gone long into the night. Rogues knew how to party.

Now, as their afternoon progressed, Kason poured coconut lotion onto his palm, oiled his wife's inner thighs. "Any regrets about getting married in the woods?" he asked.

"Psycho asked if our children would be raised by wolves."

Kason actually smiled. He and Psycho had agreed to disagree. Risk Kincaid had a more serious injury than originally diagnosed and he wouldn't return for the season. That left them cocaptains through the playoffs and a possible World Series.

With Risk on the disabled list, Alex Boxer remained in center. Boxer had slowly come into his own. His cockiness had become competent play.

The rookies had stumbled out of the gate, but gained momentum. They'd found heart, hustle, and now their souls were in the game. The Rogues remained in contention.

Starters Chase Tallan, Zen Driscoll, and James Lawless would return within a week. The team sat second in the National League East. A series win against the Raptors could elevate them to first.

Kason nudged Dayne's foot with his own. They'd had enough pool time. "I catch a six A.M. flight to Ottawa in the morning. Let's call it a day."

She tapped her watch. "It's only four thirty."

"I've other ways to spend our time."

Bending toward the pool, he retrieved the bobbing Ruckus and unhooked his safety vest. He toweled off both dogs, and the min-pin dragged the biggest towel back to the trailer.

Kason snagged Dayne's hand, drew her up. Her sexy oiled body stuck to him. He liked her scent: coconut, peaches, and sun-warmed woman. He wanted her in his bed.

"What's for dinner?" he casually asked as he emptied the kiddie pool.

"I put a small roast in the oven earlier." Dayne shut off the hose.

"Salad?" Not his favorite.

"Coleslaw."

Much better. "Potatoes?"

"Twice-baked."

"Rolls?"

"Texas toast."

"Pudding?"

"Butterscotch."

"Sweetheart, it's time to eat."

Dessert came first and dinner, hours later.

That night, in bed, Kason Rhodes broke his record for sliding home. He scored six.

Can't get enough of the Richmond Rogues?

The story of Alex Boxer is coming next month in *Ho, Humbug, Ho* featured in the *Santa, Honey* anthology. Read on for a peek.

One

Santa wore a smirk that could set Christmas back eleven months. He had the shoulders of a linebacker.

Black hair that curled at his collar.

Ice blue eyes.

A *Rogues* tattoo on his left bicep.

And abs that would never shake in laughter like a bowl full of jelly.

Confined to a dressing room at the back of the Jingle Bell Shop, Holly McIntyre faced off with Alex Boxer. He was six feet of aggravation. His testosterone set her teeth on edge.

"Here's your Santa suit." She draped the outfit over a straw reindeer statue, soon to be displayed at the front of the store. "You dress and I'll—"

The man had no modesty. He'd tugged off his navy T-shirt and shucked his jeans before she'd finished her sentence. He stood before her now, wearing black boxer briefs and a naughty grin.

He'd tried to shock her. And he had. They stood so close, his body heat pressed her breasts, nestled into her cleavage. She blushed.

Unable to avert her gaze, Holly took him in. His chest was deep and cut. His legs stretched long and muscled, the swell of his package fully loaded. She forced herself to blink, to swallow, to breathe as he stepped into the red velvet Santa pants, trimmed at the hem with fake white fur.

Alex was six inches taller and twenty pounds heavier than the previous year's Santa. The pants fit snug. The red jacket set off his six pack. There was no room to stuff a pillow. Santa looked tall, fit, and North Pole hot.

Any woman would love to have him drop down her chimney, with or without presents.

"I'm going to bust a seam." His expression was dark as he bent in an attempt to pull on a pair of black boots. His feet were big and brawny and his heel crushed the patent leather. "Too damn small." He kicked them aside, went back to his Nikes.

Santa in sneakers—they'd moved beyond the traditional image. There was nothing apple-cheeked, warm or caring about this man. He was anti-Christmas spirit.

She held up a wig and eyebrow set complete with wired mustache and full, fluffy beard. "Elastic straps go over your head."

Alex frowned. "That's got to itch."

Holly was prepared, she'd brought baby powder. She tapped talcum onto her palm, then proceeded to pat the powder onto his face. His cheeks were angular, his nose ran blade straight, his mouth set full, yet masculine.

His skin warmed and his lips parted beneath her touch. The talcum soon whitened his afternoon shadow.

A hint of powder collected at one corner of his mouth. Holly tapped the excess with the tip of her finger, and his breath broke against her palm, hot, moist, and triggering shivers.

She pulled back, annoyed that such an irritating man

could raise goose bumps. Visible bumps, that turned his gaze a wicked blue. He knew he'd affected her. And took pleasure in her discomfort.

She dusted off her hands, her voice stern. "Put on the wig set."

Alex took his sweet time. He fit the short, white curls, over his head, sneezed into the mustache, and adjusted the beard along the rigid set of his jaw.

"Glasses, stocking cap, and gloves." She handed him each one.

He squinted behind the round, wire-rimmed glasses. "My vision's blurred."

"The previous Santa was near sighted," she explained. "I had prescription lenses put in the glasses."

"Where's the old Santa now?" he asked.

"He's, um, dead."

His sharp exhale bristled every fake hair on the Santa beard. "I'm wearing a dead Santa's suit?"

"The man didn't die wearing the suit," she assured him. "It has been dry cleaned."

Alex shoved his hands in the white gloves. Gloves that didn't stretch to his wrists. "Damn, I'm squeezed into red velvet, have fake mustache hair in my mouth, and can't see beyond my nose. An unfair punishment for driving fifteen miles over the speed limit."

"You were in a school zone," she reminded him.

"It was *Sunday*."

Judge Hathaway protected his own, Holly knew. Hathaway hadn't cared that it was Sunday and the entire town sat in church. Alex Boxer had been busted for speeding. His good cheer had been left on the outskirts of Holiday, Florida.

The judge had ordered Alex to pay a substantial fine,

then tacked on forty hours of community service during Christmas week.

The service would be playing Santa Clause at Wilmington Mall. Alex had growled his objection. The hotshot baseball player had called his attorney, who'd argued with the judge.

In the end, Hathaway's ruling stood.

Alex's Saleen S7 had been impounded. The low-slung silver sports car with the gull-wing doors had quickly become a local attraction. Law enforcement opened the compound twice daily. The Salvation Army set up a stand and rang the bell for donations. Money rolled in at Alex's expense.

The one hotel in Holiday had been booked for the season, which forced Alex into the loft above the Jingle Bell Shop. The one bedroom was small, cramped, and jammed with Christmas decorations. He'd complained his feet hung over the end of the bed. And that the pillow was sized for an elf.

The small Florida town faced Christmas with a scowling Santa. There was no ho-ho-ho in this man.

Holly watched as Alex fought with the stocking cap. It was too tight. The pom-pom swung, bopped him on the nose.

Alex ripped it off. "Not going to happen." He looked around the shop, found a long red bandanna, which he wrapped as a skull cap. There was no cuddly softness to this Santa, he looked street corner tough.

"A couple of rules," Holly went on to tell Alex. "Be gentle when you hoist the children on your lap. Keep smiling even if they pee, whine, tug on your beard or burst into tears."

"Pee on me?" That caught his attention.

"Children get scared," she explained. "Peeing is a natural reaction to fear. Not every child loves Santa on his first visit."

His mouth thinned beneath the mustache. "Can the kids sit beside me and not on my lap?"

"Not an option."

"This job sucks."

"Volunteer Santas are jovial," she stated. "They embrace Christmas and bring hope and joy to children."

"I'm not a volunteer, I'm court ordered," he ground out. "I should be in Miami by now. I was to meet up with my teammates to celebrate winning the World Series. Warm weather, cold beer, and a pair of hot twins. Time to cut loose."

"Instead of your buddies, you'll spend your week with a moose, elf, gingerbread man, and nutcracker."

"Lucky me."

"I'm to write up a daily report for the judge on your cooperative efforts," she told him. "So give it your all."

His jaw shifted left, then right, and his stare turned cold. Santa had gone all silent and wintry.

She returned to the rules. "You must be as nice to the last child as you are to the first. You ask each one what he or she wants for Christmas, but never promise the delivery of the gift. Many parents can't afford what their child requests. Afterward, the elves from the photo booth will snap the holiday picture."

Alex looked down at her. His ice blue eyes were magnified behind the prescription lenses. "What part do you play in this insanity?"

"I'm the nutcracker."

"Perfect type-casting."

She ignored him. "Your Santa bag is filled with candy canes."

"I hate the scent of peppermint."

"Get used to it," she said flatly. "Each child gets a cane. There will be a decorative gift box by your chair with discount coupons from the local merchants. You'll need to give an envelope to each parent."

"You're asking me to remember a lot."

"Try to extend your mind beyond bat and ball."

He cut her a sharp look. "Stop cracking my nuts."

"Speaking of which, I need to change into my costume." She motioned toward the door. "Step outside, please."

"I dressed in front of you, feel free to strip before me."

"Not in this lifetime, Santa. Hit the door. I'll be with you in fifteen," she instructed.

Alex Boxer sauntered out. He'd have liked to watch Holly undress, it would've turned him on. He'd always had a thing for blondes with gold hoop earrings in yellow sundresses. She touched on pretty with her big brown eyes and sexy mouth. Unfortunately, she was too thin for his liking. He preferred a woman with a nice rack and curvy booty. He enjoyed the wiggle and jiggle of the female body.

He'd been looking forward to a lot of jiggle in Miami. Skimpy shorts and thong bikinis flashed a lot of skin. Spandex hugged a lot of curves. Alex and six single Rogues had booked condos on South Beach. They'd planned to raise hell between Christmas and New Years.

Instead of suntanned and oiled twins, he now faced children sitting on his lap. Any one of them could pee on him. He'd be handing out candy canes and store coupons. Not close to the wild time he'd originally planned for the holidays.

"I'm ready." The crack of the door revealed Holly to him.

Costumed as a nutcracker soldier, she could barely fit her big wooden head through the frame. Painted in the Old World style, the face had severely arched eyebrows and wide black eyes. A tall black hat topped her head. A moveable lever below her left ear opened and closed her jaw.

A red jacket with gold epaulettes hung large on her small shoulders. Baggy black pants and boots with gold glitter rounded out her outfit.

Rifle in hand, she poked him with the bayonet. "Down the hall and to your right, the door will open into Santa's Workshop. There will be hammering elves, a dancing moose, and a gingerbread man decorating his freshly baked house."

Alex backed against the wall. "Honest to God, I can't go through with this."

"You can and you will." She jabbed him a second time. "The kids are waiting for you. Move your red velvet butt."

"Careful where you poke," he cast over his shoulder. "No need to ream me a second."

He made it down the hall, even with the glasses distorting his vision. There was a clammer beyond the door, loud with pounding, laughing, and what he swore sounded like an animal's bellow. He cracked the door, squinted. He didn't like what he saw. "There's a live reindeer tied to a post beside my Santa chair."

"His name is Randolph." He heard Holly expel her breath within the hollow head of her costume. "He wasn't supposed to be here this year. He offends people."

"Offends people, *how?*" Alex wanted to know. "Does he bite? Kick? Spit like a camel?"

"None of the above."

"Then *what?*" he pressed.

"He passes gas."

"Son of a bitch," Alex snarled. "Kids peeing on my lap and now reindeer farts. Could it get any worse?"

The day went downhill fast.

Holly suggested that he give a robust 'ho-ho-ho' on his entrance. His greeting was far from jovial—it sounded low, guttural and grumpy.

His appearance silenced the crowd.

He felt captured in a freeze frame. Everyone now stared at him.

The fathers looked skeptical.

The mothers oddly appreciative.

The children shifted nervously.

One little girl started to cry.

Alex didn't mind crowds.

He was used to them. The Richmond Rogues drew tens of thousands of fans to James River Stadium. He'd been cheered and booed by the best of them.

A line of holiday shoppers didn't faze him in the least. Let the people stare. It gave him time to check out Santa's Workshop.

The day topped ninety degrees, yet the mall had been transformed into a winter wonderland. Musak blasted "Have a Holly, Jolly Christmas" above air conditioning units cranked to the max. Frost hung on the air, and Alex swore he could see his breath.

Mock snow crunched beneath his Nikes as he walked the short path to Santa's Workshop. Garlands and tiny white lights wrapped a red corduroy high-back chair. He swung the bag filled with candy canes off his shoulder, settling it between himself and Randolph the Reindeer.

Randolph didn't give him the time of day. The reindeer kept to his business of munching hay.

Cinnamon wafted from the gingerbread house.

The evergreen decorated with enormous red and green balls cast the rich fragrance of forest pine.

"Back to work." Holly the Nutcracker clapped her hands, and the elves returned to their workshop tasks. The commotion grew as Santa's little helpers put together bikes and wrapped toys for the mall customers.

Alex watched as the costumed moose danced down the line of children patiently waiting to relay their wish lists. The moose was tall, thick, but light on his feet. He played a triangle to the holiday tunes.

Alex sucked air. The sights, sounds, and scents of Christmas smothered him. He'd grown up in a wealthy household where holidays meant international travel. He'd never done small town; never sat on Santa's lap. The experience cramped his style.

"A Chippendale Santa," he heard one woman at the front of the line say.

"He's so hot he could melt the North Pole," her friend agreed.

Alex felt hot, all right. Not sexy hot, but sweaty armpit and groin hot. The Santa suit now stuck to his body in places he'd rather have loose-fitting. He discreetly tried to pry the plush fabric off his abs and thighs as he took a seat on the padded chair. He was certain to have a wedgy when it came time to leave.

A female elf materialized at his side, short, plump, and dressed in a green jumper and red tights with black patent leather mary janes. "I'll call each child forward and you can ask him what he wants for Christmas." She squeezed his shoulder encouragingly. "Maybe you could smile a little."

Smiling proved difficult. Each time he moved his lips, he got a mouth full of mustache.

The first boy to step forward came with a list a mile long. Alex heard a moan rise from those in line. Impatience could turn a crowd ugly. He'd have to hustle the kid along.

"I'm Tommy and I'm four," the boy in the denim jacket and jeans told Santa as he climbed onto Alex's lap. He held up his list, written in crayon. "Bring me these, please."

Alex scanned the list, which consisted of a jumble of letters. The kid favored the color red and the letter 'B.'

Alex patted the boy's shoulder, punted. "Books . . . do you like books?" He damn sure hoped so.

Tommy scrunched his nose. "No books on my list."

Crap. Alex went with, "A bicycle?"

The boy shook his head. "I already have one."

"Baseball." The nutcracker soldier jabbed Alex from behind, again with the bayonet. "Bat, ball, bases, Tommy's printing is perfectly clear."

Clear his ass. "You have a favorite team?"

Tommy puffed up proud. "Tampa Bay Rays."

Alex snorted. "They weren't even in contention this year."

"Win or lose, Tommy's still a fan." Again from the nutcracker.

So be it. "I'll see what I can do," Alex said, then handed the kid a candy cane.

Tommy ran back to his mother, and the nutcracker returned to handing out small bags of whole walnuts to those in line. Holly proved a personable nutcracker. She worked the lever on her jaw, spoke to every single person.

The moose danced toward Holly, gave her a quick ballroom spin. The people applauded. The moose next produced a sprig of mistletoe which he held over Holly's head. The animal dropped a light kiss on the nutcracker's wooden cheek. The crowd ooed and awed.

Alex wondered if moose man and cracks nuts were a couple. The thought irritated him. They were flirting and having fun and he was stuck coddling a drooling baby.

Definitely not fair.

Two hours passed, and Alex needed to stretch. He had butt prints on the red velvet from all those who had sat on his lap. His left thigh had gone numb. He'd yet to be peed on, which he considered a blessing. He did, however, doubt he'd recover from the blinding camera flashes. All he now saw were spots.

"Break time," he said to the elf who controlled the steady stream of children. "I'm taking ten."

The elf looked shocked, as if Alex had declared there'd be no Christmas this year.

"There are no breaks," the elf hurriedly informed him. "We work six-hour shifts."

"Not this Santa," Alex stated as he pushed to his feet. The costume was tight and had cut off all circulation to his groin. He limped his way to the side door.

"Problem?" The nutcracker blocked his escape, bayonet drawn.

Holly had lowered the lever on her wooden mouth, and Alex could see her entire face. Her blonde hair plastered her skull and sweat sheened her forehead. The collar on her gray T-shirt showed a wet ring.

She was as hot in her costume as he was in his.

He felt a flash of sympathy—but only a flash. "I'm tired of sitting," he told her.

"Sitting is part of your job," she hissed. "Santa doesn't stand or walk around, he *sits*. The chair is well padded."

He leaned toward her, his beard brushing her wooden cheek. "I need to adjust my junk." His tone was confidential.

She stepped back so fast, she bumped into the fake fireplace. The red plastic flames licked her ass. "Fine, fix it."

"Fix *them*, sweetheart, it's the full package."

Holly McIntyre couldn't breathe. She'd seen the bulge in his boxer briefs and knew any awkward shift would make him uncomfortable. He'd had kids wiggling on his lap for two hours. No doubt parts of him did need rearranging.

That he would discuss it with her made her cheeks heat. She closed the jaw on her nutcracker head, motioned him to take care of business.

He took thirty minutes to make his adjustments. Holly timed him. No man needed a full half hour to *fix his junk*. When he came back through the door, he had pizza on his breath.

"You ate lunch," she accused.

He shrugged one broad shoulder. "Got to keep up my strength."

She followed Alex back to the Santa chair. He was all slowness and swagger. Once he was seated, she unwrapped a candy cane and jabbed it in his mouth. "Fresh breath."

He gagged. "I hate peppermint."

"Then don't throw yourself a pizza party when the line's a mile long."

Damn, the line to see Santa had doubled while he'd bolted three slices of pepperoni with the mall custodian.

The man had been on his lunch break and welcomed Alex to join him.

It didn't help to have a full stomach when the kids now bounced on his lap. The really young ones jerked around like Mexican jumping beans. The bigger kids seemed to weigh twice as much as they had earlier that morning. He needed an Alka-Seltzer.

"Hey, dude, can I have your autograph?" the question came from a long-haired teenage boy, wearing a Rogues baseball jersey.

Alex took the offered pen signed *Santa Claus, North Pole* on the paper. "How's that?" he asked, handing it back.

"Get real, man." The boy flipped the paper, slipped it back to Alex. "Rumor has it you're Alex Boxer."

Not good. He'd expected word to leak out that he was in town. His sports car had become a novelty, but he'd hoped his stint as Santa would slide under the town's radar. Apparently it hadn't.

The Rogues' publicist would cringe to see his name linked to a speeding ticket should the story hit syndication. He was the man of the hour, having caught the final out in the World Series that October. He'd become a household name. He was Alex friggin' Boxer.

Sports Illustrated and GQ had cornered him for photo shoots and interviews. The last thing he needed was his picture plastered in the newspaper in the ill-fitting Santa suit. Tight red velvet was not an image he wanted to promote.

"What are you doing in line, Jerry Petree?" The nutcracker came to stand beside the teen seeking Alex's autograph. Holly lowered her jaw. "You're over ten—that's the cut off age for visiting Santa."

Jerry dipped his head, looked sheepish. "I wanted Boxer's autograph," he confessed.

"Alex Boxer is Santa for the next three hours," she said, laying down the law. "He turns back into a jock at three o'clock."

"Catch you on the sidewalk." And Jerry turned away.

She leveled her gaze on Alex. "Small smile? Little cheer? The kids believe you're real."

He looked down his body, from the pizza sauce stain on the tip of his beard to his too-tight suit. "Yeah, I'm definitely the real deal."

She nodded toward the line that swelled with children anxious to sit on his lap. "Fake it, Boxer. Impress me, and I'll put in a good word on your behalf with the judge."

"Think Hathaway would cut my community service hours by a day?" He could be in Miami by Christmas Eve, knocking back Jack and celebrating his ass off.

"I've seen the judge show leniency."

Not an outright promise, but it gave him hope.

"*Ho-ho-ho!*" His voice echoed off the walls, loud and jovial. Everyone stared, surprised by his merriment.

His enthusiasm scared the next two girls in line. The sisters broke into tears.

Holly took both their hands and led them forward.

Alex hauled them up on his lap, stiff and sniffling. He could barely get their bodies to bend.

With Holly's nudging he learned that Amy was three and Allison five. When the girls finally started talking, they went on and on. Alex got the rundown on their four older and very evil brothers.

Typical boys, he thought, they teased and played pranks on their sisters. They'd grow out of it.

He knew he'd zoned-out when Allison tugged on his beard. "Do we have a deal?"

"I'll do my Santa best."

The girls bounced off his lap, all bright-eyed and giggling. "I can't wait to have sisters," Allison sighed. "You can give our brothers to any parents you like."

Holly shuffled to his side. She'd released the lever on her jaw, her face visible, her expression pained. "Not smart, Santa. Did you hear a word those girls said? You just agreed to switch out family members."

"I'll pay more attention," he pacified her.

"And you didn't give them any store coupons," she accused. "The mall merchants need the holiday business."

Damn. "I forgot."

"Try and do better."

His lip curled. "I need to shine in your report to the judge."

"Sarcasm is beneath Santa." She stepped back, motioned the next child forward.

"I'm Louie," the boy announced as he stepped on Alex's tennis shoe in his attempt to climb on his lap. He looked six, stick-thin, and quite serious. "I want ten pounds for Christmas."

Alex lifted a white brow, asked, "Ten pounds of what?"

"Weight." Embarrassment pressed Louie's chin to his chest. "I'm skinny and get picked on a lot."

Bullies. Santa could fix this. "I have a friend, Alex Boxer, who's a Major League Baseball player. He'll be in town later this week. Maybe I could introduce you to him."

Louie looked up. "Never heard of him."

Major punch to the ego. "He's famous," Alex assured

Louie. "I could send him by your school. He'd impress a lot of kids, especially those who like sports."

"It's the kickball kids who never let me play."

"If Alex was team captain, I'm sure he'd pick you first."

"You think?" Hope shone in his deep-set eyes.

"Get with the nutcracker." Alex pointed toward Holly. "She'll set up a day for Alex to visit."

"What's the guy's last name again?"

Kid had a short memory. "Boxer, Alex Boxer."

Louie nodded. "A baseball player for Show-and-Tell. Can he come in his uniform?"

"Good possibility." He'd have one FedExed. "Alex might even autograph a few baseballs."

"Alex will be better than Mary Murphy's rabbit," Louie was excited now. "It hopped and pooped all over the classroom."

"We can only hope so."

Louie threw himself against Santa, hugged him with his skinny arms. "You look different from last year's Santa," he said against Alex's red velvet chest. "Mommy said Santa Claus has a good heart. You're not scary up close."

Alex surprised himself by patting Louie on the back. He didn't do kids or comfort. Louie slid off his lap, all bouncy and happy.

The boy's smile faded with his first step, and the air turned foul. Louie pinched his nose with clothespin fingers. "Stinks," he choked out.

"Not me, dude," Alex was quick to say.

Then who? A snort and the swish of a white tail clued them into the culprit. Randolph the Reindeer had cut the cheese.